DATURA

DATURA BOOKS
An imprint of Watkins Media Ltd

Unit 11, Shepperton House
89 Shepperton Road
London N1 3DF
UK

daturabooks.com
twitter.com/daturabooks
Black Metal Hearts

A Datura Books paperback original, 2024

Cover by Alice Coleman
Edited by Dan Hanks and Robin Triggs
Set in Meridien

ISBN 978 1 91552 307 5
Ebook ISBN 978 1 91552 316 7

Printed and bound in the United Kingdom by TJ Books Ltd.

9 8 7 6 5 4 3 2 1

MIX
Paper from
responsible sources
FSC
www.fsc.org   FSC® C013056

Marta Skaði

CONFESSIONS OF AN ANTICHRIST

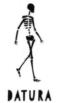

DATURA

1

You want a story? Sure. I'll give you a fucking story.

A love story. Girl meets boy, starts a black metal group, they get a record deal, have Satanic orgies, fight fascists with dildos, people die, and a church gets burned. All the typical stuff you'd expect of a Norwegian black metal love story.

But love will not win the day and there will be no happy ending. At least not in the ways you're expecting. I'm sure a life blessed with love's fulfilment, with a love returned, is a wonderful thing. But I wouldn't know about that. I loved once. Conventional, wholesome, Hollywood fucking rom-com love. And got nothing in return. My finite resources dwindled. And that's when I discovered something interesting. Without love there's nothing to soften the edges of other, more exciting, emotions that most people look down on.

Hate.

Greed.

Revenge.

In fact, when you have love denied to you, those edges become sharper. So what happens when you embrace those emotions? When you immerse yourself within them and they define your very essence? Pay attention and I shall tell you.

Those of us have suckled at a breast swollen by volume, vice and violence, those of us that have been emancipated by our hatred: we are the truly enlightened. We see the world through eyes not blinkered by convention. What we see is a world that needs to be destroyed and replaced with something new.

Aren't you sick of the music scene? Of your social circle? Of your lover? Your family? Your feelings? Politics? Religion? Emotions? Life?

I was. I reached the point where almost everything infuriated me. I'd become a ball of detestation wound so tight, if you dropped me to the floor I'd bounce beyond the moon.

Look around you. I bet that everything you see, smell, hear, feel and believe forms part of a neatly packaged product: an appliance with replaceable components that ticks along efficiently and predictably. The company that makes the car your parents drive probably sponsors your football team who in turn dictate what clothes you wear. Your phone tells you what food to eat, what books to read and what bullshit music to consume to dull your senses and make you more susceptible to eat more food, wear more clothes, and buy more crap music.

And don't pretend the rock stars out there aren't complicit in all of this. Your favorite spiky songwriter with the killer lyrics also sleeps with the influencer. Your renegade bassist dates a supermodel. The drug-addled guitarist with tattoos on his face is marrying the vapid heiress.

"But isn't that just rock'n'roll fucking the establishment," I hear you say.

Fuck no. Are you not paying attention?

They've sold you out: the rockers, the punks, the metallers. They're not about rebellion or anarchy anymore; I'm not sure they ever were. They're about rococo villas, sports utility vehicles and product endorsement. They instruct you how to vote, what to buy, who to screw and which flavor of God to suck on. They are cogs in that very same machine they encourage you to rage against. The irony is delicious, isn't it?

The love story you're about to hear is going to be unashamedly presented in all its honest, hate-filled glory. It's the story of a teenage girl who conjured up demons and specters from the depths of hell to demolish everything that most of you hold dear. And though I don't know what will

follow once the legions of the damned have razed the world to the ground, there's a good chance they will create something far more exciting than what we're stuck with now.

I'm going to lead them in destroying it all. Want to come with me?

2

So, on the night this story begins, the last of the three support bands ended up being a bland collection of circus freaks peddling the predictable zombie/Nazi shtick.

It was loud and shit and nobody cared. Texting and messaging are the most effective forms of communication in an environment like this and if the ill-judged clamor of the band could have been edited out of the mix I would have heard the muted clicks of a hundred fingers swarming deftly over their devices. Even as the vocalist was fire-eating and the bassist smeared fake excrement over his face, the sparse crowd sat cross-legged and resolute on the sticky floor of the club staring into tiny screens that up-lit their pale, bored faces with a sinister digital glow.

I had a few people to keep an eye on that night: the journalists and the man from Satan's Spawn record company. The latter wasn't going to be there yet – he was only in this for the main attraction. But the journos arrived before I did. The promise of a subsidized bar probably helped, but with four unsigned bands playing statistically at least one of the performers would go on to sell a handful of records or, better still, kill someone. The bragging rights that came from witnessing the inaugural Oslo gig of a notorious psychopath was a draw that was too much for any heavy metal hack to resist.

As you know, at the time, Norway had two magazines catering for this sort of extreme metal: *Downtuned* and *Hate Sounds*. I have no idea which of the magazines any of the

journos were writing for that night. I'm not sure they were entirely sure themselves. Movement between the titles was pretty fluid at the time and many journalists were on the payroll of both.

My first impression of Sigurd was that he was an appalling little man who had made it his life's work to do the opposite of what everyone expected. Bucking trends, championing the most awful of bands, and roasting anyone that dared enjoy a positive review from any of his peers.

Sorry, Sigurd, but you're a cock-sucking prick.

Od, was of course, his wingman. In contrast to Sigurd, I considered Od a big, wet pussy. I bet he was once a bookish teenager, good at science, eager to please, and hit puberty at the same time as he fell in love with black, death, and thrash metal along with its numerous sub-genres.

Am I right?

His reviews were always benevolent and read like the chemistry homework of an enthusiastic schoolboy with a crush on his teacher.

This is what I remember hearing:

"So how would you describe them?" Sigurd yelled over the noise.

"Goresludge," Od answered with a certainty that didn't invite discussion. Heavy metal nomenclature is a serious business and Od, having coined both the designations narco piss flange and gothsmack neo-bender (classifications that outlasted the bands to which they were first applied), was regarded as one of the foremost metal taxonomists practising in Oslo.

Sigurd wasn't having it though. He'd never agreed with anyone in his life and there was little chance he was going to start now.

"They played too fast to be sludge, Od. And didn't he say something about Satan at the beginning?"

"Blackened goregrind then," Od said, less convincing now.

Sigurd shook his head and smiled patronizingly. "But they

used a D-beat? Plus, that guitarist can shred like a petrol-engine Moulinex, so to speak."

"What are you saying then? They're blackened D-beat deathcore?"

"No. More melodic than that. I'd call them blackened D-beat power death."

"Cool." Od had to accept the wisdom of Sigurd's words. "Still shit though."

From the pictures I have seen, the crowds at Norwegian black metal gigs aren't any different from the crowds at black metal gigs anywhere else in the world; except that over here we take it all a bit more seriously. Tonight there were the usual assortment of oddballs. Boys scarred by a recent and virulent puberty with bad skin and terrible hair. Others who could tell you where any curve bisects the x-axis without breaking sweat, but who found themselves chemically incapable of speaking to girls. A slightly more sophisticated clique in the midst of a twelve-month fad who will grow out of it. One or two cute girls with far too many tattoos, who just want the love and attention of an emotionally distant father. Those who were permanently lost, not wanting to be found by anyone and seeking refuge from everything. And then you had the handful of very earnest, hideously ugly misanthropes who call themselves Satanists and hate anyone who doesn't share their particular worldview. Ironic really, as the combined worldview shared by a room full of self-proclaimed Satanists is likely to be more wide and varied than that enjoyed by any other cross-section of society.

Oh, but tonight we also got to see an aspect of Norway's metal scene that remains unique to us.

Oslo Iron had arrived. The self-proclaimed guardians of black metal.

Americans have the Hells Angels, the Brits have their football hooligans and here in Norway we have these fucks: a gang of old faux-bikers with greying beards and sagging guts who

maintain that wearing sunglasses in the dark, having a gun license, sporting the same clothes and holding the same views for decades makes them worthy of respect. Most of these guys served their apprenticeships during the second wave of black metal in the early 90s; some of them traded blows with the mainstream rock scene when black metal was born in the 80s, and two of them, regarded by the others as noblemen, earned their spurs crashing bottles into punks back in '77, before black metal had given them a philosophy upon which to justify their hatred and violence.

They arrived just as the support act finished their pathetic set and the atmosphere grew tense with an anticipatory sweat for the main event. Sigurd and Od joined me as I wandered over to the perimeter of the pit and watched events unfold on the stage.

"Fucking hell, have you seen the size of that drummer?" Sigurd said, as an enormous slab of meat and hair, with sticks looking tiny in his oversized hands, crouched over the drumkit. He looked like a bear on a child's tricycle.

"I bet that stool could disappear up his ass and he wouldn't notice," Od replied.

"He's the one I told you about. Apparently he's already killed two people."

Od nodded, like a prospective employer perusing an impressive CV. "I can believe it. From the size of him, I can imagine he probably just bit their heads off."

I smiled into the straw of my lemonade. It was bullshit, of course.

I knew Peter had only killed once.

I'd seen that beautiful beast of a drummer nearly every day of my life, so his outlandish proportions didn't seem strange to me. But I always enjoyed the reaction he provoked in those new to him.

"And look at this dude!" Od shook his glass in the direction of the bassist as he heaved what appeared to be a cuboid torso

onto center stage using a pair of short, stout legs that were poorly suited to the task.

"Jesus! I have never seen a man with a lower center of gravity than that. I bet he's never fallen over in his life."

These two unusually-shaped individuals did make for a unique rhythm section, I won't deny it. Not since the Siege of Minas Tirith had there been such an odd-looking alliance of creatures. It never seemed to bother them though: Peter the drummer and Edvard the bassist were quite comfortable in the skins nature had deigned to stretch so generously across their two opposing planes.

Peter rolled his snare and tom-toms and then gently crashed some symbols, as all drummers do, just to check that the laws of physics hadn't changed since he last tried. Meanwhile, Edvard grimaced at the kids sat on the floor and ran two tree-trunk fingers down the neck of his bass with such vigor anyone not equipped with his callused skin would have surely seared the flesh on their fingers to the bone.

Their appearance onstage provoked a ceasefire in the telecommunication combat being waged across the floor of the club. Brows furrowed, heads inclined to one side and neighbors were nudged as the crowd tried to assimilate what it was seeing.

Those that had sought sanctuary from the support bands began to migrate from the bar back to the thick of the action and the last of those seated were forced to stand up for fear of being trampled on.

It was a surprisingly big crowd for a Wednesday night.

"Lots of girls here," Sigurd commented. He glanced at me, though his gaze never climbed higher than my cleavage – which he stared at as if it was some complicated train timetable that required his analysis.

"They're not your standard metal-trolls either," Od replied. "Look at her."

He pointed at a blonde stood close to the front of the stage

with clean, straight and waist-length hair. She was well over six feet tall with a face and body lovingly chiseled from ivory.

Sigurd dragged his attention off me and redirected it stage-ward. I could see that he was forming an opposing argument, but it never escaped his mouth and quickly he was forced to shuffle uncomfortably and adjust his zipper. I suspect he had never been aroused at a black metal gig before.

"I'm pleased to see that corpsepaint is back in vogue," Od continued, staring at the band, not realizing or caring to notice Sigurd's discomfort. Sigurd himself was still too busy adjusting himself to comment.

Corpsepainting, an artistic movement that has never quite impacted on the mainstream, involves the use of make-up to give the impression that you are recently deceased. By evoking a countenance devoid of all color, with sunken eyes and sometimes even wounds or parcels of decay, it is designed to be the antithesis of glamour. But, as is so often the case, if you push off a sufficient distance from the safe and acceptable shores of fashion you will eventually find yourself crashed upon the rocks of its cutting edge. Many in this crowd were sporting a look that can only be described as corpse-chic.

The band were old-school devotees of the corpsepaint oeuvre. Huge Peter sported a full, dark blonde beard and what remained of his huge face had been painted white with eyes shaded into narcosis. Squat Edvard was also bearded, albeit much less generously than his bandmate. Even from a distance, I could discern each individual hair in his beard and moustache and map with precision their course out from his skin. With the application of corpsepaint his face looked like a salt plain populated with sparse brush.

There was a collective intake of breath as the guitarist emerged from the wings. While corpsepaint is always intended to look horrific, this confident youth was the most beautiful corpse imaginable. A celebration of strength, sex and decay.

The arrogance I knew so well was also evident in spades as he

sauntered across the stage. The man, Snorre, screamed many silent contradictions: strong of feature, yet soft of skin; clothed like a punked-up biker but with the gait of a Victorian poet; tall and muscular but with the grace of a young willow swaying in the breeze. Everything about him was overwhelmingly masculine while at the same time beautifully feminine, like a frilled cuff on a boxing glove.

He immediately noticed the tall beauty at the front of the crowd. With legs astride a monitor he loomed over her and fixed her with a stare. Everyone in the room was transfixed by this encounter – a meeting of divinities deserving of an epic poem to preserve the moment for posterity. There was an air of spiritual anticipation, as if the perceived power of their celestial majesty was such that in their coupling they might conceive a new universe.

The girl leaned over the stage. Staring up at him, she tilted her head and inhaled deeply at the side of his boot, drinking in the aroma from the leather as if were a heady intoxicant. She closed her eyes briefly, then, having had her fill, she opened them and extended her tongue, dragging it, slowly, expertly, from toe to heel.

All but one of the audience held their breath. The one was me, rolling my eyes and sucking noisily on the straw in my drink.

I waited until she had completed this ritual adoration. Raising her head as if seeking thanks, forgiveness, or some other consideration for her worship. A sly and perhaps cruel smile fractured the guitarist's face which, until that moment, had been impassive. Snorre then looked up, and with close to three hundred pairs of eyes trained upon him, he sought out mine. I greeted them with the raise of an eyebrow and a subtle tilt of my head.

He lifted his boot, resplendent with a streak of fresh saliva, and placed its sole carefully on her exquisite forehead. With a fraction more than playful pressure he pushed her back into

the crowd and she sank beneath its surface. He then turned, strode over to a guitar that was perched against an amplifier and strapped it on.

It was around then that I spotted the record company guy had arrived. I'd looked him up on one of those corporate networking sites that wankers use to show other wankers how many different wankers they know. The giveaway was the expensive spectacles that cleverly gave the illusion of depth to his otherwise lifeless eyes.

He stood at the bar with a diet coke, waiting for things to kick off.

I grinned to myself, knowing I'd got all the pieces in place.

3

Darkness began to slowly descend upon the room until a rich, ominous gloom was achieved. Then spotlights focused on the floor of the stage began a gradual illumination of the three band members.

"Oslo." Edvard the bassist spoke the word into his microphone and silence rippled across the crowd. "Praise be to Odin, Thor and the Norse Pantheon." Even from here, I could see some of the confused looks amongst those watching. *Just wait*, I thought. *It gets weirder.* Edvard magnified his voice and added, "Now… watch your backs."

All lights were then extinguished and a moment later an ear-piercing wail, without need of any amplification, split the silence and darkness open. The pitch of the sound was inhuman and of such an unusual aural texture it was impossible to place its source. It was then joined by a cacophony of abrasive drums, guitar and bass from the stage, all conspiring to intimidate and disorientate the audience with an undoubtedly illegal volume that would have caused passers-by on the street outside to flinch.

The lights came back up to illuminate three hundred very scared looking people. The source of the initial sound then made itself apparent when, for a split second, one of the lights mounted high up and focused on the stage was obscured by something passing in front of it.

Still screaming, the source of the noise came hurtling through the air from the direction of a balcony. Like that infamous fallen angel, cast out from its seat in paradise so many eons ago, it came crashing to earth in a furious turmoil. The power and direction of its trajectory was such that, on impact, a large swathe of the standing crowd, perhaps a dozen or more, were brought crashing to the ground. And those not struck retreated quickly from the seething stew of black-clad limbs that writhed like eels on the floor.

From the tangled mass, the source of the madness emerged. With blood streaming from a gash in his head, a creature – human, but only just – rose and scowled at the crowd, rabid with rage. With clenched fists held above his head, he raised his eyes heavenward and let out another unearthly shriek. In doing so, the blood that had collected in and around his mouth was given force and dispersed itself in a fine mist among the crowd.

His head then swiveled to fix on the group of Oslo Iron stood to one side. And he went for them.

Some of the men simply fled, barging youngsters out of the way or even throwing them into the path of their attacker to help their escape. Others, maybe too slow to flee, steeled themselves for the inevitable and welcome conflict.

The scream-beast was fast, agile and powered by insanity. His opponents were old, tough and strong. A good number of blows landed on the men, yet more were returned and it wasn't long before they put their enemy down. He writhed against the spilled ale and blood unwilling to accept his inexorable fate, and with a tenacity that was far more alarming than the harm that it caused, he bounced back up each time with another volley of wild and poorly aimed strikes.

Throughout the sickening violence, the band continued to play. Theirs was a soundtrack of slow, syncopated and bass-heavy riffs that pounded heads like an earthquake striving to shake the brain free of its moorings. And it was the perfect accompaniment to what was happening before them.

However, all good things had to end and once the madman

had been knocked to the ground a dozen times or more, the bassist stepped toward the edge of the stage on those short, stumpy legs of his and jumped into the pit. Using the neck of his bass to nudge a way through the crowd, he then grabbed an arm and leg of his screaming, wailing and biblically terrifying lead singer and flung him onto the stage – where he slid towards the microphone.

Under the spotlight, the beast was definitely human; albeit a strange, shrunken parody of a man covered in rags, with a hairless head and a face bloated by the cuts and weals of a recent beating.

His earlier shrieks had evoked ancestral memories of a less civilized and evolved era of mankind's past when we fought with lesser primates for supremacy over the beasts. The noise that he now made into the microphone recalled a more recent historical era where demons were known to inhabit the body of the village fool, causing a hysterical babble that would only cease upon the grateful slaughter of the devil's incumbent. It was a wild, incomprehensible diatribe delivered at breakneck speed, with wide eyes and with an intensity that demanded the attention of the audience, despite being communicated in a language unknown to anyone other than the speaker.

The music had changed too. Gone were the slow, crunching chords that had earlier pounded stakes through the skulls of the crowd with a deliberate and monotonous meter. They were now replaced by riffs that attacked the ear drum as a power-drill shatters concrete. And of the drums, all one could hear was a tinny snare and high-hat rattling together like a defective lathe.

Then suddenly it all stopped: the gibbering of the singer, the assault on the guitar strings and the battery of the drums. Silence. Silence and darkness as all lights were extinguished once again.

Had the darkness endured a panic would have undoubtedly ensued because nobody could see what the vocalist, for want of a better way of describing him, was doing. But the darkness didn't endure. Both it and the silence were broken by spotlights, a guitar in anguish and yet another new sound dragged from the throat of the freak-show that was the battered singer.

The guitar was melodic cruelty. By surrounding the circumference of an individual string with the nails of a thumb and two fingers, and then scraping up and down the neck of his guitar, the guitarist produced a sound that was at the same time tuneful and torturous. Pedals gave the sound depth and texture, and the overall effect was one of beauty against all odds, like a rainbow reflected in liquid shit. Then the vocals kicked in again, gathering in volume and intensity, a dark and disturbing sound, unlike any heard before. Imagine yanking a live goblin by its tongue from the stomach of a goat.

What beauty there was in the guitar was rendered repulsive by this hideous shriek, but combined the effect was mesmerizing in ways I still can't understand.

Both the guitarist and the vocalist went about their work with an intensity that bordered on the euphoric. The guitarist strutting the stage, embodying every aspect of the archetypal rock god, his combination of grace, looks, confidence and blatant sexuality provoking desire, envy and lust in everyone in the room, irrespective of their gender or orientation. In contrast, the singer appeared an entirely different species – a freakish diversion from the evolutionary path that the rest of our ancestors have travelled down. It was difficult to tell if he wore corpsepaint or not. The crimson streaks of blood that criss-crossed his face contrasted sharply with his alabaster complexion and that suggested that he was indeed painted. However, in the course of his beating his T-shirt had been all but ripped to pieces to reveal a narrow, concave torso of the same ashen hue as his face and resembling the broken bowl of a discarded plastic spoon. If he was wearing corpsepaint on his face, it followed he had covered his entire body with the stuff.

In aspect this man was objectively repulsive. Nobody would

deny that; not even me. But during those minutes that he shared his twisted croon with the audience he began to win parts of it over. His plaintive lament was desperately sad. Without using any ascertainable words he conveyed pain, hopelessness and loss. Eventually the drums and bass began a revival and the guitar changed pace to commence a journey toward crescendo built around a crushing, but infectiously catchy, riff.

But the vocals didn't change. The mournful song got louder, yet remained serene and heartbreaking.

A surprising number of the funereal youth now found themselves drawn back to the stage, stepping through the blood and around the beaten old men. They looked up, wary, but fascinated.

There was no shortage of girls among them. Perhaps it was sympathy, or a natural maternal instinct, or a depraved attraction of the bizarre – the same power source that any carnival draws upon to generate its charge.

I could see from the way they regarded him that some of those girls were wondering what it would be like to be fucked by that thing. One or maybe even two of them might have learned the answer to that question that night; but I'm the only woman that has ever dared go back to him more than once.

As the volume built, the horrendous beauty of the noise within it evolved. It was now a maelstrom of fear, desire, envy, lust, sympathy and sexual confusion, all swirling within a pool over which the subtle fragrance of beer, stale sweat and fresh blood hung in a mist. These were strange and volatile currents within which the crowd eddied. And there would be consequences.

Scuffles began. First between the boys, then between the girls, then all gender distinction was lost in flash points flaring up all over the venue.

Near me, a large she-goth crashed into Od, driven into him by the shockwave from a nearby brawl. Od's beer flew out of his hand and the plastic glass collapsed on the bar. The funny part was that I remember him staring at her, eyes wide with fear or anger or both. I was waiting for him to say something. To scream at her. But then she whipped her arms around his neck, dragged his head down and kissed him with a ferocity that owed more to hunger than it did to affection.

Od resisted only as long as it took for her to grab his ass, at which point he abandoned himself to the moment as men generally do. Their embrace was aggressive, and nasty, and driven by that disturbing passion that only the very ugly seem to enjoy. Their combined mass, given momentum by their crazed ardor, transformed them into an angry, throbbing, locomotive that crashed through the crowd in search of a vertical surface against which it could achieve some purchase. The moment they struck the nearest wall, four hands began a frantic search for zips, buttons or other fastenings that could be prized open to reveal something soft and yielding within. They attacked each other's clothes like starving peasants attacking a medieval fortress.

Then, once sufficient access had been obtained, and in full view of Sigurd – *oh, I remember your face, Sigurd, that was a picture too* – and everyone else in their vicinity, they commenced loud, brief and brutal sex.

It was around this time the fires started. Heaps of paper, flyers for other bands and gigs, were ignited simultaneously in three places around the venue. Pools of spilled drinks then caught fire like little lava pools and those not in a brawl began dancing around them, sacrificing scarves and T-shirts and whatever they had on them to whatever god or demon they believed had taken control of the gig.

And through it all, the band played on, building incrementally to an eagerly anticipated climax. Eventually, the vocalist concluded his alien hymn and let the others play on without him, as he leapt into the crowd to give himself over to the bloodshed.

I looked for the record company guy. He had managed to get behind the bar and, using a mobile phone, was making a film, drawing his phone back and forth across the panorama of pandemonium while grinning like an idiot.

Eighteen minutes after the band took to the stage the police, fire brigade and paramedics arrived and the building was evacuated. In the ensuing mayhem four more people were injured as the crowd was crushed through the club's narrow exits like sausage meat. The guitar and bass persisted until the authorities cut their power. Even then the drums continued to pound.

So concluded the longest and most successful gig to date for Baphomet's Agony and one that would put us within spitting distance of the record deal that would allow us to begin corrupting the world beyond our perfect little town.

4

A quick word on the naming conventions used in black metal, in case anyone is still catching up.

Band members adopt a stage name that's supposed to represent their Satanic persona. It's not meant to be an alterego because you're supposed to believe that they live their lives entirely within their corpsepainted, ridiculously named personality. It would be laughable if it weren't so often true – many in this scene abandon a perfectly sensible name, lifestyle and skin tone in preference for one derived entirely from an obscure black-and-white German horror movie.

Which is how, a week after the Oslo gig, I found myself in the kitchen of The Exorcist.

Correction, it was actually the kitchen of The Exorcist's mum, The Exorcist being the sweet, stupid, murderer (we'll get back to that later) known as Peter Suhm. My closest friend – if I would have ever admitted to having one – and the gargantuan drummer of Baphomet's Agony.

The Exorcist was the name he had picked for himself. And, right now, the terrifying, Satan-worshipping behemoth was sitting over a boiled egg, sweating and shaking with trepidation at what he was about to do. Something he'd been putting off for months.

"Mum," he said. "I have something to tell you."

"What's that Peter?"

She wasn't listening. It was obvious she wasn't listening. I grabbed his wrist and gave him a look that demanded he wait.

But it was too late. He had generated the smallest amount of momentum and he was going to drive on through.

"Mum...I'm a Satanist."

"Uh-huh," was all she said.

She was looking out of a wide window that looked over the picturesque harbor in Kragerø. Nestling on the Southern-most tip of Norway, Kragerø was renowned the world over for being among the most pleasant places on the planet. It was where rich Norwegians holidayed and, even by Scandinavian standards, it had a decent standard of living. It was clean, safe, lush and affluent.

Christ it was oppressive.

There were plenty of us who ignored its moderate climate and beautiful, clearly demarcated seasons. We hid underground from its stunning landscape. We overwhelmed the smell of pine and the sea with cigarette and hash smoke, and we buried the gentle soundtrack of lapping waves and birdsong beneath our crudely produced black metal. The relentless beauty was a blight on our lives and that particular morning Kragerø was putting on a show. It was a picture fucking postcard of cobbled streets, freshly painted rustic cottages, and bobbing fishing boats, beneath blue skies and puffy white clouds.

However, The Exorcist's mum, Mrs Suhm, wasn't drinking in the twee scenery. She had not had the huge window installed in her kitchen so she could admire the view. She didn't spend thirty minutes every morning polishing the glass so that she could people-watch.

I watched as she extended her six-foot plus height by a couple of inches, lifting herself up on her toes, as she focused hard upon something bobbing on the horizon. It was a familiar ritual and one that even I, the coldest of the cold-hearted, couldn't watch without feeling a stab of misery.

She had seen a boat approaching in the distance. There was very little wind that morning but the boat was sufficiently far out that the most subtle of ripples was causing the deck to bob in and out of view on the undulating horizon. She held a tea towel in her hands and, as the minutes drew on, she twisted it round.

Peter – sorry, The Exorcist – eventually realized she hadn't heard him and that any further conversation was futile. So we simply returned to drinking our coffee in silence while we waited.

As the small boat got closer the excitement welling up within her sought for a release and she began to move her weight from foot to foot with a clumsy rhythm. The towel in her hands had been twisted with such vigor it had become a rigid cylinder; like a relay baton. She began humming. It was a strange melody with a pitch that varied erratically, and her tune increased in pace and volume over time. As her song became stranger her gentle bounce became more vigorous. Throughout this dark routine she kept her gaze fixed firmly on the vessel in the distance.

All at once the humming ceased, the dance ended and she released her grip on the towel which spun around in her hand like a half-hearted propeller.

She let out a sigh, turned away from the window and looked at us with a deflated smile.

"Mum, did you hear what I just said?"

"What's that darling?"

She began tidying around the small table, clearing away our empty plates. She had eaten earlier, yet the table was still set for three. A full cooked breakfast sat untouched between where The Exorcist and I sat. As usual.

She left that where it was.

"I said I'm a Satanist."

Mrs Suhm carried the empty plates to the sink and resumed humming. There was significantly less insanity in the tune now and once she had placed the dishes in the sink she stopped her housework and turned to us with a look of bewilderment on her strong, proud face.

"A Setant-ist? What on earth does that mean Peter?"

"No, a *Satanist*, Mum. It means I worship Satan. Look, I've got tattoos and everything."

He rolled up his left sleeve to reveal an inverted crucifix seared into a broad forearm. It was the strong, muscular arm of a twenty-year-old youth in rude health. Beneath the pale skin I could see the rich blackness of fresh ink.

Mrs Suhm gave his arm a cursory glance before beginning the washing up.

"Yes, a crucifix, I noticed that when you left the flat yesterday. You know if you had spoken to me before you did that I could have got you a little gold one for your birthday and you could have worn it on a chain."

"It's not a normal crucifix Mum: it's upside-down. See?"

The Exorcist sat with his outstretched arm held aloft, looking like a street sign.

Only when she had finished the task and drank a small glass of water did she return to the table. She grabbed his wrist and peered over her glasses at his arm as if consulting a recipe to check the necessary quantity of seasoning.

"Well, it's upside down now but when you're playing your drums and you're tapping one of your little sticks on your top-hat it will be the right way up and I suppose that's when most people will see it."

She sat down opposite me while he looked down at his new tattoo and went through the motions of a drum-fill. She was right. I hadn't noticed it until just then, but as soon as it had been pointed out it was obvious.

"It's not a top hat Mum, it's a high-hat and an upside-down crucifix is the sign of the devil."

She smiled at me and her clear blue eyes glistened as they rolled.

"It's the sign of Saint Peter after whom you were named. You and I both know that he was crucified upside down and I think that it's sweet that you should have honored him like that."

"I haven't honored anyone!" For such a large man The Exorcist was capable of producing a squeal of surprisingly high pitch.

"You might not have done it consciously, Peter, but subconsciously you are following in the footsteps of your namesake and telling the world that you are not worthy of being compared to the magnificence of Our Lord Jesus Christ the Savior. You have shown great humility, son, and I am very proud of you. Your father will be proud too when he sees it."

Mrs Suhm glowed in the righteous heat that she pictured radiating out from her son. I too felt warm and safe at that breakfast table, but I always did feel comfortable whenever I was in the presence of Mrs Suhm with her lined and handsome face. Hers was a face that age had worked upon with great enthusiasm but with equal measures of kindness, skill and care. The finished product was ravaged by the passage of time while being thoroughly satisfying to look upon.

"Are you a Setant-ist too Marta?" she asked me.

"No Mrs Suhm," I replied. "I'm a Gemini."

She pursed her lips and narrowed her eyes in an exaggerated display of disapproval. She viewed astrology as blasphemy. She viewed science as blasphemy. She viewed television on a Sunday as blasphemy. She viewed Catholicism as blasphemy. She viewed her son, The Exorcist, the drummer in Norway's hottest devil-worshipping black metal act, as a God-fearing, Church-going boy who still had the potential for priesthood.

The Exorcist was clearly troubled by his mother's revelation. He had been immensely proud of his tattoo and I could see layer upon layer of utter confusion were being piled up behind his eyes. It was as if he was required to learn an entirely new principle of mathematics; one in which 2 + 3 = purple.

He shook it off. "Whatever. It doesn't matter anyway because that's just one of my tattoos. Look at this one and tell me that it's not Satanic."

He rolled up his other sleeve and proudly displayed another disfigured forearm to his mother.

"It's a five-pointed star Peter."

"That's right, a pentagram, and there's nothing Christian about that!"

"Of course there is! Marta can tell you. A Crucifixion Star is a celebration of Christ's suffering to save mankind."

I nodded at The Exorcist. There was absolutely no point in disagreeing with his mother on anything concerning her faith.

"It's nothing to do with Christ, mum! It's all about the devil."

"Don't be silly Peter. The five points represent the five wounds that were inflicted on Christ on the Cross."

She grabbed hold of his wrist and yanked his arm over to her side of the table.

"See." She indicated each of the points in turn with a long, straight finger. "One for each of His hands, one for each foot and one for the spear that pierced His side."

She flung his arm back to him before continuing. "Marta's grandmother used to have one over the fireplace next to a carving of the Blessed Virgin, didn't she Marta?"

My grandmother died when I was two years old. I had no recollection of her face let alone her interior furnishings, but I still nodded in agreement.

"What on earth makes you think that it has got anything to do with the devil, Peter?" asked Mrs Suhm.

The Exorcist looked at his mother, and then at me, with an expression of pantomime incomprehension, raising his hands and seeking confirmation from me that the question asked beggared belief. I didn't meet his eyes. I had warned him that something like this would happen when he had this conversation with his mother and I had initially refused to provide the moral support that he requested. I softened after witnessing the look of resigned loss on that broad, kind face of his. However, while I had agreed to be in attendance at his confession I had refused to take an active part in it. I certainly wasn't going to take his side against his mother.

I turned back to look at his face and just caught the moment that a thought arrived in his head. You could always tell when a new thought occurred to The Exorcist because his head would jolt with the impact.

"I... I don't know what it's got to do with the devil, but I know that it's something!"

Mrs Suhm placed her palm over the third untouched breakfast on the table to get a sense of how warm it was. She looked up at the clock on the wall and frowned.

"And by the way," The Exorcist continued, his cheeks reddening, "from now on, can you not call me Peter? I would prefer it if you called me The Exorcist."

"Oh, how delightful!" Mrs Suhm clapped her hands with joy. "Your old uncle Jacob would be so proud of you!"

"Who?"

"Your uncle Jacob. He wasn't really your uncle mind you. He was my cousin. He died when you were about three years old. He was a priest up by Lake Tokevann. He was the most devout Christian in all of Telemark; perhaps even all of Norway. It was he that christened you. He used to do lots of exorcisms in the 80s. There were a lot of heathens in the 80s. Peter and your uncle Jacob, who was a big man with your physique, used to hit them in the face with a club until they proclaimed Christ's glory through their broken teeth. He was a very good priest."

I laughed. I knew that Peter's attempt to come out to his mother as a Satanist was never going to be straightforward, but I hadn't predicted that it would descend into this much of a farce. And yet I felt so sorry for him too. He just wasn't a very convincing Satanist. He wasn't a very convincing drummer either. With his oversized proportions he didn't even make a very convincing member of the human race. He was in the band because Bolverk and I demanded it. Bolverk was the band name of Edvard, the bassist you met in Oslo. Remember him? Okay, well you'll get to meet him properly later on. Right now, we're still learning about The Exorcist, that perennial outsider, the Satanist in a Christian household, the Christian in a Satanic band, and the colossus that walks among us.

"No Mum, you're not getting it. I'm called The Exorcist because I'm evil."

I laughed again, unable to help myself. The Exorcist was a kind, sweet man who picked his litter up, fed squirrels and would never talk ill of anyone.

Mrs Suhm joined me in my laughter. "You're always a handful when you've not had enough sleep, Peter. But don't put yourself down, son, you're a good boy. Now, have you had enough breakfast? Would you like another egg?"

"No thank you. And I am evil, Mum. I do all sorts of evil things."

"Like what?"

He paused and sipped his coffee. "Fine, perhaps I've not done much evil stuff yet but on Thursday night I'm going out with Marta and the band to burn down a church."

I lost my good humor at that point and flashed a stern look back at The Exorcist. We were indeed going out church-burning on the Thursday night, but blurting it out like that was madness.

"Which church?" his mother asked.

Realizing his error, The Exorcist tried to stand up. His mother placed a firm hand on his arm and with the smallest amount of pressure guided him back into his chair.

"Peter." She didn't raise her voice but with just two syllables she left us with no doubt as to the magnitude of her authority. "Which church are you going to burn down?"

He looked at me for guidance. With a small nod I permitted the disclosure.

"Dønnisal." he muttered.

Mrs Suhm stood up, drained her coffee cup and walked back to the sink.

"Good," she said.

"Good?" The Exorcist and I said in unison.

"Of course! Dønnisal is a horrible heathen place. It always has been. That church was built with the remains of an old pagan stave church and no decent Christian has, or would ever, set foot in it. It should have never been built and my family was very angry when it was restored. My own mother, God rest her soul, led the campaign to prevent Dønnisal merging with Kragerø in the 60s because she didn't want the good folk of Kragerø being corrupted by the heathen influence of that Godforsaken place. She lost, mind you, but I believe that it was a success in the eyes of The Lord and I'm sure that her crusade would have assured her safe passage to The Kingdom of Heaven!"

At the point that she first mentioned her mother, Mrs Suhm began a complex ritual involving a combination of crossing, genuflexion and crucifix kissing (she always wore at least one crucifix). It continued after she had sat back down at the table with us and continued onto a new subject.

"You would be doing all right-thinking Christians a huge service by burning that church down. I only wish someone had thought to do it sooner. If I was a few years younger I'd come with you as quick as a shot, but I would probably just slow you down, what with my knees. I shall be praying for you though and with the power of prayer to fan the flames it should go up like a tinderbox."

It might surprise you to learn that I have a huge soft spot for the Church of Norway, primarily because Mrs Suhm is such an enthusiastic champion of it. To me the Church has an important role in our society because it embodies the essential madness that we each have within us. While the Satanists I know like to think that they epitomize debauchery, I know I'll find more insanity-driven wickedness within a Church of Norway knitting circle than I will within any of the covens that I frequent.

"Will you bring me back a little memento that I can put in your Special Achievements Box?" Mrs Suhm asked The Exorcist. "A charred piece of something perhaps?"

"I'll see what I can do, Mum."

"Good boy. Now Marta, you be careful if you're going to be gallivanting around the countryside burning churches down."

"I will Mrs Suhm."

"Will..." She hesitated. "Will Ailo be going with you?"

"Yes, he will."

You have met Ailo before. Remember the scream-beast from the Oslo gig who jumped down from the balcony to attack the people who'd paid good money to watch him sing? Yeah, that's him. Baphomet's Agony's very own vocalist, although we don't call him Ailo. He prefers his chosen name of Suffer.

He's also the man with whom I occasionally share a bed.

When I hinted at that earlier on, I suspect it puzzled you. You're wondering why a girl like me, who's not bad looking, has got a brain in her head and doesn't show any obvious signs of psychological damage, would allow someone as dark and damaged as Suffer any intimate privileges.

I could tell you he's misunderstood, that his offensiveness is the crude attention-seeking device of a sweet but tortured soul. But those would be lies. From what you've seen already, I know you've got the measure of him. He's a strange, ugly little man full of anger and hatred, and there is nothing soft or warm buried within him. From what I've seen, he's rotten to the core.

Mrs Suhm doesn't like Suffer because he hurts me. She's quite protective of me, but at the same time she subscribes wholeheartedly to the principle that what goes on between a man and his woman should concern nobody else. When she notices I have a new bruise, that I am limping or that I have dried blood on my tights she takes The Exorcist aside and finds an excuse to berate him for being untidy, rude or committing some sin or other. Both The Exorcist and I know she's reprimanding him for failing to look after me. There's nothing he can do about it though. The Exorcist is nearly three times heavier than Suffer and he's as bold and gallant as the next man. It's just that Suffer is a dense concentration of rage that cannot be controlled by force, law or by the exercise of any will other than his own.

You will have noticed I have not yet explained why I sleep with Suffer.

Show don't tell, my friends, show don't tell.

Mrs Suhm looked sideways at The Exorcist with a reproachful glare he avoided in favor of his fingernails. She tried approaching the subject from a different angle.

"I have been thinking about Ailo and your group recently Peter."

The Exorcist squirmed. "Suffer, Mum, we call Ailo Suffer."

"I can see why. I can't bear the boy." She placed a hand upon mine and, without looking at me, added, "No offence dear. But since this *Suffer* is such an awful singer and since you have such a lovely singing voice, Peter, why don't you sing and play your drums at the same time? I saw a drummer doing that on the TV the night before last. He was bald though. You remember how well Peter sang, don't you Marta? He has such a sweet voice and has a very high range for a big boy. Father Thomas used him as a Soprano until he was well past sixteen. If Peter hadn't gone to sea after he finished school, I'm sure that he would be leading the choir by now."

"Mum, we've been through this before." The Exorcist stood up and began gathering his things into his bag in readiness to leave. "Suffer is a much better black metal vocalist than I am."

"He's a much better drummer than you are too," I teased.

"Yes, he is." The Exorcist hesitated and suddenly there was a pang of guilt in my rotten heart. I had knocked the wind out of him. He needed time to refocus before he continued. "You may not like his vocals Mum, but there is nobody in Norway that can make the noises that he can. Between him and Decadence they *are* Baphomet's Agony."

"What on earth is a Decadence?" Mrs Suhm said.

You know who Decadence is by now, don't you? By a process of elimination you must have figured out that he's our fetching, finger-tapping and more-often-than-not fornicating, guitarist. Real name: Snorre.

"Decadence is the name Snorre has chosen, Mrs Suhm," I said.

"It sounds like a cheap perfume."

"Hmm," continued The Exorcist. "But if it weren't for Decadence and Suffer there would be no band. Bolverk and I just make up the numbers."

"That's not entirely fair," I said, digging under his skin again. "The fans love Bolverk and it's he that chats to the audience during the gigs."

The Exorcist looked at me like a dog that's just been kicked.

Mrs Suhm stood up and as she turned towards the sink another speck on the horizon caught her eye through the window. She skipped over to watch. Lost again to time.

The Exorcist sighed and pulled out a plastic lunch box from his bag. He threw it to me, I caught it, opened it and tipped the full, untouched plate of breakfast between us into it. I then sealed the thing and handed it back to The Exorcist to be shoved in his bag.

"Look Mum, we've got to go," he said. "We're helping out Snorre... I mean Decadence, at the shop."

She hadn't heard. The humming had resumed, the dance had re-commenced and the towel in her hand had begun its inexorable twist. Mrs Suhm would be lost to the world for the next few minutes.

The Exorcist slung his bag over his shoulder, kissed his mother on the cheek and we left her in a heightened state of excitement gazing out of the window.

We could still hear her song in the corridor as we left the apartment and made our way down the stairs.

5

Contrary to popular belief, black metal bands are not shat out of a volcano fully-formed, corpsepainted and spitting their hatred and blasphemy at the world. They begin life just like everyone else and their descent into hell takes place over time. That's one of the reasons I'm telling you all this. In the aftermath of what happened, so many myths were created around the band that the repeated bullshit began to acquire a polish of truth. I wanted to set the record straight, tell the truth about what happened, while I'm still in my right mind.

The day on which The Exorcist and Bolverk began their downhill journey towards hell was an April day during the Easter holidays six years ago. (My own descent had begun long before, but that's another story). Back then, the view out of Mrs Suhm's kitchen window was pretty much the same, except it would have looked out on Old Mr Suhm, the young Exorcist's father, preparing his boat for a day or two of gentle cod fishing.

I know what Mrs Suhm would have seen out of her kitchen window on that April afternoon because I was there. While her son and husband worked together, happily tending nets on the harbor and tuning the boat's engine, I loitered on the cobbles with a kid called Edvard.

Fishing is a brutal activity undertaken by difficult men. The day-to-day likelihood of death for Norwegian fishermen is ten times greater than it is for the average Norwegian, so you have to have a certain state of mind to choose that as your profession.

Old Mr Suhm was of that mind. He had served a long apprenticeship on trawlers fishing way up in the north, off the coast of Svalbard and I will always think of him as being old: a rugged, gnarly sixty-five year old with only three fingers and a thumb on each hand. He had lost one finger to frostbite and another had been ripped off by a trawler scoop, but when I was six years old he told me he had sold them to a factory that made fish fingers. He was trying to make me laugh but, like many men whose personality is fashioned in the company of brutes, he had no idea how to behave around children, women or anyone other than his kind. The joke misfired and I became terrified of him. Needless to say, I've never since eaten fish fingers and whenever I see kids at a gig, hands aloft making devil's horns, I picture Old Mr Suhm waving at me and get an unpleasant fish taste in my mouth.

Old Mr Suhm was a large, robust and simple man, who married late in life. According to my mother his marriage came as a great surprise to the townsfolk who had him down as somewhat of an over-the-hill loner. It's said he never had much in the way of ambition and was quite content to let younger, less experienced men captain the ships he worked on. When I knew him, his reputation amongst Kragerø fishing folk was one for hard work and dull wit. It was also widely held that he was marked.

According to folklore the sea will sometimes do that to a man. A man could pay her regular visits, remaining courteous and never taking advantage of her. Then, on a whim, she will take slight and exact a disproportionate revenge. The story goes that Old Mr Suhm used to be as hard a drinker as he was a worker. On one occasion he was supposed to join the crew of a trawler that was sailing out of Tromsø, way up north. This was the late eighties, just before the great Norwegian cod fishing ban that devastated the fishing industry. This was to be the last trip before the ban and the crew were preparing for a grueling month at sea. Old Mr Suhm (he was old even back then) arrived at the port two days before he was due to set sail but got so drunk in the course of a thirty-six hour binge that he collapsed at an inn and, unbeknownst to the rest of his crew, was taken in by the innkeeper. He slept for eighteen hours and missed the ship's departure. A week later the ship hit an iceberg off Bear Island and sunk. The entire crew was lost.

The Kragerø townsfolk will have you believe Old Mr Suhm should have died on that trip. From that moment on he was marked... and the sea is nothing if not a patient and cruel creditor. She will bide her time, adding interest to the debt. Then, at some point in the future, she will take what is hers and anyone unfortunate enough to be in the vicinity on the day of reckoning.

Sometimes she will mark an entire ship regardless of the innocence of her crew. Sometimes she will mark a family.

No crew would ever take on Old Mr Suhm again. He was an albatross, as far as the fishing community was concerned. On borrowed time. I remember talking to Peter and Edvard about it that very same April day.

"Peter," Edvard asked. "What did your Dad do to get himself marked?"

Peter stood on the harbor wall in silence. His habitual grin evaporated in an instant and the flat line of his lip that he produced in its place was so infrequently seen that I hardly recognized him.

"He's not allowed to talk about that," I said, instinctively trying to protect him.

"Why not?"

"His Mum said so."

I looked at Peter. He stood stock still, staring down at his toes. By that stage he was already a foot taller than Edvard and so in staring at his feet it felt to me that his gaze was much closer to our faces than it was to the floor. He didn't look sad, he looked blank. I think he had switched himself off.

"I don't think he knows anyway," I continued. "But he's not allowed to think about it regardless."

"Do you know how he got marked?"

I sighed. "There's no such thing as marking. It's just a thing that parents say to explain things they don't want to understand. His Dad isn't marked, he was just lucky that time."

Thus it was, sixteen years after his supposed marking, on that April day, lucky Old Mr Suhm went about his business on Kragerø harbor with Peter. And unbeknownst to us all, the sea prepared to take its repayment.

On the other side of the Atlantic the cold Arctic air from the north was charging headlong into the warm winds of the Caribbean and the opposing meteorological cultures whipped themselves into a ferocious hurricane. There were four ships caught beneath the howling winds and they barely lasted minutes. According to one report, the seas would have become so rough and the waves so formidable that sections of the ocean floor on the shallow banks would have probably been exposed from time to time. That would explain why one of the shipwrecks later recovered had a pulverized hull consistent with the damage that it would have suffered had it been dropped from a 150-foot crane onto the ground of an asphalt car park.

While all of that was happening Mrs Suhm was doubtless looking out of her window, watching proudly as her tall strong husband and her tall strong son worked happily together tending nets on the harbor and tuning the boat's engine.

Peter used to dream of being a fishermen like his dad and it was one his parents were keen for him to make reality. Back then, to a boy like Peter who had inherited his father's brains as well as his bulk, it was also sensible careers advice. His father wanted him to follow in his footsteps. His mother wanted him to emulate Simon-Peter from the Gospels, hoping that a new Messiah would one day use him as a rock to build their Church upon. Peter himself was just happy to do anything that would keep him close to his father and please his mother.

As I recall, even back then Edvard was intent on being a Viking. He would later be given a Viking helmet he would frequently wear to school and would often rub mud onto his face and tell people it was his beard. He also used to carry around a small sketchbook and pencil and was forever drawing Thor, or an axe or a longship, or Thor with an axe on a longship.

I won't tell you what I dreamed of when I was fourteen years old, sitting there watching Peter work, other than it was an intense, all-consuming dream that burned away all others within me, leaving such a focused desire that the dream became my obsession. Even at that tender age, my fixation with it – and the realization that no matter what I did, it could never come true – had begun to corrupt all hope within me.

Anyway. That day. As you will have noticed, I have an unusually distinct recollection of that particular day. Why? Because the monumental change in all of our lives that occurred just hours later acted as vinegar to pickle those memories and to this day I still dip back into them from time to time.

Old Mr Suhm was tinkering with the boat's engine and Peter was being as helpful as he could by passing tools. He always chose the wrong tool but his father always smiled and thanked Peter before replacing it with the correct one. As they worked, Old Mr Suhm taught Peter an ancient Norse shanty. Nearby, Edvard was sat on a bucket sketching and pretending not to listen, but his picture of Thor's hammer was eventually abandoned as he became lost in the song.

Do you know the words against,
The words against, the words against,
Do you know the words against the pain of heart, of mind and
*   body?*
Do you know the words that put,
The words that put, the words that put,
Do you know the words that put the water upon the fire?

Do you know the words that put,
The words that put, the words that put,
Do you know the words that put the restless sea to sleep?
These are the runes of our father, learned hanging from the tree.

As Old Mr Suhm delivered the line Peter's face contorted with concentration and he then repeated it back to the old man. Building up, line upon line, Peter learned the song over twenty minutes, until his father's smile cracked his weather-worn face like a fissure in granite.

"You've done it, boy."

I had been sitting with my legs dangling over the harbor wall, reading my school book and pretending not to listen, but had mastered the words and tune in less than half the time it had taken Peter. I suspect that Edvard got there before Peter too. However, we knew that Peter took great pleasure from these opportunities to learn from his father so neither Edvard nor I was going to join in the song and tarnish the perfection of their moment.

Mrs Suhm eventually arrived with a tub of food for the trip: a loaf of bread with a lump of butter, a fish pie, a kilo of cooked and oiled pasta, a dozen hard-boiled and shelled eggs, a bag of fruit and a firm, heavy cake. Old Mr Suhm and his partner were only planning a two-day/one-night trip but fishing is an activity that burns calories like few others. On some trips the pair of them would effectively eat one fish for every three they brought home.

By around three o'clock in the afternoon the boat was ready to leave. It was just a run-of-the-mill trip so there was no need for the Suhms to engage in any tearful goodbyes. Peter's mother didn't even kiss Old Mr Suhm; she was fussing over Peter at the moment he bid her goodbye and she simply waved him off without looking up. By ten past three the little gill-drifter was heading out into the sound and those of us left behind were going about our business as usual.

Meanwhile, across the Atlantic, winds of up to ninety knots were driving the waves up beyond eighty feet and, ironically, creating a seascape of peaks and troughs reminiscent of Norway's landscape of cliffs and fjords. The ferocity of the storm was as precedented as it was predicted and before long it succumbed to the inevitable draw of the Gulf Stream, was swept up into it and began its journey east.

6

I heard the news that the storm was heading toward Northern Europe on the television. There was a newsflash at around ten o'clock in the evening. I ran to tell my mother. As I re-told the words of the reporter she paled like charcoal on a barbecue.

"That was what my dream was telling me," she said quietly.

"What dream?"

"Last night, I had a dream. A nightmare. There was a woman, a banshee I think. She was rampaging through the town, throwing the folk to the cobbles. This is a bad omen!"

And though I could see the conviction in her eyes, she didn't do anything. Like so many of the superstitious folk in our town, then and now, she held fast to a fatalistic philosophy that absolved her of any responsibility to prevent the impending catastrophe. Blind faith in an unswerving destiny can rob you of any ambition and my mother was one of many victims of that criminal belief.

"It's in God's hands now," was all she said. "If it's going to happen, it's going to happen. There's nothing we can do. There's nothing that we can possibly do."

Of course there's something we can fucking do, I thought.

Old Mr Suhm had a VHF radio on his gill-drifter and some of the homes in Kragerø had them too. Edvard's home was one of them. Dressed in my nightshirt I ran to Peter's flat, grabbed his arm and, without explaining, dragged him with me to Edvard's door that I rapped upon loudly. I never told Peter what we were doing and he never asked. He just obediently followed me up the stairs.

Edvard answered the door in his briefs. I barged passed him and into his bedroom, dragging Peter by the arm and stood before the radio. "How does this thing work, Edvard?"

"Depends what you want to use it for."

"I need to speak to Peter's father. Right now. Show me how."

Edvard grumbled but set the radio to channel 16 and showed me how to call for Old Mr Suhm's boat. After a few minutes of calling a voice crackled back at us and an alternative channel was agreed upon.

"Who is that?" The voice was distant and unfamiliar. I rarely heard Old Mr Suhm's speaking voice and the only way I recognized him was by noting the hesitant tone that he shared with Peter. I could tell that he was keeping his voice down and assumed that the other crew member he was with was sleeping.

"Mr Suhm, it's Marta. I'm here with Peter."

"Marta? What's going on, is it your mother? Is it Peter? Is he hurt? Is Mrs Suhm okay?"

"No, Mr Suhm, he's fine, she's fine, we're all fine here in Kragerø. We're worried about you."

A brief pause followed.

"Why?"

"Because a massive storm is heading towards Norway across the Atlantic. They said so on the news." I looked across at Peter whose wide, sleepy face was beginning to register alarm. "We want you to come home."

A noise filled Edvard's bedroom that could have been static, but which could also have been Old Mr Suhm laughing.

"There's going to be no storm in Skagerrak tonight, Marta. You need not worry."

"There will be Mr Suhm. It's a hundred-year storm, they said"

"Marta, I know about that storm. It's all over the radio.

But you're forgetting I've been a fisherman all my life. If the storm was heading towards Skagerrak there would be signs by now and there are none. Storms blow over and they blow north and they blow south. I don't know where your storm is heading but I'll not be seeing it."

I wanted to remind Old Mr Suhm that while he might have been a fisherman for a long time he had never been a very good one. But that wouldn't have helped: fishermen pushing seventy don't like to be critically appraised on their knowledge of the sea by fourteen-year-old girls.

"Mr Suhm, please come home."

There was another pause.

"No Marta."

"Please sir."

"No. And that's the end of it." His voice had a forced certainty about it. It was an uncharacteristic and unconvincing tone coming from him, but I recognized its origins. It would have been both typical and convincing coming from the mouth of his wife.

"It's a calm night," he explained in his own voice. "And we're set to haul in a decent catch in the morning. While God is watching over us, we're staying out here."

I wasn't worried about my mother's dream. I wasn't worried about Old Mr Suhm being marked. I wasn't even greatly concerned for his well-being, with his dull brain and mangled fingers. I just didn't want Peter to lose his father.

I looked over at Peter now. His mouth was open which indicated his bewilderment, and his eyes were dancing between the radio and me which indicated his fear. Not for the first or last time, I was overwhelmed with the desire to wrap my arms around his head and hold him close. Not for the first or last time, I resisted the temptation.

Peter loved his parents but by that age even he had realized their view of the world was obscured by the twin obstacles of faith and ignorance. These vast monoliths dominated their panorama and blinded them to much of what the rest of the world could see. He looked to them for love and sustenance, while finding a curious friendship in Edvard and guidance and advice in me.

If only he had wanted more.

I handed Peter the handset.

"Peter, tell him to come home."

Peter shook his head.

"If he doesn't come home tonight, he will probably die," I persisted.

He shook his head again. It was a Suhm mantra to respect your elders and while I had no doubt he believed me, he was clearly torn between what he had been told he must do and what he knew he ought to do.

Old Mr Suhm would not stay on the radio for much longer. I swung my arm back and into his face with every ounce of my strength. Peter could have certainly blocked or avoided the slap if he wanted to, but he didn't.

I then grabbed his hair and pulled his head down to me, hissing into his ear. "Peter, you're going to speak calmly into that handset and ask your father to come home and if he refuses you're going to plead with him."

I suspect it was the determination in my eyes that caused him to pick up that handset.

"Papa."

"Peter?"

"Yes Papa. I want you to come home."

"No Peter and I'll have no more of this nonsense from you and your friends."

"Please Papa."

"No!"

I mouthed the word "plead" to him.

"Papa." At that point Peter's voice cracked. "I'm scared Papa. I don't want you to die. I don't want my mother to be a widow."

There was a long silence after which Old Mr Suhm spoke. "I have God watching over me."

"God has always watched over good men dying Papa."

"Well, if he decides that I must die, so be it."

"No Papa. God doesn't want you to die. That's why He's got me to plead with you to come home. God wanted you to be a father to me and He wants me to be a son to you. If you deny your son his father you turn your back on God."

I don't think Peter ever said anything more profound. After a long pause we heard Old Mr Suhm let out a long sigh.

"All right son. We'll come home. What time is it?"

"10.13 Mr Suhm." I spoke into the handset shaking in Peter's hand.

"Well, we're a good two hours from Kragerø. So expect us home at just gone midnight. Don't wait up."

He then shut his radio off and the three of us collapsed onto Edvard's bed. We had all found the experience shattering, both emotionally and physically, but I seemed to be the worst affected. I placed my head on the pillow and fell asleep instantly.

I woke up at eight o'clock the following morning in my own bed. Peter had carried me there and I hadn't even registered the movement. On awaking, I found my mother watching the events of the previous few hours unfold on television.

The storm had hit the coast of Norway just before midnight. It had been devastating. The sea was churned white from the tips of the waves to the very bed of the ocean. Seventeen Norwegian fishermen lost their lives in that storm. It was the worst storm to hit our shores for twenty-five years. The TV channels were competing to see which could find the graniest images of spray crashing into the biggest sea wall, the loudest wail from the ugliest wife and the most insincere condolence from the best-dressed politician.

I looked out of the living room window to see what devastation had been wreaked on the harbor.

None.

Old Mr Suhm had been right. The south of the country was

entirely unaffected. The storm was blown north and laid waste to the coast eight hundred miles from Kragerø and Skagerrak. In fact, it was a beautiful, sunny morning where Old Mr Suhm had been fishing, following a silent, calm evening with barely a ripple troubling the tranquil skin of the sea. The storm to the north had sucked all the meteorological energy out of Scandinavia to focus it on a small area up in the Arctic region, leaving it exceptionally calm in the straits that Old Mr Suhm and his partner would have been navigating the previous night. Had he been allowed to remain net-fishing in the Jutland straits that night Old Mr Suhm would have found it peaceful, pleasant and profitable.

But Old Mr Suhm's boat did not form part of the serene aspect I gazed out upon that morning. Old Mr Suhm did not enjoy a breakfast with his family when he awoke that morning. He did not say "I told you so" when next he saw me. In fact, he, his boat and his single crew member were never seen again.

In the six years that have passed since they left Kragerø there have been many theories as to what might have befallen them. There had been no storm where they had been fishing and there had been no storm between them and home. So what could have happened?

The more uncharitable among the townsfolk suggested they ran away from their wives. But any who knew Old Mr Suhm understood that his love for Mrs Suhm was pure and he would never have done that, certainly not leaving behind Peter too.

Did they get lost? Can you get lost in Skagerrak? Old Mr Suhm wasn't the sharpest hook on the line but on a calm and cloudless night those two old sea dogs were more likely to be eaten by a sea serpent than they were to lose themselves and drift off into the North Sea. So that left the theories they were killed by the Russians or Germans.

The Jutland straits are often used by vast Russian container ships transporting oil and other resources from the Black Sea westward. It is entirely possible that one of those leviathans ploughed straight through the gill-netter. If that happened there would have been no trace left of the little boat and even those on the deck of the container ship, such a great distance from the surface of the sea, might not have heard the crunch of steel against wood and then the muffled human shrieks emitted from the deck of the crumbling vessel. Even if the Russians did see or hear it happen they are unlikely to have ever reported it.

I'm going to blame the Germans though. One of the legacies that Skagerrak was left from the Battle of Jutland was the hundreds of mines that went down with the German navy. From time to time those antique incendiaries were known to bob to the surface and excite the Norwegian, Danish or Swedish coastguard. To this day they take delight in blowing the things up and I've heard stories about Swedish coastguards dragging them hundreds of miles into their national waters just so they can claim jurisdiction and detonate them.

Men and their explosions: I guess watching a bomb go off at sea in a burst of sound and spray is the quintessential ejaculation metaphor.

Of course, there was one other theory concerning the disappearance of Old Mr Suhm and his crewmate. One that was, without question, believed with the most fervor by a tall, proud woman with whom you are already familiar. It is less a theory though and more an absence of one. For Mrs Suhm maintains nothing untoward happened to her husband that night. "Old Mr Suhm is a fisherman and fishermen are often at sea for long stretches of time," she would say. As far as she was concerned, there was nothing unusual about her husband's long absence. He would be back one day with a long beard and boat full of fish. He'd get a tongue-lashing, but it would be nice to finally have him home.

Six years on and Mrs Suhm continues to lay out a fresh set of clothes on a chair in the corner of her bedroom. All the meals she prepares include a man-sized portion to be later thrown away by The Exorcist, formerly known as Peter, or snaffled off into a box to be devoured by Bolverk, formerly known as Edvard. And six years after her husband left the harbor without her saying a proper goodbye, Mrs Suhm still gets excited when a boat appears on the horizon and heads into port.

For the young Peter and Edvard, I think that event was a first glimpse of black within their otherwise colorful Norwegian lives. For my part, I had already stared into the void far earlier, mainly thanks to the man who had accompanied Old Mr Suhm into the great unknown, never to return.

A younger man than the captain, darker of temper, who left behind an arguably relieved wife and a fourteen-year old daughter called Marta.

I didn't know my father particularly well and those parts of him I did know I didn't much care for.

I didn't miss him when he was gone.

7

Having failed to convince his mother he was a Satanist, The Exorcist was in the midst of an existential turmoil. He had let Bolverk, Decadence and I convince him he was a Satanist, so how could he be anything but a Satanist? He was the drummer in Baphomet's Agony for crying out loud! He was at the forefront of a movement hell-bent on primeval anarchy, setting fire to the world, destroying every one of its institutions and then watching as dark, violent and tribal regimes arose out of the ashes.

Baphomet's Agony was to be the catalyst for chaos. On that Bolverk, Decadence, Suffer and I were agreed. It was the only thing we did all agree on.

We would focus on the gradual and careful destruction of music, as that word was currently understood. First corrupting the youth of Kragerø, of Telemark, of Norway. Then of Europe and then the world. With the backing of our legions of empowered and amoral youth, we were confident we could level all existing political, economic, religious and social structures.

Why did we want to do this? You tell me. We never really questioned it. Perhaps it was simply part of the process of descent? Perhaps it was a potent blend of trauma and rebelliousness, bottled in the dull jar of the picture-perfect town we were trapped in. Perhaps we saw through the dull façade of lies around us and we wanted to throw stones at it, crack it, break free and show everyone what the world was really like?

There are so many reasons we could give. The band never really decided on one.

The Exorcist though had always been unsure of what we were doing and his place in it. A lifetime of Christian indoctrination takes time to overcome, I guess. The relentless drip of its propaganda had gouged huge craters in his brain and although Bolverk, Decadence and I had been working hard to fill those craters with our ideas, they hadn't yet sunk fully into his consciousness.

So, yes, back to that bright summer morning, after our meeting with his mother. The Exorcist was having a crisis.

We skipped down the stairs of his flat and out onto Kragerø harbor. It was short sleeves weather, yet he pulled down the long sleeves of his T-shirt and tenderly stroked his inverted/upright crucifix tattoo through the black cotton. He was a foot and a half taller than me, but hunched and downcast he would have looked like a small child ambling, reluctantly, alongside a dominant older sibling. The Exorcist looked upon everyone that he knew as a dominant older sibling.

"Do you worship Satan, Marta?" he asked.

I knew that's what had been on his mind. "No."

"Oh, really?" He seemed confused and I couldn't blame him after everything I'd told him to try to convince him into Satanism. "But… but you believe in him, right?"

"Again, no."

"Wait. What? Aren't you a Satanist?"

For The Exorcist, confusion was palpable, like gravity, and it exerted a physical force on his body. With each of my answers I was basically attaching lead weights to hooks skewered through his nipples. He could barely walk under the strain of it all.

"Look, Peter," I began. I knew the logic behind their stage names. Hell, I was charged with enforcing their use. But one-on-one, with someone I had known for 90% of my life, it felt like my words would reach him more easily by addressing him properly. "I believe in almost nothing. I can recall much of what has happened to me in the past and I can see what is happening to me now but that's about the only knowledge that I trust. Everything else that is knowable or believable comes from other people or my own imagination. I don't trust other people and I sincerely hope, for everyone's sake, that what I imagine isn't true. Perhaps there's a God, perhaps there's a Satan but I've never seen either of them so they're as real to me as Santa Claus or Ecuador."

"Ecuador?"

"Yes Ecuador. Ecuador may well exist, but I have never seen it so I'm reserving judgment. Anyhow, because I don't believe in anything, and because I hate most of what I do know, people have called me a Satanist and that has suited me fine. It works for what we need to do. Does that answer your question?"

"I don't know. Does it?" He kept quiet for the remainder of our journey through the back streets of Kragerø.

The pearl of coastal towns, so the artist Edvard Munch, a frequent summer resident here, described Kragerø. His Scream might even have been cried out right there on the harbor. But what did he mean by calling the town a pearl? He could have called it any number of precious stones.

Why a pearl?

A pearl forms where a parasite infiltrates a mollusk and, in order to protect itself, the invertebrate covers the intruder in layers and layers of gunk that harden into the creamy gem that we treasure so. Is that how he regarded Kragerø? As a pretty gem on the Telemark coast that harbors some brooding pestilence at its core?

If so, he knew what he was talking about. Because that is exactly what it is today.

Munch himself was a violent drunk who teetered on the brink of madness throughout his life and, let's face it, The Scream is much darker than the fruit-in-a-bowl and bloated dignitaries that adorn most gallery walls. It would be fitting if

The Scream was set in Kragerø. The town has this impossibly pretty façade but behind its closed doors, in the cellars of those brightly-colored cottages and off-season in those boutique hotels, we locals scream out in twisted anguish and indulge our nasty little parasite.

It should come as no surprise to you to learn that over the last few years, just out of shot of the photos in the tourist brochures, Kragerø has allowed a Satanic black metal sub-culture to fester and thrive among its youth. In bedrooms, in one or two bars and in a subterranean record store (more of which you will learn shortly) you will find us: Kragerø's gatherings of the disillusioned. Its Hermetic orders, demon-charmers, Marxists, anarchists, covens, devil-worshipping cults, and drug-crazed misanthropes.

My people.

And the epicenter of the town's depravity? A collection of rooms that over two short years had become such a focus of our pain, lust, disgust and hatred that its connection with the surface world had been all but severed. Two years of determined effort to convene with all that is base and putrid had drilled us down deep into the infected bowels of the earth and worn away the boundaries between this world and another much less wholesome one. It had brought that particular location closer to Hell than anywhere else on earth.

The Exorcist and I were on our way there now. Which meant a necessary, but tedious, journey through the town and its unceasing color, variety and chocolate-box architecture.

To most of my countrymen the Norwegian summer is magnificent. Even down here in the south the winters are long and harsh, but they eventually yield to the spring and then the "glorious" summer. The light, the color, the sun, the moon, the wind and the smell: they all conspire to inflict on the newcomer nothing short of a sensual assault.

But like everything else about Kragerø and Norway, The Exorcist and I took it for granted. It was another beautiful day in our beautiful town full of beautiful, well-educated people with their comfortable standards of living. We were rushing through it all to get to an underground shop where we could spend the day listening to oppressive music surrounded by monochrome kids who, like us, use the darkness of the black metal scene to rebel against the security, color and affluence that generations of Norwegians had striven to provide us in this Nordic Eden.

We walked along the quay and The Exorcist nodded to the men on the dock as they hauled fish off small boats and packed them into ice boxes. The quayside was beginning to bustle with tourists looking to breakfast at the numerous cafes that jostled for space with the bars on the cobbles. For most of the year those cafes sold hearty meals that fueled the fishermen and provided them a layer of blubber that would protect and nourish them at sea. During the summer months the fat-imbued fare was replaced by delicate pastries for a more refined clientele and the fishermen had to rely on their wives and mothers for sustenance.

It was the same with the bars: for half of the year they ebbed-and-flowed with the boom-and-bust trade generated by men that would often spend weeks at sea only to blow the lion's share of their pay on a single night of drunken debauchery. Then at the beginning of the tourist season the walls would be painted and the top layer of beer-soaked wood would be planed off the tables. The whores would vacate the upstairs rooms and since childhood I always knew that spring was approaching when the smell of burning bedsheets filled the air.

During the summer months those girls who spent most of the year being ground into mattresses by drink-soaked, foul-smelling men would metamorphose into waitresses and serve cappuccinos and cocktails to customers who did not leave their torsos stained with blood and smelling of fish guts. I knew a lot of those girls. Lithe in body but dead of eye, they usually came from the Baltic, spent a couple of years in Kragerø and then headed home with a dowry to embark upon a career in motherhood. I knew that many of them much preferred those months spent wiping semen off their thighs to those spent wiping rings of mineral water off tables. The contempt of their customers that was evident in the latter was far more striking than it was in the former.

We left the port and wound our way upwards through the multicolored terraced streets. The buildings on every street in Kragerø are painted in vivid hues from a palette of yellow, red, green and blue and each is finished with the same triangular, front-facing roof with its high, sharp apex. It is another example of the delightful backdrop that The Exorcist and I let wash over us. To us the overall effect of the luminous street decoration was one of vibrant monotony: exciting counters placed on a board game that we had no desire to play.

We arrived at our destination to find it closed. No surprises there. It was highly unusual for any of us to surface until late in the afternoon. To expect Decadence, an almost exclusively nocturnal creature, to have been awake at nine o'clock in the morning was really pushing at the boundaries of science. But as I searched my pockets, I realized I'd forgotten my keys.

"Shit," I said, looking to The Exorcist and regretting the fact that I had never trusted him with a set of keys. "Shit. Shit. Shit."

A loud, clipped whistle split the air. Down the street, sitting outside a closed bar next to his motorcycle, Bolverk was smoking a cigarette. To me, he would always look out of place anywhere other than on a Viking warship with an axe in his hand. Sitting there, pretending to look casual in the 21st Century, he looked as natural as a hippo in a nail salon.

Bolverk secreted his comic in the pocket of his black leather jacket and held out a fist as we approached. The Exorcist met his knuckles with his own and Bolverk greeted me with a small nod: not an easy gesture to pull off when your chin appears to merge seamlessly into your chest.

He shifted a few inches along the bench and The Exorcist sat down close next to him. I loitered by his bike and scoured the adjacent streets in search of Decadence. I didn't want his company, I wanted his keys. If Bolverk was sitting outside it meant he'd not brought his either. In the meantime, all that fresh air was unsettling me. I needed to get indoors.

"Hey, Bolverk," said the Exorcist. "All this Satan stuff: are you comfortable with it?"

"Huh," Bolverk said. "Yes, I guess. Aren't you?"

"I mean... yes. Maybe. The clothes and the symbols are cool and who's going to take a Norwegian black metal group seriously unless they're Satanists, right? I get that it's good for us to be known that way. And yeah, Decadence draws from all that stuff when he writes the songs. But it's hard throwing away twenty years of Christian upbringing, you know?"

Bolverk had never been a Christian but he had a degree of empathy and a much kinder disposition than me, so he was better equipped than I to help The Exorcist confront his tormentor and shout "Get thee behind me Jesus!"

"Then don't," Bolverk said.

"Don't? Don't what?"

Bolverk finished his cigarette. "Don't give it all up. Just absorb it into your new point of view. Don't think you have to build little shrines to Satan and offer him sacrifices like Decadence does. You're not expected to replace God and Jesus with Satan and his minions. You don't have to turn yourself into a hate-fueled monster like Suffer and be forever committing mindless acts of violence on all and sundry. There are no rules to what we're doing. That's the point – Satan hates rules! If he had any principles that would be the second on his list after 'Satan abhors principles'."

Bolverk chuckled to himself which made a sound like an iron door being hauled over an uneven stone floor.

"So you do believe in Satan then?"

"No." Bolverk answered using the third person as he usually

did. "Bolverk believes in Odin, Thor, Loki, Freya, Balder and the rest of the Norse Gods. He's Ásatrú which means he's just a good old-fashioned pagan when it comes down to it. His faith harks back to our ancient heathen past, and he celebrates the strength and dignity of the warrior."

The Exorcist's confusion reached new depths as he looked from Bolverk to me and back again.

"So if *you* don't believe in Satan either, why do you let everyone call you a Satanist?"

"Bolverk doesn't mind being called a Satanist. Of all the jokers in the Bible, Satan seems the most Scandinavian of them all. He's a bit of Odin, a bit of Thor and a lot of Loki. Lucifer – Lukifer – Lokifer. You don't have to work too hard to connect Satan to the Norse Gods."

"Let me get this straight, you don't believe in Satan but you're happy for people to call you a Satanist because you can adapt Satanism to fit into all your heathen stuff. But surely if you can bend Satan to fit into your heathen ideas you could just as easily bend God, Jesus, Noah and Moses into place too?"

"Bolverk can't do that because he fucking hates the Church of Norway! He hates it for destroying countless generations of his heritage and replacing it with a religion that was formed fucking thousands of miles away. How can principles and cultures derived from tribes of desert people be relevant to the people of Scandinavia?"

I'd heard all of this before. It tripped off Bolverk's tongue like his date of birth. I knew we'd be getting Snorri Sturluson and The Iliad before long.

"There's been a conspiracy against the Norse faith for hundreds of years. People across Europe are taught to be familiar with the Greek and Roman Pantheon but our own much richer and relevant cosmology is pretty-much ignored. Why don't the Germans and British know Snorri Sturluson and the story of The Death of Balder as well as they do Homer and The Iliad?"

There it is. Bolverk was building up to his climax. I braced myself for the inevitable Church-burning.

"You know why the Saxons know nothing of the Norse faith? It's because of a deliberate plot to suppress the traditional beliefs of the Norse in favor of an inferior import: a Middle Eastern religion that got hijacked by a bunch of effete Italians who then spread a corrupted version across the world like a virus – a debilitating virus that leaves its victims in a state of ignorance and subservience."

I was surprised at the absence of any Church-burning. Whenever I had heard that speech before it concluded with the phrase: "a blazing steeple is a beacon to our heathen brothers!" I suspect Bolverk just forgot that bit. I bet he kicked himself later in the day when he realized that he'd left it out.

"I don't know Edvard, I really don't." The Exorcist was still lost. He was like a small child separated from his parents in a department store; a small child who was six foot six with a massive beard and tattoos. "It's easy to be a Satanist when you hate Christianity, but I'm not sure that I do. In fact, I'm beginning to think that it might be an important part of who I am."

Bolverk skillfully rolled a cigarette in his fingers and continued without looking up.

"Then just lie about it. You look more like a Satanist than the rest of us. Suffer looks like an aborted fetus, Decadence looks like just he's stepped off the set of a shampoo commercial and Bolverk looks like... like..." He clicked his fingers in an attempt to conjure an appropriate image. Such was the power in his hand that the percussive effect was almost as loud as The Exorcist's high-hat.

"...like part of the structure that holds up a bridge?" I said, enjoying being helpful. "Or like a pumpkin on a tree stump? Or a fat man's ass with a face drawn on it?"

Bolverk shrugged then continued talking to The Exorcist.

"The point is you're the only one in the band that actually

looks the part. To the average Norwegian parent with their comfortable house in the Oslo suburbs you're the hairy- oversized- tattooed- devil-worshipping-monster they've read about in the papers and who's hell-bent on eating their children. Provided you keep behind your drums and let the rest of us do the talking, you could be decorating fairy cakes back there and the rest of the world would still see you as evil incarnate."

"But could I live the rest of my life pretending to be something I'm not?"

"We both know that won't be a problem, Peter," Bolverk said.

The Exorcist's cheeks flushed. He glanced away from Bolverk, though I saw a slight smile as he turned his gaze to the ground.

"What's that in your beard?" Bolverk asked as he got up from his seat, walked over to The Exorcist and brought his hands slowly to his face. Then he grabbed his beard with both hands and pulled his head down, twisting it into a headlock.

"OK Altar Boy. Let's start this conversation over."

The Exorcist squirmed but knew from years of experience his strength was no match for that of his stocky friend, even when he was messing around like he was now. The more he wriggled the tighter Bolverk squeezed his head.

"Do you embrace Satan and all his little goblins?"

"No!"

"Pledge your allegiance to the goblins!"

"No!"

"The goblins man! Do it for the goblins!"

"Get a room boys."

A new voice had made itself heard. It was a voice that Bolverk and The Exorcist had often heard sing and shout and argue and laugh. It was a voice that I had also heard weep, scream out in orgasm and whisper tender entreaties for a love that I had never returned.

8

Bolverk released The Exorcist and turned to face the tall youth who had spoken and who was almost upon us. His clean, mathematically-straight hair fell over the back of his black leather jacket and continued half way down his back. The yellow, gold and white strands reflected the sun like quartz.

He had his arm around a thin, pale girl whom he carefully positioned so we could take in her proportions unobstructed.

"Snorre!" Bolverk raised both arms in an elaborate welcoming gesture to the guitarist.

"Call him Decadence," I barked. It was important to me that, at the very least in the presence of outsiders, we respected the band's naming convention.

"Decadence then. Praise be to Odin, Thor and the Norse Pantheon!"

Decadence rolled his eyes. "Bolverk, I didn't even praise *her* this morning after I had defiled her in unspeakable ways right the way through the night, so I'm certainly not going to offer any praise to your imaginary friends."

The girl wore black lipstick and eye make-up to match her straight, dyed black hair. If you wiped away the make-up there might not have been a face underneath it. Her features were not unpleasant, just devoid of character, and I suppose what is there not to like in the blank page of a book?

But Decadence was far prettier.

He slept with a lot of girls. In fact, sex with him was a "must-do" in many a black metal guide for young women. Girls would travel from all over Europe to stay in Kragerø for a few days knowing that in the course of a five-day visit they had a good chance at sleeping with him at least once. He even had a website (he was the only one in the band that did) where girls could get preferential rates at many of the local hotels. Decadence took a percentage of the click-through revenue, so everyone was a winner. He spent more days a week in Kragerø hotel rooms than he did in his underground crypt. His penis was a vital part of the local tourist economy. It certainly saw more footfall than the town's museum.

Given his singular looks these transient partners were always going to be less attractive than him – and this skinny bitch was no exception. I wondered how much money he had taken from this one. Often girls would be as quick to open their wallets to him as they were their legs but whether the cash was taken consensually or surreptitiously they never seemed to object. He averaged a few hundred Krone from each of his conquests; in addition to the revenue share from the hotels and sundries like drinks, meals and drugs.

The girl nuzzled him, pretending to hide her face from us. It was an ostentatious display of false modesty. I'm not going to say that the gesture caused me to hate her: hate is too strong word for it. I simply, and immediately, consigned her to the ranks of the pathetic, needy and irrelevant.

"So, my dark Angel." Decadence was talking to the girl but looking at me and Bolverk. "Let me introduce you to two of the most high-ranking Adepts within my Satanic Order. Here we have Frater Bolverk: our bass-wielding Norse warrior so beloved of the dice-throwing, war-gaming and bedroom-dwelling among our fanbase."

Bolverk raised an eyebrow but didn't object.

"And over here we have Madame Marta: Theosophist extraordinaire and Grand Mistress of Norway's Chapter of the Blavatsky-Sprengel School of Diabolism."

His whore looked me over in that critical manner that skinny girls so often adopt. I can tolerate men looking at my tits but when skinny girls do it with that air of evolutionary superiority it makes me want to take the wrong end of a hammer to them. Or any end.

I don't get on very well with skinny girls. It's my firm belief that if you shed lots of weight it will come off your brain and personality before it comes off your thighs.

The Exorcist sat up straight and rubbed his neck from the headlock Bolverk had pinned him in. Decadence glanced down with barely concealed contempt. The same he always reserved for Peter.

"Oh there's him too," he added, as though it was an afterthought. "I'd forgotten about Peter."

"The Exorcist," I said.

"Right, right. And what the hell's wrong with him now? He's got a face like a slapped arse."

"A faith wobble," I said. "It's been a difficult morning and in a moment of weakness he might have just sold his soul to Christ. Is there any chance that you could ask Satan to perform him a miracle to restore his faith?"

"Huh. Okay then, listen up Peter –"

"He's The Exorcist you cock-sucking prick," I interrupted again. "Fucking call him *The Exorcist*!"

I have always liked that image: a cock-sucking prick. I picture a circular phallus with a head that goes down on its own root. It reminds me of the sea serpent that Bolverk bangs on about all the time – the one that encircles the world and bites on its own tail. One day I'm going to get a ring made that depicts a cock-sucking prick. Perhaps it will be the icon around which I will build my religion.

"All right Marta, fine. Just chill out will you? *The Exorcist…*" Decadence eyed me warily, "…think of it like this. Is your God a forgiving God? Yes, of course He is. In fact, your God goes fucking mental over a repentant sinner doesn't he? More than anyone else."

"I guess."

"While the Devil, Satan, he resides here on Earth doesn't he? And if you give yourself over to Him on Earth, He will reward you with Earthly riches, right?"

"Yes, sure."

"There's your answer! While you're alive here on Earth screw yourself stupid and debauch yourself to the point of self-induced insanity. Provided that you remember to renounce Satan on your deathbed and seek mercy from your ever-forgiving God you'll be able to jump the queue to Heaven ahead of all the schmucks that have lived righteous, pious and boring lives." Decadence looked very pleased with himself. "It strikes me that if you accept God is forgiving, it's illogical to pander to him now. You're much better off paying your dues to the Devil, having an exciting, no-holds barred life, and saving God the bother of forgiving you all this time until you actually need his forgiveness. All good now, The Exorcist? Great, let's go!"

He pushed his girl away and tapped her backside, allowing his hand to linger on the pocket of her black jeans. "Off you go my dark Angel." He only called girls dark Angels when he'd forgotten their names. "Maybe I'll see you at the next gig."

The girl took hold of the hand that hadn't quite been removed from her rear and raised Decadence's fingers to her mouth. "I thought I could maybe hang out with you in the shop."

"You can if you want. But it's going to be busy so don't expect me to talk to you much today."

She took two of his fingers into her mouth and began to re-enact events that had no doubt taken place the night before. Which bothered me more than I thought it would. I got up and moved closer to Decadence, stared him in the eye and slid my hand indulgently into the tight open corner of his jeans pocket. It wasn't an easy thing to do: his jeans are tight at the best of times and with the pressure building gradually from the inside I suspect that getting my hand in there involved more friction than the two of them enjoyed from any of their no-doubt varied unions over the preceding hours.

The girl knew she couldn't beat me. She had his fingers in her mouth, right down to the knuckle, but his eyes were fixed on mine. With the tip of my tongue between my teeth, I pushed my hand deeper into the balmy cotton of his jeans. As I brushed my fingers ever so firmly against the warmed shaft I had been seeking, I gazed intently at him. I could almost see the memories of our former intimacies playing in low-resolution across his retinae.

Then, in one quick, violent move I wrenched the keys to the store out of his pocket. His yelp was loud, but it was soon buried beneath the satisfying shriek the girl let out as, in reflex, he ripped his hand from her mouth and almost took her tongue-stud with it.

I didn't see the look on either of their faces. I was too busy striding back down the road to the shop, waving the keys in the air.

9

The keys I snatched from the pocket of Decadence unlocked a door. It would have been an unassuming metal door had it not been for the sigil cleverly etched into the rust that covered its surface. Stenciled into the very fabric of the metal was that Norse serpent that bites down on its own tail. Encircled within it was the head of a goat contorted in pain. The source of its misery was an inverted pentagram that had somehow found its way inside the skull of the goat and then contrived to burst out of various parts of its face. It was Baphomet and he was in agony.

The door opened onto what looked like a treacherous flight of dilapidated metal stairs over which hung a buzzing and flickering neon legend:

Abandon hope all ye who enter here.

Except the stairs were perfectly sound and the electrics worked fine. We had spent a lot of money creating an impression of peril and decrepitude. The lighting had been cleverly designed too, so from street level the staircase appeared to descend into an infinite gloom.

Where did the stairs lead? We didn't ever refer to it by any name. When I come to think of it, we never needed to. It was the only place there was so it was just understood that that's where we would have been and where you could have found us.

It began life as a record shop that also sold a few occult books and black metal T-shirts, but over the years the numerous aisles, alcoves and claustrophobic passages had been filled by us with an eclectic mix of goods. Clothing was the first and most obvious product range we expanded into, usually involving a combination of leather, PVC, rubber, string, industrial metal fastenings, zips, crucifixes, pentagrams... yeah, you get the idea.

The clothing section then merged seamlessly into bondage and fetishist accessories, before eventually leading to dildos, vibrators and synthetic vaginas. Adjacent to the sex racks you would, naturally, find the porn section.

Jewelry and drug paraphernalia (along with the drugs themselves, if you asked the right questions) could also be purchased down there. And, for a while, we also had a tattoo parlor in one of the alcoves, but it didn't last long – the health and safety regulations and the visits from council officials in cheap suits just didn't fit our carefully curated aesthetic.

I flicked on the lights. What natural light did once penetrate that dungeon had long since been banished and replaced with bulbs designed to flicker unnervingly and the occasional fluorescent tube projecting hellish shades of crimson into the many corners of the booths and alcoves. I went straight to the "Den" to make coffee.

The network of tunnels we occupied honeycombed beneath a large swathe of the town. We could never figure out why this elaborate complex of open spaces and passages existed or who was their legal owner. Above it was a semi-occupied warehouse belonging to a pension fund that knew but cared nothing for what we did beneath ground. So, whenever we needed more space, either for the shop or for the private quarters where Decadence lived, we simply opened up a wall, buttressed the ceiling and expanded. The Den was the largest space we had and was big enough to accommodate tables, chairs, sofas, a bar and even a small stage for the occasional live performance (music, performance art, sex... whatever took your fancy).

I use the term "we" here but in the main I mean "I".

I conceived the sigil on the door, I commissioned the staircase, I expanded the goods from records to clothing, to sex toys to filth, and I arranged for the regular expansions of our Kragerø netherworld. Decadence chose to introduce a tattoo parlor and, to give him credit, it did prove to be viable as a business. But I was the one who decided to move it to separate premises, where it now thrives without compromising our diabolic integrity with its attendant bureaucracy.

Looking back I'm proud of what we achieved. In less than three years we had created an underground culture beyond reproach in terms of its credibility while being beyond compare in terms of its profitability. Everything we sold was ludicrously overpriced but the kids would fall over themselves to buy it. They would travel down from Oslo and from all over Norway to just soak up the atmosphere and buy stuff they had calculated would justify the largest branded carrier bag for the smallest outlay. It was precisely for that reason that the money we made from old vinyl too scratched to be played made up a significant part of our annual profits.

I was pivotal to the cause, but I had to do all of that invisibly. The black metal world is famously sexist. It's also famously racist, ageist and intolerant of just about everything that distinguishes one person from the next. That's misanthropy for you.

The sexism though: that was a problem for me as the manager. A black metal band or hang-out run by a woman could never be successful. So I hid in the background, manipulating the limbs of Decadence, Bolverk and The Exorcist as if they were my black metal marionettes – which, of course, they were. I can't say the same of Suffer. He did as he pleased and answered to no one.

For the most part, I used Decadence to front my activities. He was widely regarded as the business guru behind the success of the shop and the band but, although he was smart enough, he was incapable of setting aside his gratification to actually do any work. I acted in his name and paid myself generously for my efforts. None of the band complained. They would have been nothing without me.

As I brewed the coffee in the Den, The Exorcist, Bolverk, Decadence and his girl arrived and draped themselves over the furniture.

"Could you remind Bolverk why he's up at this ungodly hour?" Bolverk asked.

"We're supposed to be Satanists," Decadence said. "All of our hours should be ungodly."

"Then replace the word 'ungodly' with 'early' and answer the fucking question."

"As usual you're all here to help me help you," I said. "The staff are all a bit jittery about the threats they've heard Oslo Iron have made against us. Those pricks have never liked us and the Oslo gig was the final straw. Apparently they're going to come down here, smash the place up and kick the crap out of you all."

"Is that all? Bolverk could do with the exercise!"

Oslo Iron never liked Baphomet's Agony from the start. Like all ignorant peasants they were fundamentally opposed to change. We were taking black metal some place new and they were dead-set on keeping it precisely where it always had been. They especially disliked Decadence and Suffer. I suspected with Decadence it was because of his confusing beauty, stirring a homoerotic confusion among their ranks that they refused to confront. They didn't like Suffer because he was a Sámi. They saw him as a savage Lapp polluting the Nordic purity of black metal with his "Eskimo filth" (as I'd heard them refer to him). And after the pasting he gave them at the Oslo gig, he hadn't exactly endeared himself to them.

"Is Suffer supposed to be coming here this morning?" The Exorcist asked.

Bolverk lay on his back on the sofa, staring at the ceiling. He snorted. "Do you think there's much chance of that vampire doing anything before sunset?"

"Actually, he's in Court this morning," I said. "On that assault charge for the tourists."

A silence followed in which I suspect that we all revisited the memory of Suffer's unprovoked attack on the poorly-dressed couple. It all happened shortly after Suffer told us that he had decided to kill "an innocent".

"The slaughter of an innocent is the most heinous crime against God and man of which I can conceive. Unless I am prepared to make that commitment to evil I cannot fulfil my true destiny." I think those were his precise words. And then, on cue, as if we had stumbled onto the set of a Hollywood farce, an obnoxious, white American couple materialized behind us.

It was The Exorcist who held Suffer back from stamping on the unconscious woman's face after the beating the singer had inflicted on them.

"Is he going to jail for good this time, do you think?" Bolverk asked, not sounding very hopeful. "He gives us eternal hassle, Suffer does."

"There are some in this band who are replaceable," Decadence mused. "And there are some who are not. Suffer gives us a danger and demonic charisma we couldn't get from anyone else. Besides, someone needs to keep Marta occupied in the bedroom or she might come after one of us!"

I didn't look up as I spoke. "Not all of us measure their self-esteem each week by calculating the amount of skank they've fucked. And no, I don't think he'll go to jail. I think he'll get let off. It's his first time before this particular Judge which means that the sob-story about his folks leaving their Sámi tribe for the south will be new to them."

That was all true. Middle class Norwegians can't help but feel guilty about a kid raised by alcoholics forced out of their tribal homes to build a power station that now fuels their television sets.

"Even when he is very clearly a fucking psychopath?" Bolverk asked.

"*Especially* when he is very clearly a fucking psychopath."

Decadence looked at me. "Whether he gets off or not, he's not here now. What are we going to do if Oslo Iron turn up? There are at least thirty of them, give or take the few who die of old age each year."

"I'm having a panic alarm installed in half an hour," I said. "This was just a heads up. None of you need to stay unless you want to. You could go into the Crypt and get some practice done if you want. The Bergen gig is just a day away and we all know there is a record deal on the horizon. Put on a performance again and it might just seal it. But... you know... come running if I sound the alarm."

The Crypt was within the inner sanctum of our Hades, within the space where Decadence lived. It was accessed through a locked door in the Den and was a multi-purpose space used interchangeably as a rehearsal room, recording studio, crash-pad, Satanic temple and love-nest. In contrast to those of the shop, the walls of the Crypt were painted red with black fittings and it was decorated with the spoils the band had plundered from its numerous raids on local churches and graveyards. Things like statues, crucifixes and even an ornate gold tabernacle nestled amongst headstones and human remains, all arranged in a seemingly random fashion around the room like an undiscovered Pharaoh's tomb.

Decadence and I had taken great care in our curation to produce the optimum dramatic effect but in a way that made it difficult for the rest of the band to notice that items moved in and out of the collection with a degree of fluidity. Decadence and I were known to frequent the blacker parts of Oslo's black market.

I finished my coffee and began getting everything ready for what promised to be a brisk day of trade. Since the Oslo gig takings had been up and with Bergen the following day – the gig which could finally cement our record deal – I needed to capitalize on the interest that was snowballing around the band.

By midday the shop was busy. The Exorcist had helped me with chores, Bolverk had smoked cigarettes and slept in the Crypt, and Decadence spent his time chatting to groups of girls that congregated in the Den. The girl with whom Decadence had spent the previous night lasted until about eleven o'clock. She stormed out when he asked her for a pen so he could write down the phone number of another girl.

We always sold a shitload of porn, but the sex and smut aisles had been unusually active over the preceding week: the unseasonably hot weather had apparently been keeping everyone frisky. Just before lunch I took a clipboard and went to investigate what had been selling. As I had predicted, DVDs had been flying off the anal shelves like shit from a well-oiled asshole.

It wasn't long before Decadence joined me, mischief curling up the corners of his mouth.

"I was touched by your display of jealousy this morning, Marta. With that girl. It turned me all the way on and I'm still feeling the after-effects of a crotch burn. Want to soothe it?"

I barged past him towards the sex aids. "Fuck off, Snorre, and don't flatter yourself. I never give you a second thought."

"You know I still often think of you," he said, following me. "Normally when I'm with other girls. I imagine your face on their bodies." He looked around quickly to check we weren't being overheard and then, turning his back to the rest of the shop so that only I could see his face, he lowered his voice. "It needn't be like this, Marta. We could get back together any time you want. If you want it to be our little secret, then nobody else need know."

There was something in his change of tone that took the edge off my resentment. I couldn't help it. I smiled up to him, into that strong, smooth face with its pale eyes twinkling at me like Swarovski crystals. I wondered if anyone else had ever declined his advances. I suspect not.

"You and I finished a long time ago, Snorre."

His smile changed a fraction. "It wasn't that long ago was it? I don't need that good a memory to remember the night of the Oslo gig."

Oh. I'd forgotten about that.

"Look, that was just by way of a reward for a good gig, Snorre, a little bonus payment. Don't read anything more into it and don't imagine it's going to happen again."

"Really? Well then. I wonder what Ailo would say if I mentioned it to him?"

I kept my smile in place under the threat of being ratted out. Put the clipboard down on a shelf and slowly raised a hand to Decadence's face. I cradled his strong jaw and then stroked my fingers through his soft hair. He half closed his eyes and gently pushed his face into my palm.

"Do you really think you can play a game like this with me and win?" I continued to caress his cheek. "You've already failed twice. Once because you're assuming Ailo would get angry with me if he found out what happened between us last week. The truth is that he wouldn't give a shit if you told him. He wouldn't give a shit if he discovered I'd dug up his dead Dad and fucked him."

I haven't, in case you're wondering.

I continued, "You've also failed because if you're going to blackmail somebody you need to be confident they haven't got any leverage they can use against you. In my case I know your deepest, darkest secrets better than you do."

"I doubt that," Decadence said, his eyes still closed, savoring my caress.

At that point I pulled his head down gently towards mine. We were so close I could smell his skin.

"I know all about the drum machine you bought last month and keep hidden under your bed," I said. "I also know about the vocal coaching you have every Tuesday afternoon. Uh-huh, that's right. Now *there* are two things the rest of the band would be very interested to hear about don't you think?"

Those eyes of his opened and then widened with astonishment, "How did you know about that?"

I continued smiling, brushing my nose sensually against his and allowing my lips the lightest and most delicate of contact with his.

"There's nothing you say or do that I don't know about, Snorre. In fact, there's nothing you say or do that I don't make you say or do. I own you so completely that if you ever tried to sell your soul to the Devil you'd find there's nothing there to give him, except perhaps a receipt with my name on it."

I checked nobody was looking and then yanked his head towards mine and enveloped his mouth with my own. I spun my tongue in a quick half-moon circuit behind his front teeth and then, as I pulled away, I punched him hard in the stomach.

He doubled over and leant for support on the inflatable-doll shelf while I sauntered off to check on the stock of vaginal jewelry.

10

Was Decadence always such a vain and promiscuous cock-sucking prick? No, I don't think he was. It took me time to shape him into what he eventually became. Have I told you how we first met him? No?

It was the first day of school term when we were all fifteen. There was a new form teacher that year called Miss Tveitan, a mouse with a constitution so fragile it was like she was made from crepe paper. As a consequence, the boys' natural tendency to torment their teacher was tempered by a pity for her physical and emotional weakness and they neither respected nor resented her.

I found Miss Tveitan pathetic. Years later, I persuaded Decadence to fuck her one Christmas Eve. He claims that she hummed carols while he took her from behind and brayed like a horse when she came. It was the trophy fuck of which he was the most proud (until recently that is when on consecutive nights he seduced the daughter and then the wife of a Baptist minister visiting Norway from Ohio).

"Ladies and gentlemen," Miss Tveitan said in her feeble voice that would have made barely any impact upon the rowdy, excitable classroom had she not entered the room with her hands placed on each shoulder of a new arrival. "I want you to welcome your new classmate."

The classroom went from boisterous accounts of summer bravado to a perfect silence as we contemplated the most beautiful girl that any of us had ever seen. Shimmering locks of spun gold hung over a face of such delicate beauty that I found it acutely painful to even look at her. That skin! It looked so soft that just to touch it you risked tearing a hole. It was as if she had wrapped her skull in a cloud. Even with her rather long, square jaw she made the best-looking girl in the class look like a diced turd.

"Say hello to Snorre Lant," said Miss Tveitan.

"Snorre?" Peter said in disbelief. "But Snorre's a boy's name?"

The class laughed and the girl-boy flashed two bejeweled eyes towards Peter with a loathing that gave their shimmering beauty new, dark and exciting depths. It was a look displaying a capacity for hatred of which I was immediately impressed. It was followed by a crude inhalation and then a loud inverted snort. Had we been outside it would have undoubtedly been concluded with some glutinous spit on the floor. It was an aggressively male gesture and the revelation of our new classmate's masculine gender left the entire class speechless.

I looked across to Peter and Edvard. Peter had been pierced by the bolt of distilled hatred that Snorre had shot him and was downcast. Despite the revelation of Snorre's gender Edvard, on the other hand, remained glassy-eyed with a look that mixed wonder and reverence and spiced it with desire.

During that first week the boys, girls and teachers could neither look at Snorre nor tear their gaze from him without suffering anguish. He provoked strong emotion in everyone that passed close to his orbit, but the truth is none of us could have predicted this shy and delicate doll would, within four short years, mutate into the conceited, amoral sex-obsessed prick that you have come to know.

In later years, Decadence would learn to use his androgyny to his advantage. By overlaying it with an arrogant swagger he transformed a feminine countenance into an effective sex weapon that devastated women and intimidated men. But back then he had yet to tap into the power harbored in his looks. He was shy and embarrassed by his features. He wore his hair long because of his taste in music (which we will come to shortly) but his locks also gave him a screen to hide that beautiful face behind.

A group of three older boys had surrounded him in the playground that first lunch break. With his hood up and his face downcast Snorre had been attempting to hide from the world, but beauty that forceful is impossible to conceal and attempting to do so is like using sunglasses to forestall the break of day.

The usual homophobic slurs followed, accompanied by one of the boys knocking Snorre's bag off his shoulder and then another delivering a poorly executed punch to the ear, though it was enough to knock Snorre to the floor.

It was at that point that Edvard intervened.

"Hey Ademec!" he called to the ringleader. "If you wanted to play tickle with someone from our class you should have called for Edvard."

By fifteen, Edvard already had a reputation for being indestructible. And with Peter at his side, standing at well over six foot, any numerical or age advantage Ademec and his friends had was entirely academic. Edvard pinched one of Ademec's nipples through his shirt.

I have experienced one of those pinches (although, thankfully, not to my nipples). The strength in his fingers is so great that you fear that he has the ability to condense your flesh until the individual cells pop.

Ademec squealed. "Lay off it Kittelsen!"

"Are you kidding?" Edvard said, enjoying himself. "Edvard is just beginning to see why you like this game so much."

He pinched the other nipple. I fully expected Ademec's teat to burst and splatter flesh and perhaps a little lacteal fluid against the inside of his shirt. He shrieked in agony, before Edvard then compounded matters by pinching the boy on the inside of his thigh, just below the groin. Ademec began to cry.

"That's round one to Edvard I think. Now. What do you reckon Ademec? Best out of three? Or would you and your girlfriends prefer to just fuck off?"

They decided to fuck off.

Peter walked over to help Snorre up, but the boy slapped his outstretched arm away.

He then got up and dusted himself down. Standing near a window, he caught his reflection in it, adjusted his waistband and used his fingers to comb his fringe down over his eyes.

As he was doing this, I picked his bag up off the floor and contemplated the patchwork of death metal insignia that decorated its surface.

Peter, Edvard and I were already listening exclusively to heavy metal, but our tastes had not progressed beyond the safe and sanitized thrash beloved of teenagers throughout the world. Our bedrooms broadcast the same tunes you would hear leaking from US baseball stadiums at least one night a month and our clothes and walls were festooned with images of tattooed forearms and logos that could be seen on billboards everywhere.

The imagery that adorned Snorre's bag was altogether different. He had not yet arrived at black metal (the destination at which you will inevitably arrive if you pursue an interest in extreme noise to its conclusion) but he had been on his musical journey far longer than we had and his quest had brought him to a terrifying place that lay well beyond the borders of the relatively sterile musical state in which we were residing at the time.

The patches on his bag depicted graphic images of death and violence. They were arranged as if to convey their own disturbing narrative like The Stations of the Cross; only rendered in brutal tableaus of torture and sexual deviance.

Despite the unashamed misogyny, or perhaps even because of it, I found the imagery captivating. One image in particular held my gaze: three bloodied, headless zombie-type creatures were nailing a bride face down to a crucifix while a leprous dwarf, having previously amputated the bride's leg, rammed the severed limb, foot first, inside her.

"What's that all about?" I asked, pointing to the picture as I handed Snorre his bag.

He gave me a strange look. I suspect he had never before come across a girl who showed any interest in his musical tastes. He reeled off the expletive-ridden name of a band I would later learn were among the more notorious on the Hungarian death metal scene, then tilted his head as if he were unsure if my interest in heavy metal was sincere or sarcastic. I held his gaze and eventually he realized I was sincere. He pulled out his phone, found a track and played us a snippet.

Through the single speaker of his phone it sounded like a herd of oxen marauding through a warehouse full of bone china while a road was dug up in the background.

"I can't hear any tune in there," Edvard said.

"That's because there isn't any. Tunes are for choirboys and cheerleaders."

I stared into the eyes of our pretty new paradox and raised an eyebrow. He would have made for a textbook choirboy and a very convincing cheerleader. But then, looking back, that was probably precisely why he found himself drawn to the extreme, cartoon machismo of death metal.

"Where are you from Snorre?" I asked.

"I was born in Newcastle, England. But my parents moved to Bergen when I was little."

"You're English?" Peter asked.

"Does Snorre sound like an English fucking name?" There again was that spike of aggression directed towards my Peter. "No wonder your dad left you. Idiot."

I smarted. I heard a little switch clicking in my head in that moment. There was a finality to it, like a branch snapping. I secretly filed away Snorre's response in that area of my brain where I house grudges and vendettas (which, by fifteen, was already a richly populated database).

"He didn't leave," I told him. "And it wasn't just his father that disappeared that day you know. You'd have a different outlook on life if you had lost a parent too."

Edvard stepped in to defuse the tension. "So how come you moved here?"

"My mother is a Kapteinløytnant in the Royal Norwegian Navy and she happened to be stationed in Newcastle when I was born."

Ah. Snorre's mother. She had to make her debut in this story sooner or later.

Unlike me, Peter and Edvard never really got to know Snorre's mother that well. They knew that she was a beautiful and formidable naval officer who was always immaculately (and perhaps obsessively) well dressed and whose job it was to train recruits in the art of maritime navigation. They knew that she had as much personal warmth as snowfall on a polystyrene kerb, but they also knew Snorre was devoted to her.

They might have enjoyed getting to know Snorre's mother and perhaps, despite her foibles, they might have come to love her as we all did Peter's mother. But, sadly, that wasn't to be. Before Peter and Edvard ever got the chance to see much of Snorre's mother, before they got a chance to form their own opinion on her, Peter killed her.

11

Back in the shop, Popcorn Lady arrived at lunchtime. She and The Wheelchair Goth were among the more memorable of our regulars. The Wheelchair Goth would arrive alone, made up in a heavy application of corpsepaint like a sadistic panda, and loiter upstairs until someone volunteered to help him and his wheelchair down. He would then spend the day in a darkened corner scaring the shit out of people who happened to stumble across him sitting in silence between L and the M in the vinyl racks. We would often forget his presence and he would sit there in the dark overnight.

Popcorn Lady was a diminutive woman (she was too old to be described as a girl). She might have been Japanese, she might have been Korean. What was certain was that she was a long way from home and irretrievably lost. She had very bad skin that she disguised under a heavy layer of white foundation which gave her the complexion of curdled milk. She arranged her hair in two large bunches that sprouted out of her head like pom-poms and she always wore white lace gloves and bright, flowery dresses that finished just above the knee. Fluorescent tights or stockings and stacked heels finished off her strong and very creepy look. She didn't speak any Norwegian but she chatted incessantly in her own peculiar language.

Popcorn Lady was the most promiscuous person I have ever come across. She was pathologically promiscuous. Not even Decadence could keep up with her. She exercised absolutely no judgement when choosing a mate and would simply approach every male that passed her with an appropriate gesture (or inappropriate gesture, it depends on your viewpoint). At least once a day she could be found bouncing between the L and the M racks astride The Wheelchair Goth. The terrifying sound of her painful orgasm (fake or real, I couldn't tell) rang out from the toilets and alcoves throughout the day with a mechanical frequency. But despite their horror, those screams made for a welcome respite from her irritating natter.

She was called Popcorn Lady because that's all she would eat. She snacked on the stuff all day. I don't know how long she had existed within this nightmare, but it was taking its toll. She was emaciated, her teeth were rotting and her breath stank. When she was still a novelty Decadence would sometimes take her for a ride. He told me she insisted on keeping all of her clothes on (she wore no underwear and if wearing tights she would cut a slit into the crotch to enable unobstructed access). He had glimpsed sight of deep scars on her wrists.

By the time Popcorn Lady had arrived, Decadence, Bolverk, The Exorcist and I were at the circular cash desk, from which the aisles spread outwards like the spokes of a wheel.

Bolverk had devoured Old Mr Suhm's breakfast within a minute of The Exorcist throwing him the box earlier in the morning (he didn't use cutlery, he just tipped the contents straight into his mouth) and was asking about Decadence's lay from the previous night.

"It's a shame about her," Decadence said. "She was cute enough, and quite filthy with it, but too skinny. She needs to indulge in some other sins of the flesh. It could only do her good to binge on something other than sex once in a while. It's no good indulging in lust alone and neglecting the other six deadly sins. Therein lays the path to ruin."

"Are you going to lecture us on sin again?" I asked.

"All I'm saying is that if you fully embrace all of the deadly sins you will never have any problems. If you overdo lust at the expense of gluttony, like she did, you'll be too thin to get anyone decent to fuck you."

"Evidently."

Decadence ignored my jibe. "Of course, it's only acceptable to be a glutton if you have sufficient vanity and pride to check your physical decline." At that point he glanced disapprovingly at Bolverk.

"The ameliorating effect of pride is criminally overlooked."

Bolverk considered his three empty sandwich packets, shrugged and ripped open a fourth. The rest of us watched him consume the entire thing in just two bites.

Both Bolverk and The Exorcist were sturdy, grim-faced men who never really excited the band's female fans and who never seemed to get excited by them. The Exorcist was handsome – at least I'd always thought so – but he hid his features behind his beard and hair because he was shy. Bolverk, on the other hand, had a face like offal that nothing short of an iron mask could camouflage and he was anything but shy. Nevertheless, he was surprisingly repressed for a self-proclaimed Pagan with Satanic leanings.

Then there was Suffer, with his hideous looks and even more offensive behavior. Some were lured by his unique horror, but only the strangest, troubled and lost women ever allowed him to have his dark ways with them.

All of which suited Decadence. If his bandmates were better looking or any more appealing it would have diluted his allure: a light always shines brighter in the dark.

"You know you ought to indulge more in the carnal delights that the black metal lifestyle has to offer," he said to Bolverk. "When was the last time that your little longship went to war? Or does the warrior code of the Vikings only permit sex in the context of rape and pillage?"

Bolverk emptied the better half of a foul-smelling packet of potato chips down his throat before replying.

"For the true warrior ejaculation is a wasteful release of

aggression. It should only be undertaken with carefully chosen mates in order to breed a more warlike generation."

"Didn't your Vikings have wives to love them and entice them back home after they'd laid waste to a nation?" I asked.

"Love is a much worse vice. During the Viking era the best warriors were required to kill their mothers, wives and children in order to prove that they were merciless and to avoid the risk that anything might conflict with their focus on the campaign at hand." I wasn't sure if that was true, but Bolverk didn't wait for anyone to question his Viking knowledge. Sucking the salt from his fingers, he continued, "Talking of which, that skinny girl of yours, Decadence, looked like she could have executed you on the spot this morning."

"Oh, she'll thank me for it in time," Decadence said. "I emancipated her. She was laboring under the Christian myth that the physical union of a man and a woman is a small part of wider and lifelong relationship. I tried explaining to her that it was, of course, a spiritual thing that we did: sharing our bodies like that. But it was also a perfectly complete magickal episode. I enjoyed myself in those moments as I'm sure she did and one day she'll realize that a full and happy life involves sharing as many moments like that with as many people as possible."

Bolverk walked over to where Decadence was sat on a stool and with uncharacteristic tenderness placed a large hand on each of his shoulders.

"That's beautiful man."

He then leaned in close and belched into his face.

12

Shortly after lunch, while we were all still congregated around the hub, we heard a commotion at the top of the stairs. Kids often stood on the street near the doorway to smoke cigarettes. There were raised voices and by the sounds of it a scuffle had broken out. The three band members and I exchanged anxious glances; the threat of the Oslo Iron reprisals was hanging over us and it seemed likely, to me at least, if they were going to lay waste to us they would begin by attacking the stragglers on the street before focusing on the shop and anyone in it.

I heard a girl's muffled scream as if a blow had obstructed its sound mid-way through the shriek. I instinctively retreated behind The Exorcist, putting him between me and the staircase. The stale air of the shop became charged with an electric tension, before the door to the street crashed against the wall and something began to tumble down the stairs.

The Exorcist leapt over the desk and raced towards them. Somewhat slower, but with the same sense of urgency, Bolverk ran around the counter after The Exorcist as fast as his little legs would carry him.

Decadence stayed with me. My plan was to run into the Crypt at the first sign of trouble and hole myself up in there until it was safe to emerge. I suspected he had something similar in mind.

A seething, writhing mass of black leather, cotton and hair cascaded over the last step and spilled over the floor of the aisle. The Exorcist reached it first, plunged both hands into its midst and extracted two human(ish) forms. The less human of the two was Suffer. The other looked like a young fan of the band decked out in more than two thousand Krone's worth of brand-new Baphomet's Agony kit, replete with factory creases.

"I just wanted to shake your hand!" the kid cried. "I'm a fucking fan for Christ's sake!"

"Don't touch me!" Suffer growled. "I'm not one of you!"

The Exorcist was holding the two apart. Suffer's face was red and choleric with a familiar and eerie sheen about it. To look at him you would have thought that someone had brought him in from the cold and immediately applied a glossy lacquer to his features. He aimed a kick directly into The Exorcist's shin and, when the drummer roared in pain and released the singer to nurse his leg, Suffer launched himself at the fan again.

This time Bolverk intervened. He shoved the fan out of harm's way with one arm and then swept up Suffer with the other, locking him into a bear-hug. This was a familiar scene to us all. It was the only way to restrain Suffer when he had got himself into this state.

With Suffer's arms pinned to his side, all he could do was scream, writhe and spit into Bolverk's face as the bassist squeezed the oxygen out of his brain. He contorted his scraggy frame into shapes unknown to human anatomy and angles new to mathematics, trying to escape, but all to no avail. His impenetrable babble drifted into murmur and his thrashings settled into inertia.

Once he had been rendered unconscious Bolverk threw Suffer over his shoulder, took him into the Den and dropped him onto a sofa.

That episode was not unique. I had witnessed Bolverk take Suffer under on numerous occasions. We all knew one day the monster would try to kill again. In the preceding six months The Exorcist and Bolverk had saved the lives of numerous unsuspecting victims by intervening in a fight and restraining him. He kept on about wanting to kill an innocent.

It was important that it was an innocent he killed too. Killing in self-defense or if provoked was no good to him: that might be justifiable on some level. It was important to him that his victim be undeserving of his or her death. It was only with an entirely unjustifiable killing that Suffer could rid himself of his last remaining vestige of humanity.

I watched Bolverk dump Suffer on the sofa and then wandered over to look at him. Gazing down as he lay there, I could see he was at peace, for a short time at least. Awake he would always be either on the brink of, or in the midst of, a rage. Only when unconscious, and presumably upon his death, would he enjoy any tranquility. Even when he slept his features would twist and spit like a stirred pot of simmering gruel.

We'd had sex numerous times, but spent the full night together just once. I'd laid awake all night in terror, watching his face contort, and tried to imagine what it was like to exist within his frame, in his pain and with his curse hanging over me.

Of course, I conducted my studies in silence. Suffer was a light sleeper and if I woke him I risked being beaten or, worse still, subjected once again to his peculiar and savage take on sex. I much preferred a straightforward beating. With a beating at least my injuries were external and could be easily treated.

Suffer and I very rarely engaged in conventional sex. Vaginal penetration held very little interest for him but on the handful of occasions we tried it we never used contraception. He refused to entertain the thought of it. He insisted that he was infertile so there was no risk of us conceiving a child. The only time I did ask him to use a condom I underwent my inaugural beating at his hands.

From what I've just said it would be natural for you to assume that maybe he beat me because he was infertile, that his beating of me was in response to his own sense of shame and inadequacy. You're wrong. Suffer was fiercely proud of his infertility.

He once told me he believed Christ was infertile. It was one of the few times I'd seen him truly lucid, despite his train of thought leaping the tracks of logic as he explained it all to me. I won't go into the details here, lest you think me insane. But there was a lot of talk of the paradox of God's sperm, God's own lack of ancestry, how this meant He had no self-replicating genes (indeed it would be a blasphemy to argue otherwise because if He had, it would leave open the possibility there could be more than one God), and therefore he couldn't have passed any down to His Son.

Suffer liked to think on this, because he had long held the view that if Christ was the son of God made man, so the Antichrist would be the son of Satan made man.

And, if Christ was infertile, so it *must* be that the son of Satan, the Antichrist, would be infertile.

Can you see where I'm headed here?

Yeah. Suffer thought he was the Antichrist.

The thing was, I thought he could be too.

13

The fan Suffer beat the shit out of ended up bruised and shocked, but there was no long-term damage. We gave him a free 12 inch vinyl record that Decadence, Bolverk and The Exorcist had signed and he seemed placated as he hobbled away dripping only a little blood.

It was almost a shame, because had it happened a little later that day, the Satan's Spawn company man would have been there. He would have witnessed the ferocity of Suffer in the lair of Baphomet's Agony. And we might have got that record deal earlier. But then there was always the risk that Suffer would have focused his attack on the one man we most needed to impress.

No matter. I can't control everything. As much as that really pisses me off.

Anyway, where was I? The band had been making tapes and pressing and releasing E.P.s and demos on vinyl for over a year. Recording sessions could be erratic, much depending on the mood we found Suffer in on the day, but when it all came together we could create a masterpiece in loosely structured chaos. It's hard to describe the Baphomet's Agony sound, but imagine you have an infinite number of pigs and an infinite number of tractor engines. Now, take the engines apart, place the component parts carefully in a steel drum with the smallest parts closest to the surface and group the pigs together in tightly-packed clusters of around fifteen. From a height of about eight meters drop the engine parts slowly onto the pigs and make a sound recording of what happens. The sound of the steel drum emptying, the pigs squealing and the components smacking into swine flesh will be horrific. But, if you do it an infinite number of times, at least one occasion will result in the combination of sounds creating a repulsively recognizable rhythm and melody.

A successful Baphomet's Agony recording sounds like that.

When he wanted to, Suffer could lay down formidable vocals. Unfortunately, he rarely chose to do so. There was only a 50/50 chance he would turn up for a recording session and, even if he did grace us with his presence, he wasn't always prepared to be recorded. However, the songs were solid and the performances of Decadence and Bolverk were always strong. The Exorcist was a shit drummer, but I'd convinced the others that an element of ineptitude was essential in black metal. Decadence never really understood and despaired at The Exorcist's failure to keep time in the most straightforward of rhythms, but I had trained him not to say anything.

We made good money on the recordings. In fact, a release always sold out within a few weeks of launch through an informal network of specialist shops across Scandinavia, Germany, Poland, Switzerland, Russia, Canada and (bizarrely I've always thought) Brazil.

Initially, I'd hoped social media would help create a digital web of bile and hatred through which we could channel our music and ideas without the need to use traditional music industry distribution networks. I was sorely mistaken. We had a Twitter account for one hour and twelve minutes. The first response to my inaugural post compared the band to one of the black metal bands of the second wave. The second post defended us in the kind of illiterate, childish way I assume fans talk about their manufactured boy band crushes. So I closed the account immediately and we've never repeated the experiment.

If we were going to explode the pillars of polite society, I realized that we needed to use a medium that relied less on the brainless dialect of social networks. We needed a record deal, with its investment and associated distribution network.

Cult status was all well and good, but world domination required us to infiltrate the mainstream and use its machine for our nefarious purposes. That was why, pretending to be Decadence, I had been chatting online with the talent scout from Satan's Spawn and had managed to convince him to attend the Oslo gig.

To be honest, as good as that performance had been, we hadn't heard from him since. Not until that day in the shop, following the new editions of *Downtuned* and *Hate Sounds* hitting the shelves. Both had reviews of the Oslo gig from our friends Od and Sigurd. Remember them? Of course you do.

I kept the clippings.

All Hail The Baph!

At 9.47pm last Thursday I think I witnessed the dawn of a new era in black metal. That was the moment Baphomet's Agony arrived on stage through a fug of blood and sweat, to a fanfare of brain-splitting metal and in the midst of an orgy of sex and violence.

...

In their guitarist, Decadence, Norway's Satanists have an ESP-wielding hero to raise up on a pedestal comprised of Metal Masters, Fuzz Boxes

The Mysteries of Shit-nas

Another Thursday night and another evening of tedium lifted momentarily by a brief interlude of fire-eating and shit-smearing from a promising support.

...

Baphomet's Agony are the latest over-hyped black metal embarrassment to waste my time on a night I could have more entertainingly spent picking grit out of the soles of my shoes.

...

and Ibanez Tube Screamers. Whilst in vocalist, Suffer, they have a terrifying new deity to add to their diabolic pantheon. Bolverk, the bassist, was a solid slab of iron that hammered out complex time-signatures as if his heart was beating 7/8 time. Disappointingly, and in contrast to the groundbreaking sound of the rest of the band, the drums were at best pedestrian and occasionally woeful.

…

There were super-hot babes wall-to-wall (and one certainly up against a wall – I can vouch for that!).

…

It was a seminal performance. I don't recall having attended a black metal gig with as much excitement and tension in the air as this one.

…

Gig of the year I reckon and let's hope we see a lot more of these guys in the months to come.

…

There's very little I can remember of the performance: I think the singer might have fallen over once. Otherwise, it was derivative stuff from a conservative band performed in front of a bored-looking crowd composed entirely of Oslo's hardened black metal fetishists who would probably turn out to watch Cliff Richard if he wore black jeans.

…

I did like the drummer though. Harking back to the golden era of black metal here was a man that decried technical proficiency in favor of the pared-down, minimal, garage sound that the movement was built upon – all credit to him for bucking the trend and keeping it real.

…

Take it from me, the bubble has burst. I wouldn't bother.

Sigurd

> Kill your granny to get tickets for the upcoming Bergen gig - it's going to be carnage!
>
> **Od**

Did I like these reviews? That's a hell of a question to ask me. "Reviews aren't for the bands," isn't that the saying? But, yeah, sure, as the manger I needed to know these things. And you might be surprised to learn I was particularly pleased with Sigurd's review: criticism that harsh from him would have sent a strong message to the industry that the gig was phenomenal.

No offence, Sigurd.

These reviews were the final piece of an intricate jigsaw I'd been putting together for nearly eighteen months. At any point in the career of the band I could have got them a record deal, but they would have been with small-time labels keen to add Baphomet's Agony to their roster of bands with ambitions as limited as the funds the labels made available to them.

We needed Satan's Spawn. They had kept it quiet but I knew behind the scenes it was financed and run by the biggest media conglomerate in the world. We needed a beast of that scale and with that many tentacles to spread our hatred and filth around the globe.

As luck would have it, within hours of the magazine reviews hitting the shelves, those slime-coated tentacles found their way down our perilous stairs.

It was the silence of his arrival I liked the most.

Our regulars tend to clatter down the stairs in heavy boots and in cheap leather jackets that creak like old floorboards. In contrast, the supple hides of the A&R man's boots and jacket were soundless and movement rippled on their surfaces like a breeze across a pond. He must have sourced his leather from a special breed of Ninja cattle.

His sudden presence provoked massive anxiety amongst our customers. And some anger.

"People like you aren't welcome here."

The rangy teenage kid making that observation had colorful tattoos sprayed up one side of his neck. He looked as if he recently visited a wallpaper factory and been shoved into a roll while the ink was still drying.

The A&R man paused and smiled.

"I'm not convinced you know everything there is to know about me."

"I know enough." The wallpaper-kid twitched and sniffed.

"How about you stick to just knowing enough and let people like me worry about the rest that there is to know?"

The A&R man strode over to where I was sat with Decadence and The Exorcist.

"Decadence, isn't it?"

Lounging diagonally across two seats Decadence nodded.

"I'm Péjé Swartz from Satan's Spawn."

He spoke with a well-educated Swedish accent and tossed a business card onto the low table in front of us before settling himself into a sofa. Suffer lay unconscious a few meters away but the man gave him no more than a cursory glance.

"Satan's Spawn?" Decadence said, clearly confused.

"Yes. You and I have been corresponding for a month, remember?"

Decadence looked across at me like a child who has waded into the mud too deep and needed a hand out. Péjé was quick enough to notice and turned his unnerving smile to me. His pale, damp eyes didn't change the smallest fraction.

"I recognize you from the Oslo gig," he said.

"There were lots of fans there."

"True. But not all the fans were directing the guys on the lighting rig and the mixing desk from their phones."

I didn't respond.

"Look," he continued. "I don't really care who's working who behind the scenes. The fact is I was impressed with what I saw that night. I've listened to a couple of your E.P.s too and I'm quickly approaching the stage where I going to want to sign you."

"For how much?" Decadence asked. I kicked him hard in the shins, hard enough to cause him to jump up and walk off the pain.

For that I got the smile again.

"We can talk about that later. First, introductions please. I recognize the big man here. The drummer, yes?" Péjé glanced over at The Exorcist before looking down again at where Suffer was slumped. "And I've seen this thing before. Is it dead?"

"Suffer is dead to the norms of society, morality and popular culture," I replied. "But I'm guessing your question was made with reference to his biological state, rather than anything more philosophical? In which case, he's as alive as the rest of us."

"That's a shame. A good death early in a band's career can do wonders for record sales."

I caught Decadence nodding in agreement.

"So what's wrong with him?" Péjé continued.

"He was squeezed unconscious about twenty minutes ago. He'll come round in another ten, give or take."

Péjé didn't seem to like the idea of being here when that happened, so the introductions were made quickly, each member of the band finally using their given names. Which would have been great, except the record company guy wasn't impressed.

"Are you sure you're entirely happy with the names you've given yourselves? Even you?"

Péjé looked at The Exorcist.

"Yes… why?"

"Because it's ridiculous. It's just not evil, is it?"

"Not evil?" *The Exorcist looked crestfallen.* "Are you saying a girl with a rotating head, who's possessed by the devil and who stabs at her thingy with a crucifix isn't evil?"

"But the exorcist in the movie was a priest who banishes the demon," Decadence explained. "That's the opposite of evil."

"Oh."

"Will you change your name now?" Péjé asked.

"I guess. Although it took me months to come up with that one. I suppose that I'll have think of a character that's evil.... Maybe Darth – "

"For fuck's sake, show some imagination will you?" Decadence interjected. "You don't have to name yourself after someone else. Just think of something evil and then build a name around it."

"Like what?" asked The Exorcist.

"I don't know. Think of something that Satan would do. How about The Nun-Fucker?"

"Gross!" The Exorcist shuddered and looked at me. "Does Satan really fuck nuns?"

"Probably."

Péjé closed his eyes and then opened them to look at his watch.

"Okay, so it needs to be something wicked and gross, right? Like eating vomit?"

"Jesus," Decadence sighed. "If you're thinking about calling yourself The Puke Muncher then you're out of the fucking band."

"Leave him be," Bolverk said, turning to Péjé. "Can you live with that name?"

"If it enables me to catch the train leaving Kragerø in fifteen minutes then yes, I can live with it." Péjé went to the door. "Look boys, I'm going to be at Bergen tomorrow night. This is it, this is your chance. If you can show me something special, then you can find yourself a lawyer and we can discuss terms next week. Deal?"

"Deal," the boys said.

I showed Péjé out and when I got back to the Den all three of them were grinning at each other. They could feel it, just as I could.

We were on the cusp of something. And everyone else needed to worry about it.

14

I think you should hear more about Snorre Lant now.

Not Decadence – you've seen enough of him for the moment and he looms large in the rest of my story. No, it's his earlier incarnation as the young Snorre, the shy and sensitive outsider, that you need to understand better. It is in the story of his early friendship with Peter, Edvard and I that the seeds of what he became were sown.

Snorre, the timid she-boy that had located his masculine identity within the ugly misogyny of death metal, had been granted entry to my small collection of Kragerø's teenage curiosities. I kept him in a pickle jar on a shelf alongside the simple, elongated and fatherless specimen that I called Peter Suhm and the sardonic pocket-Viking with moveable limbs that was Edvard Kittelsen.

Outside of school we would hang out together in bedrooms or cellars filled with Edvard and Snorre's hash smoke and listen to ever-darkening heavy metal. We spent a lot of time at Snorre's parents' house because it was so much bigger than anyone else's. The other great advantage, for Edvard and Snorre at least, was that Snorre's father would not only tolerate them smoking pot, he would encourage it – and sometimes join in. Mr Lant had spent much of his youth in Christiania: a hippie commune in Copenhagen. I think that was his undoing.

I have a problem with hippies and to be fair I was already uneasy about them before I met Snorre's father. When I was a child, I took against the indolence of their lifestyle that set them so far apart from my own fishing community where the men, women and children always seemed to toil so hard just to get by. It never seemed fair to me that these well-spoken offspring of liberal wealth could get away with doing so little.

I suppose more than anything else it's their hypocrisy that gets me. They preach love and tolerance but then look down on anyone that chooses to work hard and achieve a goal which, after all, is simply an alternative to their alternative. What's more, they always rail against capitalism and wealth but couldn't exist without their trust funds and welfare and where do they suppose those funds come from? For a long time, I sincerely believed the word "hippie" was a diminutive form of the English word "hypocrite" and that they wore their hypocrisy with pride.

Snorre's father was an archetypal hippie: lazy, self-centered and decadent with a vocabulary peppered with the acrid jargon of spirituality. His wife, Snorre's mother, earned a good wage and the navy always provided them with a decent home wherever she was posted. As a result, Mr Lant wasn't required to work, so he didn't. And as Mrs Lant was often away, she would never know if he was faithful or not, so he wasn't.

To this day he has never been put under any pressure to do anything constructive with his time, so he hasn't. All he did was hang around their spacious home, watch television, smoke pot and hit on girls. Even if they had only just turned sixteen.

"So Marta, you want a beer?"

"No."

"You want to maybe smoke some pot?"

"No."

"You know, I can see why Snorre and those other two want to spend so much time around you. You're a cute, smart girl and for someone your age you have a fine –"

"Thanks," I said quickly, not wanting to hear the end of that sentence.

He continued regardless. "But those boys don't appreciate you. It takes time for a man to learn to truly appreciate a woman, I think. Especially one as special as you. To them you're just a hot chick that's fun to be around. They wouldn't have a clue what to do with you. But to the more experienced man you could be something amazing, you know? Like a muse. A more experienced man could unlock all sorts of potential within you."

"And I guess you've got a key that might fit my lock?"

"We'd have fun finding out wouldn't we?"

I almost gagged. I suspect in his mind this seduction was going well. In reality, I had always seen him as a prick and the more he spoke to me the more I imagined him arching over trying to suck on his own cock.

"How about we split from the kids and you and me just hang out upstairs?"

With those words his circle was complete.

"I have a better idea," I said. "A Buddhist Guru from the deserts of the Sahara once told me you cannot begin to help someone know themselves unless you truly know yourself."

"Deep man, real deep."

"So before you unlock anything within me, I think it would be super-hip and cool for you to use that mystical key of yours to unlock your own potential."

"I like it! I like it! Can you help me with that Marta? Could you guide me like my Holy Guardian Angel?"

"Sure."

"So how do we do it?"

"Well you go upstairs to your bedroom."

"Yes."

"Get undressed and slip between the sheets."

"Uh-huh"

"And go fuck yourself."

All Mr Lant had going for himself was his looks. He had those long, square features in which the ravages of age find themselves pleasing angles and crevices upon which to build handsome sculpture. His eyes might once have had the shine and luster that Snorre's had but by the time that I looked upon them they had been overlaid with a milky lens composed, it seemed, from the marijuana smoke that had coiled over them for the past twenty-five years.

I can only assume that Mrs Lant was young and naive when she first met Snorre's father. His looks would have doubtless been sufficient to create the initial attraction but what it was that could have persuaded her to set up home and breed with him I cannot guess. It wasn't just that he was a cock-sucking prick: the two of them inhabited entirely different worlds, they operated on different planes and they spoke different languages. They were two life forms that shared as much common DNA as a Christmas tree and a koala bear.

She too was beautiful, but her beauty was like cut glass: light would reflect from the faultless surface of her face and dazzle you but there was no warmth in the sensation. She managed to radiate light without heat. There was nothing about her that would make you want to touch her. I always sensed that were I to stroke her cheek I risked slicing my palm on the sharp fold of her jaw and if I touched her hair those glistening strands might pierce the skin and become impaled upon the bone in my fingers.

And she knew that. From the way that she looked out on the world I could see that she felt trapped within her immaculate splendor. Somewhere deep inside that crystalline fortress a plain girl, capable of at least some degree of warmth, was lamenting the ill-fortune that had seen her encased within unattainable physical magnificence.

On our first meeting I saw immediately that she was ignorant of the subtleties of human interaction: those tiny, almost imperceptible cues that the rest of us process and that enable us to navigate past each other without thinking.

I found that interesting. And, potentially, of great benefit to me.

Her relationship with her husband was appalling. I once witnessed a chance meeting that they had on the street outside of their home. She was leaving the house while he was returning from one of his occasional trips to score drugs. They were forced to interact because they had almost collided but there was none of the surprised jollity that acquaintances or even mere strangers would share in the same predicament. Instead, they both shook their heads and gave each other an unnecessarily wide berth.

It was in her interaction with Snorre that the suggestion of something human trapped within Mrs Lant could be seen. Snorre treated his father with disdain. It was impossible to respect Mr Lant because he had achieved nothing, he aspired to nothing and there was not even an underlying principle to which he subscribed that justified his pursuit of nothingness. He was just a detestable slob. Edvard and I could see it and I suspect it was so obvious even Peter had noticed it. Snorre was certainly aware of his father's failings and was acutely embarrassed by them. It was in his mother, therefore, that he invested all of his filial pride, respect and affection.

Being slightly less charismatic than a combination boiler, she was the unlikely focus for anyone's devotion. However, Snorre had deep reserves of feeling that he drew upon to fund his love for his mother and, in his view at least, the trajectory of her career was something to be greatly admired. That's what I call the Decadence Paradox: he is a man that continually chases after superficial liaisons and one-night-stands, yet I know he is in search of the rich and profound emotional attachment that has eluded him his entire life.

Snorre's devotion to his mother could not have been more intense even if it were actively Oedipal (which I don't think it was, but I guess you never know). He would relish the opportunity to raise the subject of her in conversation, at which point the animation in his speech would increase exponentially. In her presence he would literally bounce like a cartoon rabbit.

And while she would never reciprocate his gestures of affection, she never sought to curtail them. She wouldn't encourage him to dote but there was something in her tolerance of it that indicated to me that if you peeled back the callous layers of resin with which she had overlaid her heart, what beat beneath it would resemble the same organ that powers each one of us.

I saw her once, stood alone on the harbor staring out to sea. It was a blustery day when the grey in the sky and the sea matched that of the concrete wall on which she stood. The windscale had nudged just beyond the boundaries of what was acceptable for that time of the year, like a playful child who, with the best of intentions, hits his sister too hard among the horseplay.

There Mrs Lant stood, contemplating the bedlam wreaked upon those shallow waters by the elements. Maybe she was applying her nautical and scientific mind to the motions of that ocean and improving her mastery of its navigation.

I wasn't. I had other things on my mind. By then, I didn't fully understand why Mrs Lant had to be punished. But that she would need to be punished soon, was well beyond doubt.

15

I have spent many hours on that harbor, leaning over the rails and contemplating the sea. When the wind and rain blow hard and the waters churn I can stand there transfixed, just watching the infinitely complex physics at work beneath me. That interplay of sea, wind and rain, each of them charged with their own distinct energy, is so intricate it would require an algorithm of inconceivable complexity to calculate and predict the movement in just one square meter of ocean. If you extrapolate and attempt to comprehend the number of minuscule forces at work across just Kragerø harbor your mind will begin to swim and you risk inducing a state of mind approximating vertigo.

How then is it possible for a single entity, even a divine God, to be the architect of the madness of the oceans? The concept that some unseeing hand manipulates our every move and the machinations of all things is laid bare as a lie by the chaos of the seas. So formidable is the task of choreographing even the smallest expanse of open water, it would leave a divinity little time to achieve anything else, even if He had an eternity to work on it.

"Ahh!" I hear you say. "But God has infinite time and capabilities so just because a task of infinite complexity is beyond our capabilities it doesn't mean it is beyond His."

True. But if God is so infinitely powerful and capable that He can conduct the oceans while at the same time juggling the ways of man, how come the seas are managed with such sublime perfection yet mankind, the most beloved of His creations, is such a fuck-up?

No. The sea doesn't need a God and neither do I.

The same, however, cannot be said of Mrs Lant. She was in dire need of a divine power to protect her from the malignant forces at work in the darker recesses of Kragerø, but, unfortunately for her, none would come to her aid.

I don't know what faith Mrs Lant had. I didn't care, to be honest, but if she did ever have any gods watching over her they were derelict in their duty that day I found her alone and looking out over the harbor. Any loving power would have sent a thunderbolt down and burnt me crisp before I could go and do what I did.

I had only recently been introduced to Mrs Lant by her doting Snorre. We didn't know each other that well, only in passing. Yet for some reason I couldn't quite explain I was drawn towards her that afternoon. In the years that have passed I have convinced myself that I saw my opportunity to cause mischief but I'm not entirely sure that's true. Another part of me might have been looking for happiness. It might have been looking for an extended hand to haul me up to the surface.

I learned later it was earlier that very day she'd been told her stay in Kragerø would be prematurely cut short and she was to be posted to Suffolk, on the east coast of England. On the face of it she was not a woman susceptible to any form of human weakness, but I could sense I was catching her at a vulnerable moment and even at that tender age my powers of manipulation had been finely honed.

I carefully chose my spot at the same railing, watching the sea, knowing the slightest turn of her head would allow her to see me. Which she did and then gave me a nod and a smile. It was the most subtle of greetings but it allowed me the opportunity to move closer.

For a minute or two after that, we kept watch as the waves

crashed over each other until finally she spoke to break the silence between us.

"Marta, do you like Snorre?"

"I don't hate him as much as I hate most other people," I said.

"Do you think he's happy?"

"I've known him for two months. You've known him since he was born and presumably for the nine months before that too. You tell me?"

She pondered that. "I admit he seems more settled here in Kragerø than he has been anywhere else. I think it's because he has found friends like you here."

I said nothing, a little taken aback. I too had enjoyed the preceding months and her comment gave form to a thought I had refused to acknowledge: that perhaps Snorre had something to do with my happiness.

She was dressed immaculately in her uniform with her blonde hair sculpted round to the back of her head in whirl of petrified honey. She embodied serenity, order and calm: she was a triumph of structure, of rationalism. I could see her as an effective teacher, one who could explain the precise mathematics of navigation in clear and efficient language that left no room for ambiguity or humor. She wasn't an easy person to like but, then again, neither was I.

Our similarities were as obvious as the contrasts between my own mother and myself. Between my own mother and her.

"Is Snorre popular?" she asked.

"Not really. He wants to be popular, but boys our age measure their worth by their prowess in sport and fighting. Snorre doesn't do any of that. He's different to the other boys. And his looks hold him back too."

"Oh. I always thought that he was handsome?"

"He is, that's the problem. Girls are jealous and boys get so confused they resort to brutality to realign their hormones."

"I see."

I didn't know if she really did. Was this woman capable of understanding anything on an emotional level?

I looked at her face and tried to imagine how spectacular those features would have been in the prime of her youth. Age seemed to have paid scant attention to her as it waged its relentless campaign against all other life forms on the planet. Up close her skin had a shiny, plastic texture which exaggerated her inorganic demeanor and removed her further from the animal kingdom. In contrast Snorre's skin was so soft that it was more conceptual than real: it had the suggestion of substance to it but you wouldn't bet money on it actually being there. Snorre's was an ethereal face you wanted to touch, if only to confirm whether or not your eyes were deceiving you as to its existence. If Snorre's mother had possessed his intangible complexion as a teenager perhaps it would have brought her closer to the rest of the population, but at the same time would have provoked anxiety, desire and hatred in her contemporaries. Perhaps the memory of that meant she could empathize with Snorre's predicament?

"Can anything be done to help Snorre become more popular?" she asked.

"I suppose if he was more confident around people, and engaged with them, they would be able to get over his looks and like him for what's underneath."

"And how does one go about acquiring confidence, do you think? I have neither had it nor lacked it."

In that moment I saw clearly everything I lacked, everything I could gain and everything I stood to lose. Where Mrs Lant had been burdened with the unasked-for and yet unquestioning love of her son, I existed without the only love I ever sought. Where she suffered an absence of emotion, I was burdened by a surfeit of the shit. But it needn't be like that. Mrs Lant was trying to overcome her nature in order to bring some light into her world.

Could I do that?

Here was an opportunity to shift my perspective, to change the plan and to pursue joy over despair.

No. I must not do that.

That moment of weakness was fleeting. Then, as now, happiness must always remain an abstract concept to me. I could describe it, I could see it in others and I could even give it to others. But I had resolved to never experience it on a personal level. Happiness had refused to bend to my will and I had made it my enemy.

It was noble effort on the part of Mrs Lant – she showed me an alternative future in which I might have been happy with Snorre. But, sorry, that's not the plan. I have a much greater ambition than to live a merely happy life. And in return for trying to help I began to form my plan to destroy Mrs Lant and everything she cared for.

I had always been able to persuade adults to trust me. The secret is in responding confidently to anything that they say. It doesn't really matter what you say or whether or not you answer the question asked of you, you just need to be able to speak fluently and adopt the tone of someone answering the question. It's pure style over substance and the best lesson my mother ever gave me was when she told me "Never bother to study a subject if it's easier to master the teacher."

I could see Mrs Lant trusted me. Good. Having established trust – a positive – I was now free to inject a few negatives in her like doubt, fear and shame. It would be easy for an artist like me whose palette consisted exclusively of shades of black and grey – I would have no difficulty in fashioning the required canvas of gloom and despair.

"Snorre is trapped in a cage," I said bluntly, my words confident in the face of the raging sea before us. "The bars of this cage are formed by you. You need to set him free."

There was no surprise, merely a pause. "I wasn't aware I was confining him?"

"I'm afraid you are, Mrs Lant. Snorre and I have spoken of it often. As much as he loves you, he feels you are a constant presence in his life, watching over him, criticizing him and chastising him whenever he seeks to do anything you might disapprove of, anything that you wouldn't do." I waited for a moment, letting it sink in before I continued, "You may not have intended it, I'm sure you didn't, but it's what you've done. For instance, the other night, we were invited to a friend's house for a party. Peter, Edvard and I said we would go but Snorre did what he always does – he asked 'Would my mother go to this party?' and then he decided the answer to that question was no, so he stayed in his bedroom at home while the rest of us went out."

That was entirely bullshit. Back then none of us ever got invited to parties. But I knew this thought would serve well as the embryo for the nasty little idea I had just planted in her head.

"Why would he do that?" she said. "Why would he want to be like me?"

"Because I suspect he looks at his father and he looks at you and he feels that given that stark choice of lifestyles yours is the one to aspire to. It's ironic really. If he were more laid back and open like his father, I suspect he would be more popular with girls and with boys."

Mrs Lant stared out to sea for a while as I stood looking at her face. Curiously, there had not been the faintest ripple of curiosity, shock or delight to upset the uniform dignity of her features throughout our exchange. As she stood looking out over the harbor not even the boisterous wind blowing across us could distress her apparent tranquility. She seemed not even to blink at what I was saying, yet I knew she felt it. Misery can sense misery.

"You do not lack confidence do you, Marta?"

"I don't let people intimidate me if that's what you mean, Mrs Lant."

"And yet outside of Snorre and his two friends you are not popular."

"I don't draw strength from the approval of others. I'm happy with the friends that I have."

"Do you have sex with Snorre and his friends?"

Bizarrely, the monotone delivery of the question ensured I did not take offence at the question. I shook my head.

"And do you have sex with my husband?"

"No."

"Has he attempted to seduce you?"

Both the delay before I answered the question and the hesitancy in its delivery were deliberate.

"Yes."

With that, I witnessed the first tiny crack in her mask – a minuscule and momentary fissure on that elegant and impassive face.

Perhaps all those years ago when she met him, Mrs Lant had seen in Snorre's father a way to escape her emotional confinement. Perhaps he had used on her those same lines about unlocking her potential he had used on me. He was full of bullshit, but with women like that it is often only the bullshitters that ever have the audacity to approach them. It would be tragic to suppose on the one occasion in her life where she gave herself over to the moment, the one occasion where she chose hope over sense, she found herself duped by a cock-sucking prick. It would be tragic, but I suspect it was true.

"Would you lie with Snorre if he attempted to seduce you?"

"Perhaps," I said, honestly. "But it's not likely to happen unless Snorre begins to take his life lessons from his father, which he won't do while he remains devoted to you. And more his father, your husband, seems entirely incapable or unwilling to exert any paternal influence over his son. It's as if he has been drained of all vigor, of his very life force. I do wonder what could have happened to Mr Lant to have emasculated him in that way."

We stood in silence for a while before she turned and looked down to me. "I must speak to Snorre. It's not too late for him to change."

"Oh, no. I wouldn't do that if I were you, Mrs Lant. Snorre is stubborn. Once he has decided upon a course of action nobody can alter that course but him."

"Then what can be done?"

Here it was. My chance.

"It's not through words that you'll persuade Snorre to change his ways," I said. "It's through actions. You need to do something to force a change of direction upon him. Something drastic."

We both stared back out towards the sea. Empowered by the rowdy wind, the water's surface was rocking in all directions and across all plains and dimensions. I took great comfort in knowing the same was happening within Mrs Lant.

16

Fast-forward to that afternoon in the shop and all four of the boys had retreated into the Crypt to practice, leaving me on my own at the shop counter.

The prospect of a record deal had put them in a good mood. Well it had put three of them in a good mood. Suffer had regained consciousness but his mood was trapped in a perpetually contracting vice in a lake of fire located deep within a mountain of pain... so not particularly upbeat.

The new alarm had been fitted earlier in the day and I was feeling as secure as possible given we had been marked for death by Oslo Iron. The shop was quiet and peaceful when four guys walked cautiously down the stairs.

It would be significantly less peaceful when they left.

I had never seen this group before and my suspicions were not immediately aroused on their arrival. They looked as if they were in their early 20s, certainly metallers, but more conventional than our usual clientele. Their jeans were blue and they wore long hair and white trainers, but that gave very little away. They could have been retro-rockers, glam metallers or just plain, stupid, stadium-cattle.

They might also have been death metallers and two years earlier that would have caused me concern. Death and black metal, genres that to the uneducated had very little between them, had in fact been at war for decades. It was the inevitable conflict between devout followers with a shared ideology but with subtly different dogma: like Protestants and Catholics; Shia and Sunni. In the early days we did once get firebombed by a death metal crew but one of the first items on the Baphomet's Agony agenda was the bringing together of these two tribes (that was another thing that Oslo Iron held against us – they liked to take their vendettas to the grave). It had taken a couple of years, but we had been successful. If these kids were death metal devotees I had nothing to worry about.

They weren't.

New arrivals tend to explore in excitable groups, with gasps and superlatives shared at their first sight of each new shelf. However, on arriving, these young men split up and explored the aisles on their own.

That, in itself, didn't cause me any great alarm and neither did the exclamation that one of them emitted when he chanced upon The Wheelchair Goth. The new arrival muttered something at him but I was too far away to hear what it was. All I saw was the long, slow blink The Wheelchair Goth gave him in reply. From a distance, the black make-up around his eyes made it seem as if each eyeball hung suspended, in defiance of gravity, within a fist-sized hole punched into his skull.

No, my suspicion over the group of visitors was not aroused until I noticed they were looking less at the stock and more at each other as they prowled the aisles. At first I felt indignation. I had put a lot of time and creative effort into the construction of artfully pleasing shelf displays, each designed to trigger deeply-rooted purchase impulses. The least that these fuckers could do was look at them!

But then bitterness gave way to trepidation as they kept looking at each other, as though waiting for something.

My finger hovered over the alarm button.

Could they be Oslo Iron? It seemed impossible, they were far too young. But what if I'd underestimated my opponents? Word would reach us very quickly if a gang of fifty year old Oslo Iron were headed our way. Perhaps they had anticipated that.

Perhaps they had sent these guys in to do some reconnaissance in advance.

The more I peered at them, the more I worried. Patches covered the denim they wore over their leather but I didn't recognize the bands featured; the logos depicted none of the beasts, blood and blasphemy I was used to. That too was puzzling. I knew, and stocked, merchandise from most underground metal bands and the imagery of commercial thrash and heavy metal was of course known to me. To discover advocates of an entirely new scene startled and professionally embarrassed me.

The youngest of them, the one that had encountered The Wheelchair Goth, had edged closer to the counter and was flipping through the "S" vinyl. He had long ginger hair and tattoos on the palms of his hands. I couldn't get a clear view of them but they looked like crude Xs etched onto each palm. On seeing that I thought these guys must be straight-edged.

I had always thought the straight-edged scene was a strange one. These were bands and kids that eschewed drugs, alcohol and sometimes sex in favor of regular exercise and a macrobiotic diet. That's not to say that they were benign, peace-loving beatniks – their music was fast, ugly and aggressive and their politics was often fascist. You throw those ingredients into a sweaty venue and add a PA system and you soon discover that straight-edge gigs can be among the most violent on the planet. Without drugs and alcohol to dull the senses, the pace and hostile thrash of their metal turns a straight-edge mosh-pit into an impromptu bout of near-professional kickboxing.

Straight-edge devotees often scrawl the letter X on the backs of their hands in recognition of the convention adopted by venue management to indicate the cross-bearer is underage and should be denied alcohol. I had never seen the X tattooed onto a palm before, but I figured if someone was crazy enough to devote his life to abstinence then nothing was beyond the parameters of his insanity.

We tended not to see many straight-edged kids in our Satanic enclave. Theirs was a philosophy that did not sit too well alongside the unbridled debauchery of our own. I was not aware that any of the straight edge militias had spoken out publicly against Baphomet's Agony and it seemed unlikely they would have struck up an alliance with Oslo Iron.

I soon decided they couldn't be straight-edged kids. First, they all had the long hair and heavy metal aesthetic which was inconsistent with the military crops and hardcore punk styling of straight-edge. Second, one of the patches I could see looked like it featured a figure waving a wine glass in the air. Straight edge doesn't do irony.

It was a puzzle and, I must admit, I was enjoying the challenge of pigeon-holing these specimens. I guess it gave me the same sort of buzz that a zoologist gets when she finds a new frog in the Amazon.

But I was about to discover that my newly discovered genus carried a toxic venom.

As I stared at one of them he pushed some of his hair behind his ear and there was another clue: a tattoo. This one was a symbol of some sort drawn onto his neck, just under his lobe. Most of it remained hidden behind his hair but what I could see looked like a triangle, with one side missing, attached to some larger symbol.

Triangles could denote an affection for the occult, Egypt, Freemasonry, 70s Prog Rock, Bermuda, the list is endless. A triangle told me nothing.

What the hell was it? Who were these fuckers?

I didn't have long to wait to find out. With his three companions positioned at key spokes around the hub the larger of the four looked wide-eyed at each of them. Disgust was still contorting his flabby cheeks, making him look like an octopus sucking a lemon.

"Ready?" he said loudly in English, tossing his hair back and allowing me to see the entirety of his neck tattoo.

The blood in my head drained leaving my face cold and without any means to convey expression. It all emptied into my stomach where it welled and immediately began to fester causing me to feel simultaneously light-headed and nauseous.

The tattoo was a fish. When I saw that, everything fell into place.

Those weren't Xs: they were tattooed stigmata. The figure holding the wine glass was a priest. The fish was Ichthys.

These guys were our worst possible nightmare.

Christians!

"Holy Unblack!" screamed the large Christian as he tore down the contents of a vibrator shelf, burying Popcorn Lady under an avalanche of mechanical phalli. Before I had even triggered the alarm the contents of three more shelving units had been scattered.

Product crashed to the ground, packaging burst and yet the loudest noise of all came from the English verse recited in a monotone unison by the arseholes.

"Yea, though I walk through the valley of the shadow of death."

Bongs cascaded to the floor and shattered, dispersing fragments of colored glass like fluorescent candy wrappers.

"I will fear no evil."

Vinyl representing forty years of heavy metal history from "A" to "C" (one of the most richly populated segments of the metal alphabet) was hurled across the room.

"For thou art with me."

An entire wall of pornography was ripped from its moorings and two hundred DVD sleeves tipped slowly towards the floor in a tsunami of naked flesh and sodomy.

"Thy rod and thy staff they comfort me."

The entire verse had been recited by the time the door from the Crypt burst open and The Exorcist began a stampede towards me with the might of a steam locomotive at full-tilt. Yet before he got anywhere near me, Suffer spun across the room like a tornado. His eyes were larger than I had ever seen them, terrifying globes that looked fit to burst within their sockets. While rivers of effervescent drool rode channels down either side of his mouth.

It was the face of a murderer.

The Exorcist continued his charge. He didn't register the pandemonium, the assailants or Suffer's murderous intent. He looked straight at me and when he saw I was unharmed in the eye of the storm his features lost some of their tension and he slowed down.

However, as any physicist will tell you, an object of The Exorcist's mass travelling at speed takes time to come to a rest. Unfortunately for him, one of our Christian Soldiers was stood slap-bang in the path of my de-accelerating savior. He turned in time to see The Exorcist bearing down on him, but didn't even have time to utter a mitigating prayer for leniency.

The Exorcist attempted to avoid the collision and failed. The impact sent the Christian flying through the air towards the counter behind which I stood. I screamed as he flew straight towards me, but as his feet clipped the edge of the counter and flipped him upside down I had just enough time to dodge him. The airborne Crusader crumpled in a heap precisely where I had just been stood.

The Exorcist leaned over the counter and, with sincerity, offered his apologies to the man, while making sure he wasn't badly hurt.

Suffer had no qualms about inflicting harm. I had seen that look of his before. It was the look he'd had when he attacked the tourists, which was the same look he'd had when he launched himself at Oslo Iron the previous week, which was the same look he'd had the first night we spent together when he broke my jaw. Remembering the pain of that attack I felt a sudden empathy for that stupid Christian kid who was about to die.

"Ailo!" I yelled. "No!"

Suffer turned those eyes on me, eyes that hadn't blinked for as long as I had been watching him, and through bared teeth he hissed. Then he soared through the air towards his victim's head.

With his customary slowness, Bolverk then appeared to join the fracas. Bellowing a hearty cheer, he dipped his head and charged around a corner towards the largest Christian.

Now, take my word for it, that Christian was as huge as you could fathom, but he was all amorphous blubber whereas Bolverk was constructed of a dense, brick-like substance, like pagan dark matter. So when the unstoppable force of his charge met the immovable object of his god-fearing opponent, the impact was cataclysmic.

It was fortunate our bassist didn't have a neck, because if he had it would have folded in on itself like an accordion. I swear I witnessed his whole head, right down to his shoulders, disappear beneath the surface of the Christian's stomach and then re-appear when the Christian sprang-off his shoulders and catapulted backwards down the aisle towards the stairs.

Meanwhile, Suffer had landed on his Christian and somehow engulfed his head and face within his sunken torso. It was almost as if the kid was wearing a Suffer-themed balaclava.

Suffer began a boa-like squeeze. The victim didn't know what was happening and panicked. His attempts to use his hands to remove his assailant were of no avail; Suffer held tight to his scalp like a yeast infection. The Christian began crashing around, hoping a harsh impact against a wall or other hard surface would dislodge his attacker. Again, it served no purpose other than to encourage Suffer to squeeze more tightly.

Suffer was killing him, of that I was sure. I was pissed we had been attacked by this God Squad but I didn't want anyone to die down here. It might be good for the band's infamy later, but we needed that record contract and to get it we needed our vocalist. The lawyer I'd found to represent Suffer was good, but even she might struggle to wriggle him out of a murder conviction in time to sign the deal.

I grabbed The Exorcist's arm.

"You'd better save him, Peter," I said, pointing to Suffer's victim. "I think his God is about to forsake him."

Suffer's Christian had fallen to his knees. What little oxygen he had left was being diverted away from his limbs in an attempt to maintain his vital organs for as long as possible before death. I suppose it must have been like drowning for the poor guy. Drowning in a sea of Suffer.

Once the kid had keeled over, Suffer released his grip and scuttled on all fours towards a display of swords and axes that adorned the vertical surface of the hub. Bolverk's Folly is what it had come to be known as. The collection of arms looked ridiculous and entirely incongruous, but Bolverk had insisted we keep it there as a shrine to Odin or Thor or Voldemort. I forget which.

These tacky stage props were pinned up with small bits of wire. Suffer knew he could snap them with just one good yank. However, just before he got to them, The Exorcist reached down one of his long arms and grabbed Suffer's collar. Then with the other hand he reached over the counter, grabbed his own now-conscious Christian and with one deft move hoisted him over the counter and brought his face close to his own.

"Take your friends and flee," he suggested, trying to keep his grip on the struggling Suffer. Then he flung the young man towards his comrade.

Once his second hand was free, The Exorcist gave himself a second point of purchase on Suffer's waistband, swung him around and like a ten-pin-bowler hurled him down the aisle back towards the Crypt and away from the Christians.

By the time Decadence arrived at my side, the group's footsteps on the steel stairs were echoing off the walls. I had grown accustomed to the myriad expressions he could beam across those handsome features of his: scorn, lust and self-satisfaction were the most frequent of them but during our more intimate past I had also glimpsed flashes of fragility, longing and, dare I say it, love.

However, the look that he gave me as he sidled up towards me through the chaos of scattered black-metallicana was entirely new to me. It was the look of awe you would give a tractor if it beat a superbike off the lights.

I returned his stare with my customary disdain at which point he diverted his eyes to the ground near to where I was stood. I followed his gaze and shrieked at the sight of the fourth Christian, the young ginger one, lying unconscious at my feet; his head leaching blood onto the floor from a wound by his ear.

It was then I realized that in my right hand, clenched tightly, was the hilt of a gigantic dildo, stained with blood.

17

In the weeks following my windswept conversation with Snorre's mother on the harbor wall, I had numerous opportunities to position myself in front of the sun and cast long shadows across her.

I had divined two chinks in her armor. The dual flesh spots exposed on the belly of the dragon were an anxiety about Snorre's future happiness and a vague guilt concerning what had happened to her marriage. I could see she harbored a memory of happier times with her husband many years in the past when, presumably, the balustrades on her emotional defenses were less formidable. I could also discern she felt responsible for the deterioration of her marriage and the resultant sloth and depravity of her husband.

I then set about exploiting those weaknesses.

"I was talking to Mr Lant the other day," I told her. "He was telling me how the two of you met when you and some friends spent your break in the countryside just outside Copenhagen."

That was bullshit of course. I never communicated with Snorre's father unless it was absolutely necessary and even then I managed to get by with a narrow vocabulary of shrugs and grunts. What intelligence I had about their courtship I gleaned from Snorre himself.

"Yes," she replied. "I was with my friends Suuvi and Rebecca. We had a month's leave that we spent on a campsite on the shores of the Øresund Sound."

I noted with interest the ever so subtle hint of nostalgia that animated her speech.

"Is it true back then he was energetic and athletic?"

I can't say with confidence that a smile passed over her lips, so perhaps it was the halogen light of the Lant kitchen that somehow managed to find a reflective surface in her aluminum eyes sufficient, just, to provoke a moment of sparkle.

"Yes. Back then we both shared a passion for fishing and camping."

"Really? Mr Lant?"

"It's true."

"He once made a crude remark to me about having a tent pole in his pants but from the way he behaves now I would have never thought him capable of enjoying a vigorous outdoor life," I said. It wasn't a comment that required a response. It was just another barb under her skin. "I guess he was chasing after all three of you girls on that trip."

"No. Back then he only had eyes for me."

I contrived an expression of skepticism.

"It's strange isn't it," I said with feigned contemplation. "The way people can go from one extreme to another over the course of a short lifetime. Was it a gradual change with Mr Lant or did it just happen overnight?"

"Perhaps it was gradual. I don't recall."

"You don't recall? But there must have come a point when you first realized that there had been a change in his attitude towards you?"

"When I was younger I used to spend a lot of my time at sea. The Navy would take me away from him and from Snorre, sometimes for months at a time. It's difficult to maintain any kind of intensity in a relationship when there's so much distance and silence between you."

"Distance diluted the intensity between you, then...?"

My comment hung in the air between us. I watched as her

sparkle faded and she processed the meaning of what I had just said.

I left the Lant household that day with a spring in my step.

Mr Lant's degeneration was a useful and frequently called-upon subterfuge for my heinous plot against Snorre's mother, but on other occasions I used a different contaminate to poison her reservoir. Her son's prospects for a contented life was the other wooden horse, packed full of assassins, that I regularly wheeled through her gateway.

"You look sad Marta," she said on a later visit.

Fuck right I did. I'd been practicing that face and gait in front of a mirror the entire morning. By the time I deployed it all in front of Mrs Lant I had almost managed to convince myself I was depressed.

I shrugged.

"What is troubling you?"

I looked away from her and forced moisture from my eyes. This artfully manufactured display of emotion clearly unsettled Mrs Lant and, as expected, she didn't know what to do. She wanted to comfort me but I'm not sure she knew how. From her safe distance she eventually stretched her arms out their full length and cradled my jaw in both her hands. They felt hard and cold upon my skin, but there was strength in her fingertips.

"Tell me, Marta. What is it?"

Having fought to encourage them I then fought to contain my tears. Using as punctuation the sobs that pulsated through my frame I embarked upon my well-practiced speech.

"I have come to enjoy the time that I spend with Snorre; we all have. It will be difficult for Peter, Edvard and I to leave it all behind and move on."

"Move on? Marta, what are you talking about?"

"Snorre says he's uncomfortable being around us. He has decided it's not right for him to have so many friends."

"But he's been so happy recently. What could have made him say that?" Glad for the opportunity to do something practical with her hands Mrs Lant pulled a handkerchief from her pocket and wiped the tears from my cheeks.

"I hope you don't mind if I speak frankly Mrs Lant... and in confidence?"

"Please do."

"He is just so anxious to be like you!" I blurted out, letting the words tumble out of my mouth as if they had built up behind my lips with such pressure the stress had bucked my teeth. I paused and took a well-rehearsed breath, then continued. "He watches you from a distance. Tries hard to copy your mannerisms and adopts affectations that in his eyes make him sound or look like you. He even studies your old photo albums, searching out new secrets that might give him a greater understanding of your methods." I sighed theatrically. "He's got it into his head you achieved your success by shunning your friends and withdrawing into yourself. By his reckoning, Peter, Edvard and I are obstacles in his path to emulating your accomplishments. You never wasted your time on friendships so he insists he shouldn't either. He has decided that he must abandon us. But please don't tell him I told you that. I want to make the most of the time we have together and if he hears that I have told you about this he will shut us down immediately. I couldn't cope with that."

When Mrs Lant eventually spoke again I could hear a wretchedness corrupt her voice like sand mixed through butter.

"If I had my time again, I would probably work much harder to preserve the friendships that I enjoyed in my youth," she said. "It certainly wasn't a conscious decision of mine to close them down. That it happened nevertheless has been a great regret."

I saw then that my moment of triumph was fast approaching. I've said before it is my firm belief the only time previously anyone had succeeded in penetrating Mrs Lant's defenses (literally and metaphorically) was when she opened her heart to her useless, beatnik husband. On that occasion she was swindled by a parasite on the hunt for sex and for a host from whom he could leach a life of lethargy. Ironically, on the occasion it happened next – the occasion I am describing to you now – her predator was motivated by a different kind of selfishness. One intended to drive her away and tear a hole in Snorre that would ensure his decline was irreversible. That would be success. That would ensure he could never make me happy.

"Whatever," I said with weary resignation. "That's what Snorre thinks. He wants to get rid of his friends."

"Then this must stop."

"Yes, but you won't stop him by confronting him about it. If you do that it will serve as fuel for his fire and he will entrench."

"But something must be done, Marta?"

Scanning the shelves close by where I stood in the Lant living room my gaze settled on a photograph of the Lant family taken many years earlier, when Snorre was newborn.

"You look so happy together there," I said, feigning a smile while my mind raced ahead trying to find new pits and traps into which I could shove my unsuspecting victim.

Mrs Lant followed my gaze and then took the frame from the shelf in order to see it better. A young and devastatingly handsome Mr Lant held his son with visible pride while Mrs Lant looked on adoringly at both of them.

"We were so happy then," she said, smiling down at the photograph.

"But no longer," I replied, puncturing her smile with the rusty nail of truth as I took the frame from her hands. I turned it over thoughtfully in my hands. "You know, if Snorre spent more time with his father, and if he were somehow persuaded to be more like him, then, paradoxically, it could result in all three of you being happier."

"Oh," the older woman said. "Do you think so?"

"I do. If Snorre indulged in some of life's pleasures, with just a fraction of Mr Lant's enthusiasm, it would do him no end of good."

Her heart may well have been carefully concealed deep within the impenetrable fortress that she, or perhaps circumstance, had built around it, but I am fucking dogged when I need to be and little by little my intensely focused laser beams of darkness began to find their mark.

"Perhaps you are right Marta. Perhaps it is time for me to leave Kragerø and allow the two of them together for a while."

There. That was what I wanted. Except... now she'd said the words I'd wanted to hear, they were no longer enough. I needed her departure to be far more final than that.

Let's get clear what I was trying to achieve here. I wanted her to go; to leave Kragerø for good and to sever all ties with Snorre. Snorre was used to her leaving him with his father for months at a time so more of that was no good to me. I required Snorre to have full and unambiguous closure on the maternal relationship that made him happy.

Still holding the frame, I released its backing and slid the photograph out.

"Snorre will turn sixteen soon. How can you avoid the possibility he will follow you rather that remain here with his father?"

"That I don't know, Marta."

Staring intently into Mrs Lant's eyes throughout, I ripped the photograph down the middle, permanently separating her image from that of her son and husband. I then handed her both halves of the photograph, slowly turned on my heels and left the room.

More time passed and I continued to litter Mrs Lant's path with my emotional landmines. Nothing too obvious: cryptic little hints that, despite his father's encouragement, Snorre was still ignoring the girls at school because he didn't think his mother would approve of him having a girlfriend. Targeted little questions about her engagement and early married years, designed to reveal pleasant memories in my presence, but that would leave behind lingering guilt and shame bombs that would eventually go off when she was on her own.

These skills of manipulation, formed during my apprenticeship in the Lant kitchen and honed in the years since, have served me very well in my career. I can now make almost anyone within my gravity do pretty much anything I want.

Yes, I know you know that. Why else do you think you're here, talking to me? Anyway, don't interrupt.

To be clear – my need to punish her was not down to any personal grievance. I quite liked her. It's just that I felt a compulsion to remove her from the picture. It didn't work out the way I planned, but by Christ did it work out!

It all came to a head one October evening of our sixteenth year.

Peter, Edvard, Snorre and I were sat in Snorre's basement listening to speed metal as Snorre attempted to keep pace with the chord progressions on his beloved guitar. Back then he had an ESP EX-260, a brash and ostentatious parody of the classic electric guitar. There were no soft and sensual curves or sunburst designs on this device, it was all spikes and jagged edges rendered in black with a headstock sharpened to a deadly point.

Despite Snorre's tendencies towards the darker shades of metal, he had us on a balanced diet of punk, sludge, death, speed, thrash, grindcore and, only occasionally, black metal. If you know how the metal scenes work and intertwine you will appreciate that kids fed from that eclectic a menu will, relatively speaking of course, be of an optimistic bent.

It's only when you polarize into one particular metal sub-category that you begin to isolate yourself from the wider metal community, retreat from its light and head towards the dark corners. Once you have sworn allegiance to one particular tribe you will begin to display your affection for it in your detestation for everything else. It's simple psychology really: kids with poor social skills can only communicate positive emotions like friendship, appreciation or happiness through negative media like hatred, scorn and violence. And if the particular metal sub-genre to which you pledge your allegiance is black metal, you will find your flames of hatred have themselves a jet-powered fan so formidable even a minor irritation can be whipped up into an all-consuming and murderous rage.

If you choose black metal it is not a dark corner of the heavy metal cave you will find yourself hiding in, it is a deep well with smooth walls. And while at that point in our career we knew of the existence of the well – indeed we peered over its edge with curiosity from time to time – we still exercised caution when we played nearby. It took the events of that evening to pitch us headlong into the abyss.

In one corner of the basement in which we often spent our evenings the Lant family kept its luggage. The suitcases were sturdy, sensible and well-used, and stamped with an anchor surmounted by a crown – the insignia of The Royal Norwegian Navy.

Early in the evening Mrs Lant appeared and, in silence, retrieved three of the cases from the shelves before taking them upstairs.

Whenever it was possible for Snorre to gaze upon his mother he would do so and therefore his eyes remained fixed on her throughout this activity. Yet, unusually, on that occasion she went out of her way to avoid all eye contact with him.

I felt a tickle in my uterus. I had sensed all day something momentous was going to happen and the retrieval Mrs Lant's luggage was a good sign. Luggage equals travel, equals departure, equals looming despair for Snorre.

An hour later Snorre decided we all needed coffee. I agreed to help him prepare it so the two of us went upstairs to the kitchen. He often walked around his home with his guitar slung around behind him with its neck pointing downward and that evening he did just that so I was forced to give him a wide berth as we negotiated the corners – that spike on his headstock was lethal.

As we passed through the hallway we saw the three suitcases lined up by the front door in a neat order determined by their relative size. A quizzical frown upset the flawless surface of Snorre's features while another tingle of excitement shot out from my abdomen and pulsed right through my virginal body. I recall how my buttocks clenched with an energy I would later discover was deeply sexual in its origins.

In the kitchen we found Snorre's parents in the midst of an argument.

"Suffolk?" Mr Lant said in disbelief. "I don't get it. How can you decide to up and leave at a moment's notice to start a new life in Suffolk of all places? What's got into you? What about us?"

"Leave?" Snorre asked. "Who's leaving and what's Suffolk?"

"Your mother is leaving us, Snorre. To go and live in some English backwater."

Snorre edged away from his parents towards the units that surrounded the kitchen. His guitar clattered against a cabinet and his hands instinctively reached up to hug his arms.

"Mother?"

Mrs Lant shot me a momentary glance before turning towards a spot a fraction to the left of her son's face. "I'm leaving you," she said hesitantly. "I'm.... I'm fed up with you, with both of you."

Emotion of any variety sounded peculiar in Mrs Lant's tone, but the irritation that she contrived sounded downright bizarre.

"I don't understand." Snorre's voice was small.

Mrs Lant took a deep breath and began what was clearly a well-rehearsed speech.

"I've spent the last sixteen years wasting my life with you and your father. I have not been happy since the day I married. I should have spent my youth having fun with my friends." Her gaze flicked to me momentarily and I nodded as if giving her my approval. "Instead I focused on my career and on you, Snorre. That has ruined me. It has turned me sad, bitter and cold. Lives are meant to be lived to the fullest, son. My life these last sixteen years has stagnated and it's time for that to change. There's still time left for me to turn my life around, to start afresh and to experience the happiness that I should have allowed myself in my youth."

She turned to her husband. "You won't need to worry about money. I will still provide for you. You just won't ever see me again. I want a divorce and in the meantime you can go off with whomever you want and live as you please."

The anxiety that had been so evident in Mr Lant's tense arms and bit lip vanished in an instant and he almost slumped to the floor in relief. Snorre, meanwhile, was folding in on himself like a paper ball crumpled by an invisible hand.

My emotions were more complicated. I was ecstatic of course, but my joy was multi-faceted. I was thrilled that my carefully executed plan had borne fruit and was proud of myself in succeeding in breaking through the surface of someone as thick-skinned as Mrs Lant. I was a little irritated Mr Lant had prospered from my efforts, but I figured I would work on manipulating him to disappear soon enough. However, I had to swallow all of that down and feign ignorance and sympathy while the episode was still being acted-out in front of me.

"Don't leave me, Mother."

Mrs Lant turned away from her son. Again, just for a moment, our eyes met. There was doubt in hers, conviction in mine. In that split second of communion, I pulsed fortitude over the intervening space between us and she fed on the strength I offered her.

"I *must* leave Snorre. You'll both be fine." Mrs Lant turned to her husband. "You'll find yourself girlfriends and between yours and his you'll be able to replace me with something more much suitable." She then addressed both of them. "I have failed you as a mother and I have failed you as a wife. Whomever it is that comes to you next can only be an improvement on me."

That feeling came back to me again, an exquisite tingle beneath my stomach that sent a wave of condensed joy rippling through my abdomen and then out through to the extremities of my toes, fingers, nose and ears. I staggered from the intensity of it and required support from a chair placed fortuitously close-by. It was a complete sexual satiation the likes of which no man would ever provide me.

However, the sensation was short lived. It was soon replaced with doubt, fear and anxiety.

Snorre began to cry. His small sobs grew quickly into shoulder-shaking wails.

It wasn't compassion for Snorre's plight that caused my anxiety. It was fear of the reaction Snorre's tears provoked in his mother. She began to falter. She wanted to go to him, she wanted to comfort him. I could see her resilience was failing her. I could also sense that she was fighting to keep her eyes away from me again. The battle was raging within her and she knew just a glance in my direction could determine its outcome.

"Mother I love you!" Snorre wailed. "I love you because of who you are and had you raised me differently I couldn't possibly love you any more than I do. If you leave me, you won't free me, you will… you will… destroy me."

Mrs Lant's eyes – eyes that had remained as dry as a desert for over sixteen years – began to fill. When the tears eventually fell there came a monsoon and the smooth surface of her adult cheeks came to know the sweet, salty fluid that cascaded down her face.

Snorre opened his arms to her and she ran to him.

Shit, I thought.

Until that moment (I would later learn), Snorre had no memory of his mother ever actually touching him. And in that embrace, sixteen years of withheld maternal love was unleashed at once in a torrent.

My heart sank with sickening velocity. The kind that only comes when hope has been quickly raised and instantly dashed upon the rocks of failure. I tasted bile as it rose up into my throat and its vapor filled my mouth.

But in the wake of my nausea came some clarity of thought. Snorre was stood with his back to the kitchen door, his long limbs encasing the slim, athletic body of his mother who sobbed and whispered long-repressed expressions of love and devotion into the ear of her fragile son.

I saw the door, anticipated its swing and applied some quick, crude mathematics to the numerous angles, arcs and levers displayed before me. For a moment I ceased to see the room in three-dimensional Technicolor and instead interpreted my field of vision as a blank page filled with pencil lines and geometric indicia.

I pulled out my phone and sent a text to Peter:

"Help! Come quick! Now!"

I then walked casually towards the two-headed, Hydra-like mass of Lant flesh that was still blubbering by the door.

"I think we could all do with some coffee," I said and, under the guise of gaining better access to the kettle, I placed both my hands on the waist of Mrs Lant and carefully repositioned both her and Snorre closer to the door.

As I filled the carafe I heard some of what Mrs Lant was whispering to Snorre. In retrospect, it was a beautiful little speech of motherly love and promising she'd never leave him. The kind of speech that leads to happy people and happy lives living happily ever after.

Usually.

In this case, her final words were obscured by the sound of Peter thundering down the hallway right on cue, displaying the blinkered concern for my well-being I had carefully provoked by my text. I turned just in time to see the door burst open.

It all happened very quickly but what followed was a short sequence of events the macabre choreography of which will remain engraved into my memory forever, with a groove deeper than that of a first kiss.

The kitchen door slammed open and hit the body of the inverted guitar still slung over Snorre's back while he embraced his mother.

The guitar was spun down and around in a powerful arc.

The pointed headstock swung up and pierced the back of Mrs Lant's skull.

It entered just above the nape, embedding three of the six machine heads in her brain.

As far as I am aware, Mrs Lant was cremated with the headstock still stuck in her head. When I last saw the corpse, being zipped into a green bag in the Lant kitchen, the headstock had been sawn off the neck of the guitar, but it remained protruding from her skull. It meant that when she was laid on her back, her head would tilt forward, giving the impression she was focusing intently on her stomach.

Was Peter responsible or was it my fault? That's an interesting question. But that's neither here nor there, simply a minor detail in the story, okay? Let's not dwell on who was the principal and who was the agent or whether it was homicide or a gruesome accident. She died, Peter took some of the blame and although not the intended execution of my plan, the results were the same.

A kid like Snorre would not emerge out of that experience with anything resembling positive mental health. The terrifying prospect of happiness had therefore been removed from my path and some major foundations had been laid for the mayhem that Baphomet's Agony would go on to generate.

18

To my surprise, the dildo emerged unscathed from the blow I delivered to the Ginger Christian to render him unconscious. Apparently, the craftsmanship that goes into the manufacture of twenty-four inch, double-headed, battery powered, latex-sheathed vibrators is second to none. Once the blood had been wiped off it was as good as new.

As The Exorcist knelt over the young man, trying to determine just how badly he was hurt, Decadence and Bolverk chatted, clearly overjoyed at the afternoon's fight.

"Did you see how that guy somersaulted over the desk?"

"Yes, but you did you see what happened when Bolverk rammed that fat fuck in the gut? Cunt never moved so fast in his life!"

"What about the one that Suffer nearly killed? He was all over him like a swarm of bees."

Suffer wasn't stood with the rest of us. He walked in a small circle within one of the aisles muttering to himself intently and gesticulating randomly. At one point he gripped hold of his skull as if his brain were pulsing uncontrollably within it.

I walked over and laid a hand on his shoulder. The contact extracted him from whatever nightmare had enveloped him, but I received no thanks. Rather, he spat at me and shoved me against one of the few intact shelves left in the shop. He then turned to the rest of the band.

"Are we done?"

"Are we done what?" Bolverk asked.

"Are we done with the practice for the day?"

"Yes, we are," Decadence replied.

"Good," Suffer said. He pointed at me as I righted myself and rubbed my bruised back. "You come see me tomorrow."

I nodded.

Once a week I was required to defile Suffer in new and disgusting ways. If I succeeded in finding a way in which to humiliate him, he would cum and I would be spared. If I failed to make him cum, he would finish himself off as best he could which might then result in me sustaining injuries. Under those pressures it's amazing just how inventive one can be.

Having set up our oh-so-romantic rendezvous, Suffer scampered down the exit aisle and, on all fours, bounded up the stairs on to the street.

Bolverk, Decadence and The Exorcist watched him leave in silence and then all three of them looked at me with a mixture of wonder and horror. Only Decadence found a way to bury his discomfort.

"Well, that was an eventful end to practice. I feel like I've got half the Columbian coke harvest coursing through my veins after all that. What are we going do now?"

"We need to clean up," I said.

"Shouldn't we get this guy to a hospital?" The Exorcist asked, still leaning over the incapacitated Ginger Christian.

"Fuck him," Decadence said.

"Fucking him is one option," Bolverk said. "Alternatively, we do something a little more permanent. Our Gods have been kind to us today. Perhaps they deserve a sacrifice?"

Decadence's eyes managed to find what little light there was in the basement and sparkled with excitement.

"It's about time," he said. "Let's give the priest a call."

19

There was a short investigation into the death of Mrs Lant, but it concluded that it was simply a horrible accident and no charges were brought against anyone. Peter explained his enthusiastic entrance into the Lant kitchen with reference to my text message, which I convinced everyone was just a plea for assistance in carrying the biscuits downstairs – which, in retrospect, was perhaps a little over-dramatic. But hey! I was a teenage girl that played with three pubescent boys, *of course* I got a bit carried away from time-to-time.

Peter was initially shaken up over the incident and his mother and her Church were no help. They both rallied to his assistance but did so by mounting an unnecessary defense and counter-attack rather than by offering him the psychological support he actually required. Where they should have given Peter a hug, they instead sent him on an intense bible-study retreat with a bunch of strangers out in the frozen wastelands in the north of the country. Where they should have offered Peter counselling to help him through his trauma, they instead spread the rumor he was doing Christ's work in ridding us of sinful heathens. And instead of helping Peter mend his relationship with Snorre and his father, they instead dug up dirt about Mr Lant's extra-marital activities and broadcast it from the pulpit.

Having said all of that, Peter eventually emerged from the episode largely unscathed. He was a simple boy who had already been damaged more than most, so I guess the additional emotional scarring barely made an impression on his already toughened and lacerated soul.

It was Snorre who was the scathed one.

As I'd hoped.

When the neck of his guitar caved-in his mother's skull, Snorre was still locked in an embrace with her. The impact crashed her forehead into his face, cracked a cheekbone, left a permanent scar on his chin and knocked him out. He came to in a hospital bed and on doctor's orders the news of his mother's death was withheld for forty-eight hours. When he was told what had happened, he apparently closed his eyes and remained very calm and silent. This pleased the doctors who took it as a sign he was handling his grief well. What they didn't know was his calmness was in consequence of his entire store of energy being focused on an intense and silent fury that left him without any resources to expend on external displays of emotion.

Snorre was off school for a month and when he eventually returned he had metamorphosed. Gone was the butterfly with its iridescent wings and in its place was a beautifully ugly, scowling larva that sat apart from everyone at the back of the classroom burning away any joy in the room to fuel its wrath. His hatred for Peter was all-encompassing. He didn't speak much during this period but what he did say was normally hate-filled and directed towards the person he held accountable for his mother's death.

I was proud of the transformation I had caused in him, although the Peter loathing, whilst inevitable, was an inconvenience that I needed to fix. However, it did come with an unexpected consequence.

I found myself drawn to Bad Snorre.

I had set out to dim his light, to corrupt it. Yet now it was gone I became captivated by the void in its place. The brooding, sinister ghoul lost in his grief, prowling the school corridors consumed with rage was intriguing. That new darkness cast a shadow over his face that made him infinitely more beautiful in my eyes than he was before. The stink of his mother's death that clung to Snorre in the following weeks acted as a pheromone I found quite compelling.

During this period, I once saw him standing on the harbor in exactly the same spot I had found his mother a few months previous. I kept my distance and watched him from the warmth of a cafe on the adjacent wall of the squared-off harbor.

For two and a half hours he barely moved. Like his mother, Snorre seemed immune to the forces of nature that attacked everything around him. I watched others being buffeted by the harsh winds that charged off the sea and then tore round the harbor. Yet wearing just jeans, T-shirt and leather jacket, Snorre seemed untroubled by the elements. He just stood there, letting the wind sweep his long hair from a face solemn with grief. He wore it well.

Until, suddenly, his expression changed. Morphing in an instant to one of unrestrained violence. He ran to one side, ripped a plastic garbage can from its moorings and, whirling it and himself five hundred and forty degrees, spun the entire thing out to sea. Colorful litter arced like the tail on a comet as the can flew through the air. Panting, with shoulders rising and falling in competition with the slap of the waves on the harbor wall, Snorre watched the can bob up and down on the water's surface. As it sunk beneath the surface he spat into the sea, turned on his heels and ran away.

There was a power and madness in that rage. I felt something stir within me. A sexual something, but there was inspiration in there too. I hadn't bargained on this new, dark Snorre. I sensed if I could channel for my own ends some of the dark power he was generating we could achieve something significant. At the same time, I saw an opportunity to bring him under my control and tone down his enmity towards Peter. All of these ideas led me to the same conclusion.

Snorre's bedroom had a small balcony that overhung a side

street. I knew on a warm night the glass door that led onto it would be open and at midnight, about six weeks after Mrs Lant died, I arranged for Peter to meet me underneath that balcony. I readied myself by standing very still and tense and then Peter crouched down, grabbed my ankles and raised me straight up in the air, thus achieving a sufficient height for me to scramble onto the balcony.

At just gone one o'clock I emerged onto the balcony and jumped down into the arms of Peter who had been instructed to wait for me below. He had no difficulty in catching me; over the years he must have got used to my size and shape which has never tended to fluctuate wildly. On that particular night, what weight I had shed from losing my virginity in the intervening hour I had probably gained back by taking Snorre's.

20

Father Jacobson was a rotund priest of about fifty years of age. He had one of those perpetually reddened faces that would have you believe that it had just emerged out of the cold. He wasn't really a bad man or even a bad priest, except of course in this one respect: he would regularly officiate at Black Masses where, powered by the massive consumption of narcotics, he would preside over a crowd of copulating hedonists as they made sacrifices to Satan.

He needed the money, you see. Rumor had it when he was a teenage seminarian he was tricked into lying with a prostitute. It happened just the once, but if fate decides to shit in your cycle helmet that's all it takes. The prostitute fell pregnant and ever since he has secretly maintained his hidden family. For that he required funds.

Nobody knew where he came from or where his parish was. His name was almost certainly a pseudonym too. He was just a pay-as-you-go mobile phone number that got passed around those high up in Norway's Satanic pecking-order.

He'd got quite good at his job over the years. Clad in his dramatic black robes and cowl, with a rich bass tone to his incantations, he could really camp it up. He wasn't the only priest in the municipality that would do that sort of thing, and he certainly wasn't the cheapest, but he was definitely the best.

I always insisted on being the one to pay him, cash in hand, before the sordid events. I enjoyed watching him the moment he took the money. I suspect he had trained himself to dissociate the amiable, bumbling rural clergyman (no doubt beloved and well-fed by the septuagenarian womenfolk in his parish) from the wicked blasphemer who would conduct the Black Mass with such malevolent aplomb. Payment was the transition point. While the money was in my hand he was edgy, nervous and wracked with guilt so tangible that he could have done with a leash to keep it under control. But the moment the cash was in his hand his anxiety would evaporate and a louche sensualist would take the place of the apprehensive prude. In an instant, his look of shame would be replaced by one of lechery.

Securing the services of Father Jacobson was the first stage in our preparations. A cryptic message beamed out to the faithful over a few social networks came next, and then we prepared the Crypt.

Our particular Black Mass involved the services of three naked women. I always left it to Decadence to source them, seeing as he had a long list of eager, nubile groupies that would have jumped at the chance to perform. In recent months he had fallen into the habit of using two in particular to form the Pillars of the ritual: a tall Ethiopian girl with a shaved head who, barefoot, was almost as tall as The Exorcist; and a slightly shorter white girl with immense breasts.

On this occasion, the girl that Decadence used as the Altar that sat between the Pillars had a familiar face: it was the girl who licked his boot at the Oslo gig. I learned later she was the daughter of a government minister. That didn't surprise me. Well-heeled teenage girls of wealth were often drawn into our circle, but only ever briefly. They would be attracted to the air of gothic romance Decadence fashioned around himself like a cloak, but once they had appalled their parents and shocked the neighbors they would tire of the scene and spin out of it, back to their lives of high fashion, dinner parties and banker boyfriends. A stint as a Kragerø Satanist was becoming as much a part of the Oslo debutante life-cycle as voluntary work in Africa or an unpaid season at a New York auction house.

Early that evening, as the Black Mass got underway in the Crypt, the Altar and the Pillars took up their position on the elevated stage. With the aid of soporific opiates procured at great cost from a hospital in the Oslo suburbs, they would then remain motionless, impassive and naked throughout the night's festivities.

Did they know how they were going to be used that night? Perhaps, perhaps not. Their parents certainly didn't and I would have loved to be a fly on the wall if they ever found out.

"Off out again darling? Is it the private party at that new contemporary art gallery?"

"Not tonight, mother."

"Where then?"

"Well Mummy, I'm off to the underground lair of some Satanic black metal band, where I'll be voluntarily drugged and stripped naked, and will form the backdrop to what I've been told may be a human sacrifice. Don't wait up!"

I'm sure it sounded something like that. And, yes, you heard me right. Human sacrifice. Although it's perhaps not the kind you're thinking of...

By around ten o'clock that evening a lively throng of freaks and weirdoes had poured into the shop and amassed in the Crypt, and the wine was flowing. Many of the crowd wore elaborate animal heads: goats, wolves, snakes, pigs, bulls and lions. Everyone with the exception of Popcorn Lady wore black. Many were in rubber suits, exposing nipples and genitals. Some were already eyeing up their partners for the night, while around them firebreathers and dancers wandered as a precursor to the main event.

Wheelchair Goth was there: silent and sullen as ever, his chair rolled against a wall.

We had a strange soundtrack that night. Decadence was giving us the usual mix of metal with an emphasis on its darker shades, but in a departure from what I had come to expect he mixed the metal with an occasional electronic track or an abrasive piece of industrial dance music. It wasn't conventional by any stretch of the imagination, but it suited the night perfectly.

By twelve, the crowd was drunk, high and horny but, being respectful of certain unwritten conventions, no actual penetration had yet occurred – although every act falling short of it had become commonplace.

"Thou shall not be lain 'til the beast is slain (so just give head 'til blood is shed)." That was our oft-repeated mantra.

At the stroke of midnight the huge gong that dominated one wall of the Crypt was struck and as its echo trailed off it left behind a silence. After a short period (necessary for the generation of the optimum quantity of drama) a door on the opposite side of the Crypt swung open and the crowd let out a collective gasp.

Father Jacobson led the robed forms of Bolverk, The Exorcist and Decadence (Suffer never attended these soirees) in a solemn procession across the room to the Altar behind which the Baphomet's Agony logo adorned the wall. The boys carried a full-size wooden crucifix, upon which the now conscious and visibly terrified, naked – but gagged – Ginger Christian had been hung.

Father Jacobson stopped in front of the Altar with his back to his congregation (a stance he maintained throughout the ceremony that followed, as wherever possible a Black Mass seeks to reverse the conventions of its Christian sibling). The Exorcist and Bolverk placed the crucifix upright against the wall and retired to take their place among the faithful. Decadence remained with his back to us, just to the left of Father Jacobson.

It was at that point a realization of what might happen to him dawned on the Ginger Christian. Looking out across the narcotic miasma of the Crypt, he would have seen a room full of outcasts eagerly anticipating bloodshed and patiently awaiting the diabolic display of blasphemous pageantry of which he was the centerpiece. He would also have seen a table to the right of Father Jacobson that had been festooned with bejeweled daggers, scalpels of polished steel and a spectacular (and incomprehensible) array of implements of surgery, torture or a combination of the two.

The sacrificial victim would have had a clear view of them all.

All credit to him though, a lot of people would have soiled themselves in his position. Naked and strung up on a pair of hastily conjoined oak floorboards he didn't have an awful lot of dignity left, but what little he retained he managed to preserve by avoiding the temptation to shit himself.

That had certainly happened before.

"Hail Satan!" boomed the priest with arms outstretched over the now gently writhing Altar.

"Hail Satan!" the congregation boomed back in unison.

With his back to them Father Jacobson continued in his most sonorous tone, "We have been gathered here together in hate to celebrate the profane, to renounce what is righteous and to worship at the base of what is most base. Hail Satan!"

"Hail Satan!"

Father Jacobson gestured to the Ginger Christian.

"We have before us a guest. Let us welcome him into our repugnant midst. He is a child of light wandered into the shadows."

The Ginger Christian looked down upon Father Jacobson with something approaching hope. "Surely an ordained man of the cloth would not permit a God-fearing child such as he to perish at the hands of a Satanic mob," he must have been thinking. "Surely a man of the cloth would intervene to save him."

Not this man of the cloth.

"As children of the night it is incumbent upon us to plunge him into an eternal darkness. As the enemies of all that is good and pure, we must rid the world of the kind, of the meek and of the righteous. We must stain the unstained and corrupt the incorruptible. Poor and blameless child, look your last upon the world through innocent human eyes."

Here Father Jacobson paused. We all stared at the Ginger Christian with a strange combination of pity and acute, excited anticipation. In return, his wild eyes flashed from one face to the next – from ox, to goat, to pig, to wolf. But not even the human faces before him returned his beseeching look with anything other than an eagerness to witness what was soon to befall him.

Father Jacobson turned to Decadence and gave him a small nod. Decadence stepped round the nearest Pillar and retrieved a silver goblet from between the legs of the Altar. The concoction within had been mixed earlier in the evening. It consisted of equal parts cream sherry and human blood to which some herbs and brown sugar had been added before the potion had been gently warmed (but not boiled), sieved and then left to stand for an hour before three droplets of LSD were added from a pipette.

Decadence handed the goblet to Father Jacobson. I was never sure how much of the cocktail the Good Father drank. I suspect he just moistened his lip before handing it back to Decadence who greedily consumed the remainder of the draught. He always insisted it tasted delicious but I'm sure that there's some mind-over-matter in there.

We all knew what was coming next. We were poised on a sacrificial precipice.

"Please!" the Ginger Christian said in a faltering whisper. "Please don't!"

"Silence!" Father Jacobson shouted with such force that everyone flinched. "We are not a congregation in which pity or mercy is respected, we are not susceptible to thanks and we deplore kindness. Unless you are prepared to bribe us with material wealth or sensual pleasure you must remain silent and preserve your energy so that the spectacle of your sacrifice is not compromised."

Father Jacobson spoke in Norwegian, of which the Ginger Christian appeared to speak none, so the meaning of the sermon was entirely lost on him. The victim continued with his pathetic pleading for mercy.

"Please! Please don't!"

But the moment of sacrifice had arrived.

What happened next? Sorry, but one of the rules of a Black Mass is that the precise details of the sacrifice may not be disclosed to the uninitiated. Anyway, no amount of me explaining to you will actually convey the sheer depravity of what followed.

Did he die? Sadly not. However, we certainly broke his soul. Sacrificed his spirit and changed him forever.

Or, rather, Popcorn Lady did.

"My sinful and foolhardy children," Father Jacobson said as the ritual concluded. "The moment of sacrifice is complete and I invite you to bid farewell to the innocence of this young man. With that, our mass is now at an end. You are now free to satisfy your animal desires. Go forth and fuck, fist and felch. Indulge until you puke. Revel in your vice, fulfil your most depraved of desires and leave no hole unfilled. So it is done. Hail Satan!"

There was no response this time, as the crowd immediately took his advice and leapt upon one another. I watched as Decadence pulled one of his chosen women up off the floor where she had collapsed on the finale of the "sacrifice" and pushed her back over the Altar. With his right hand he ripped off the last remaining traces of her underwear and with his left hand he unfastened his robe. As the gong sounded her legs opened and, along with many dozen more around the Crypt, they remained open until sunrise.

For one of Baphomet's Agony it was to be a sunrise of exceptional and devastating significance and for everyone in our Satanic circle it was to be the last sunrise before the dawn of a new age.

21

After he had spent an hour or so hanging over us as our debauched Messiah, The Exorcist, Bolverk and I took the Ginger Christian down from his crucifix.

I expected him to gather up his clothes and flee. But he didn't. First, in very polite English spoken with a deep southern accent, he asked for a beer. We don't permit beer at a Black Mass (red wine lends much more gothic drama to proceedings) but I gave him a glass of wine that he sank in one gulp. Refreshed, he then sought out Popcorn Lady, and to her obvious delight, and with cheers and a round of applause to accompany him, he lowered her gently to the floor and proceeded, with great enthusiasm, to embrace his inner demon.

"Bolverk is honored to have such a prestigious guest to help him celebrate his Blót," Bolverk proclaimed to the Ginger Christian when he'd finished. The convert grinned and nodded. "Skaal!" he said back at him. This joyful toast was the only word of Norwegian he knew, apparently, but his use of it pleased both of them more than any words of love or thanks ever could.

Bolverk quickly took the Ginger Christian under his wing, introduced to him whichever girl he pointed towards and then plied them both (and himself) with wine. Bolverk insisted on drinking from a horn which, for reasons I can no longer recall, only I was allowed to fill. The problem with drinking from a horn is that you can never put it down, but that didn't seem to bother Bolverk a great deal – he had the capacity to drink gallons of wine with little discernible effect.

"So Bolverk," I said, as his new friend found and locked into an embrace with yet another girl. "Any of these raven-haired beauties float your longboat?"

"To be honest with you Marta, Bolverk is turned off by the whole dyed-black hair trend, you know?" He took a long drag from his drinking horn. "We're not a race of dark-haired people. We're blonde and we're red-haired. Dyeing your hair black is very un-Norwegian."

"What about her then?" I said, pointing to one of the pretty rich girls down from Oslo whose expensive school no doubt prohibited hair dye. "She's blonde."

Bolverk waved the thought away with forced contempt. "You modern Norwegian women are like cod: flaky, layered in fat and easy to catch. Where's the sport in that?"

"Come on, aren't you ever tempted to join in any of this?"

He turned those thin, flimsy eyebrows on me and literally bent them into question marks. Poor Bolverk. Here was a man who should have had long locks of hair spun from auburn wire and a beard like rusted nails. If you shut your eyes and just listened to him speak you could imagine a face so thick with growth it could sustain its own ecosystem. But when you opened your eyes you saw he had in fact been allotted just a fraction of his hairy dues. Whimsical, that's the best way to describe his beard. You'd find more hair on a bar of soap.

"You'd better hope that Bolverk never gets a taste for it, Marta," he said. "If he ever did, he'd set about it as he does most things and you and every other woman in Kragerø would never sleep safe again."

I smiled and turned to gaze out over the low budget flesh-flick that was being acted out before me. Decadence was of course the star of the feature. He was still in his robe and was sat by the Altar resting between girls and building up his strength for another conquest. Two more girls formed an orderly queue to his left.

As was usual at these events, Decadence took great care to ensure he knew where I was at all times and that I could see what he was doing. He smiled his stupid smile at me when he saw I had glanced in his direction. It was a little pathetic.

Then I noticed Bolverk watching him too. "What about a bit of man-on-man, Edvard? Have you ever wondered what music you could make with another guy. Maybe Snorre?"

"Be careful where you toss your insults, Marta! You know what Bolverk thinks about that."

"I don't actually. Enlighten me."

"It's just wrong."

"But isn't all that 'a man shall not lie with a man' stuff just more Christian propaganda? Why don't you rail against that as you do any other Biblical dogma?"

"It's not a religious thing. Vikings don't regard homosexuals as evil or perverted: they are just ragr."

"Ragr?"

"Yes; or seiðr."

"Seiðr? Edvard, are you having a stroke?"

"You unbelievers might call it weak or unmanly. You see, the Viking is the epitome of manhood. He is strong, he is a leader, he is a father, he is a hunter, a provider. A man who subjugates himself before another man in bed will do the same in battle or in the hunt and no Viking legion can afford to have a man like that in its ranks. What's more if you accuse a Viking of being ragr he has every right to kill you to disprove your allegation so just be careful what you say to me on this subject."

"Ah but what if you're the active partner rather than the passive one? There's no subjugation there: quite the opposite."

"Of course! We Vikings have a proud history of sexual aggression and the taking of your enemy, irrespective of gender, is a noble tradition. But Snorre is not Bolverk's enemy and if he fucked him he'd then have to kill him and you'll doubtless agree with him that that wouldn't be good for the band."

He playfully nudged me with his elbow. Given the force he had behind him, I did well to stay upright.

"You know," I said, "if for just one day you could stop

believing in your dragons and fairies, climb down from your banquet in the clouds and allow yourself to exist in the 21st century, you might enjoy yourself and we might discover you're not such a Viking relic."

I grabbed his ears, pulled his head towards me, and kissed him hard on the lips. The Hungarian Merlot was having an interesting effect on me. Realizing this, I thought it best to bring a curtain down on my performance within the evening's festivities.

"See you later losers," I said. "I'm going to bed."

"Will I see you before we leave for the Bergen gig?" The Exorcist asked.

"Probably not. I'm seeing Ailo at noon, you're going in the truck early in the afternoon and Edvard's taking me to the venue on his bike later in the day."

The Exorcist cringed as he often did when reminded of my relationship with Suffer. I let him think about what horrors I might be subjected to for a moment before approaching him.

"If you don't like it, change it," I said and beckoned him down from his great height. Once he was within reach I grabbed his ears even harder than I had Bolverk's and kissed his mouth with deliberate aggressive passion. There was a parasite of hopefulness within that pearl of a kiss. Perhaps the last time I would feel it.

But when we were done, nothing had changed.

With his ears still in my hands, I pointed his head towards Bolverk and spoke loud enough for them both to hear.

"Keep an eye on him, Peter," I said. "If you see him trying to fuck Snorre, make sure there are no sharp implements close by because if he decides to honor the Viking way and kill him afterwards, we lose our guitarist and we all lose our meal-ticket. The Bergen gig is tomorrow. Our gateway to corrupting the masses is within our reach. Let's not fuck it up, okay?"

Peter nodded and immediately did as he was told, staring wistfully at Bolverk.

I stiffened. "I'll see you in the morning," I said, and left quickly.

22

Snorre was a sensitive, almost feminine lover who would often lose himself within a prolonged, languid caress. Back when we were sixteen, he was just as happy to be held by me as to fuck me.

Almost the instant I started sleeping with Snorre his widow's veil began to drop and he emerged out of his mourning. He was still dark and angry, but his rage had been softened by less abrasive emotions and his hatred was no longer all-consuming. Snorre was capable of deep and intense hatred, but I soon realized he was also capable of deep and intense love. However, his take on love had been fashioned during the bizarre relationship he had shared with his mother. For Snorre love was something that you gave without expecting anything back in return. He didn't need to be loved, he just needed to love. For that reason our union seemed a match made in heaven.

I am not a girl given over to public displays of affection (or private displays of affection come to that) and, aside from our regular and thoroughly satisfying sex, I don't recall ever instigating any intimacy with Snorre. But that didn't bother him in the slightest. As long as I was prepared to accept his love he was prepared to give it and his resources were infinite. Unfortunately for him my capacity to receive his love had its limits and my concerns over what it might be doing to me began to nag.

After our two weeks of clumsy, experimental sex, Snorre

was able to re-enter the Kragerø community. We already had a wealth of damaged souls in our town who disguised their psychopathic, sadistic or perverted tendencies behind smart clothes, smiles and successful careers so adding another variety into the mix would barely register on Kragerø's scale of fucked-up-ed-ness.

I had to work harder to get him over his fixation with Peter though. I knew he really wanted to kill him and I wasn't going to let that happen. I needed to find a way to bring them together and bridge the rift. Which was when I came up with the idea for a band.

Yes, that's right. The band initially started for that very trivial reason, although it soon became clear fate had put this idea before me for many reasons.

Snorre needed a distraction from wanting to murder Peter in revenge for his mother, plus music seemed a good way to hone his interesting new darkness. Edvard needed to focus on something other than food, Viking role-playing games and marijuana. And Peter needed to find a vocation that would keep him out of a lifetime of low-paid jobs or, worse still, the priesthood.

Plus, a band would be an outlet for my own corruption – the most brutal, hateful and evil black metal band the world had ever seen would be an interesting platform on which to launch my own career.

A boy is so easy to manipulate, especially when you're fucking him. As Snorre attempted to sow his seeds in me, I planted little seeds of my own within him. Only mine germinated and after a few days of subtle hints and unspoken suggestions Snorre decided it was imperative he form a band with him on guitar and Edvard on bass. Meanwhile I instructed Peter to take up the drums, persuaded his mother to buy him a small and inexpensive drum-kit, and then stole into the music room at our school one night and vandalized the only other drum kit in Kragerø. Overnight I reduced the pool of potential drummers for Snorre's band to just one.

Soon, Snorre, Edvard and Peter had gone forever and Decadence, Bolverk and The Exorcist had risen up, undead, rank and putrid, from their graves.

From the word go the band showed promise. I can't say that the sound they made was pleasing to the ear. It was like somebody driving a bulldozer through a scrap yard full of abandoned washing machines. But there was a compelling sense of newness and energy to it all, even during those inaugural practice sessions in the Lant cellar. It sounded fresh and original but at the same time was a sound I felt had always existed and had somehow remained undiscovered until that moment. In some respects, it sounded as if it had been around for so long it had begun to decay.

Despite what a guitar had done to his mother, Decadence had continued playing – he admitted it was a way to feel close to her – and was by then an accomplished guitar player with a knack for creating sinister and slutty hooks.

As for Bolverk, for a short, fat man who refused on principle to ever dance (dance, apparently, was unbecoming to the Nordic race), we discovered he had a deep groove carved into his spine that someone had filled full of funk. As he progressed, he began to accompany Decadence with dirty, chunky bass-lines, tapping into something elemental that had been vibrating through the world's darkest shadows since before the advent of man. And then once he had etched that groove into your mind so firmly it altered the beat of your heart, he would abandon it and spin out an alternative riff that slipped in seamlessly underneath a chord change.

Meanwhile, The Exorcist's drums were shambolic but he made enough noise for it to work. If anything, his ineptitude improved the whole ensemble. His crass errors and inability to keep time added an element of chaos to the band's sound and kept the tamed beast feral.

In those early sessions, all three of them tried out their vocals. Decadence and Bolverk couldn't carry a tune (or a screech, growl or bark). The Exorcist could sing but his technique, honed over eight years in his mother's Church choir, was ill-suited to the angry cacophony Decadence and Bolverk were scratching out of their amps. What's more, The Exorcist could only just manage to walk and speak simultaneously: expecting him play drums and sing was as realistic as expecting a teenage metal-head to have a favorite musical.

It was equally exciting and frustrating. None of us had expected the three of them to have the chemistry that they did, but we all (with perhaps the exception of The Exorcist) saw there was something missing from the band. Something of fundamental importance.

There was a big hole in the band, just the right shape and size for a psychopathic Sámi Anti-Christ.

23

Suffer came to Kragerø in his and our sixteenth year. Back then he was just known as Ailo.

By then, Snorre, Edvard and Peter had adopted their grimacing, sub-human alter-egos, but it was all for show. Behind the characters they were not quite the satanists I continually told them they were.

Ailo, however... he was a different story. And while he eventually changed his name to Suffer when he joined the band, he never needed to affect an evil persona. Ailo was always Suffer; Suffer was always Ailo, and he was always evil.

We never knew where he came from or what his upbringing had been like before he appeared in our lives. He never spoke of anything in any kind of coherent detail, dropping only hints and stories that conflicted from day to day.

He had been born in the gutter. He had been born into wealth. He had been in and out of abusive foster homes for years. He was rebelling against an overbearingly loving family. His family was dead, killed in a tragic accident. His family cooked him meals every night and his mother did his washing. He didn't know his family. He didn't *want* to know his family.

We speculated over which was truth, which was lie. We never figured it out. But in the end it didn't matter.

On the first day he arrived at school he made his mark. Small as he was, only a fool would have looked in his eyes and then picked a fight with him. As luck would have it our old friend Ademec was just such a fool.

Ademec spent two months in hospital and required reconstructive surgery on his face. He's a weird looking guy now. You would look weird too if your nose had been bitten off and somebody had tried to push your eyes into your skull sockets with their thumbs. It's only because Bolverk ripped Suffer off him that Ademec is now only partially blind.

So by lunchtime on his first day at school Suffer had become Kragerø's most dangerous pariah. I knew then that I wanted to know more about this peculiar creature but I didn't know that I would be recruiting him into the band, I had no inkling that within two years I would sleeping with him and I didn't guess that in so doing I would be sealing all of our fates.

In the weeks following his introduction to our school – and then his immediate suspension – I became mildly obsessed with Ailo. I had only seen him briefly the morning he arrived like a street riot in our town, but that fucked-up visage of his lingered at the front of my mind like a migraine.

I followed him one afternoon after school, into the evening, until he reached a cliff on the Southern part of the island of Øya, just off the coast of Kragerø. It was up on that cliff I first heard Suffer yoik. I had never heard one before I heard Suffer's strange hymn that night, but it reminded me of playing a record backwards in search of hidden messages, shadows, and demons. That eerie tone and the clipped ending to the vocal are evident in both yoiks and backwards British heavy metal.

Perhaps there were lyrics in there rendered in an ancient Sámi dialect. Suffer's yoik contained no words I could understand, but I did feel something else there, much more primeval than language buried in his wails – an overwhelming sense of isolation, pain and loss.

The band already had energy, chaos and violence.

I knew then Suffer would add terror and pain.

24

Suffer didn't need a great deal of persuading to join the band. He showed little interest in the kind of music we were playing, but once I put the band and the music within the context of my campaign for world desecration his interest was piqued.

As soon as Decadence heard Suffer's yoik, he was excited the missing piece in the band had been found. Bolverk took some convincing to let him join, but once I had drawn out the similarities between Suffer and the Norse God Loki, Bolverk began to warm to him too.

I was less successful convincing The Exorcist. It's fair to say Suffer didn't bond with any of the band in a significant way, but there was something about The Exorcist's bumbling innocence that caused Suffer real pain and led to huge friction between them. To make it worse, Suffer had never had formal training in any instrument but he took to the drums instantly and he found it greatly frustrating The Exorcist had such difficulty remembering the rhythms that came so naturally to him.

The feeling was reciprocated too. I had never known The Exorcist to fear or dislike anyone – he was always capable of seeing the goodness in people. But with Suffer there *was* no goodness. He was rotten all the way down to his core.

At the time, I convinced myself that a healthy degree of friction in the band could only be a good thing for their success. In the end, as you know, I was proved both right and wrong.

With Suffer brought into the fold, all the diabolic elements of the band fell into place. Suffer didn't just add his vocals to the band's sound, his detestable appearance, energy and unpredictability completely changed the dynamic and the outward perception of Baphomet's Agony. Overnight they became blacker than the void before the dawn of time.

Looking back at those early gigs, it defies all logic the band didn't explode on take-off. In practice sessions, if Suffer turned up, if everything came together just right and if his mood-swings didn't derail the session straight off, the band might manage two minutes of sustained genius in the course of an hour. Yet despite that track record, we all agreed it was time to inflict our madness on an audience.

The first gig took place in the school hall on a January evening of the first year that Suffer arrived in Kragerø. The band came on to the small stage halfway through a line-up of earnest musical performances from the school choir, the orchestra and a handful of the more talented cellists and boy sopranos.

During the interval I helped set up the drum kit with The Exorcist while Decadence and Bolverk set up their amps and the microphone. Suffer stood in the back corner of the stage facing the wall and scratching his arms compulsively. When everything was ready and the audience had returned to their seats I went to sit with Mrs Suhm on the front row. She was brimming over with excitement, clad in her Sunday best and, despite the loud complaints made by some of the other parents, she made sure to keep the seat on her left free should Old Mr Suhm make a late appearance (a note had been left on the kitchen table telling him where she was and what meal there was for him in the fridge).

The band hadn't found their look by that point. There were no beards, no corpsepaint and Decadence was the only one of the four that owned a black leather jacket and black jeans. Mrs Suhm had forced The Exorcist to wear a suit and bow tie which made him look like the doorman at a strip club. Bolverk just wore his school uniform and his Viking hat and Suffer; well, we'll come to what Suffer was wearing shortly.

"Doesn't he look handsome Marta!" Mrs Suhm beamed with pride at her gargantuan son as he crouched over his three-piece drum kit. Imagine what a hippo would look like if it were forced to sit upright and handed two chopsticks and a small bowl of rice: that's the spectacle that we had before us.

"He does cut a dashing figure Mrs Suhm."

"What are they going to play for us tonight?"

It was a question I couldn't answer and it had generated a great deal of debate over the preceding days.

Bolverk was keen to do a song he had written lyrics for called "Asparagi Morti" which was all about a farmer who buys some asparagus seeds from a mysterious figure and when the farmer refuses to hand over his firstborn son he is impaled upon the asparagus spears.

But Decadence had his doubts. "As fruit and vegetables go," he said, "asparagus just isn't very, you know, evil."

"You want to smell his piss after Bolverk has eaten asparagus," said Bolverk. "Right there is the smell of unadulterated evil. Anyway, Bolverk wasn't aware there was a heavy metal hierarchy for fruit and vegetables."

"Satan tempts Eve with an apple. Could we switch the asparagus for some apples?"

"For fuck's sake. You can't impale anyone on an apple!"

It was left to me to point out that none of this mattered – Suffer would never even look at any of the lyrics penned for him. The yoiks, screeches and howls he laid over their accompanying music differed each time they practiced, so they just needed to pick a few riffs, string them together and leave it to Suffer to improvise the rest.

Once everyone was ready, the music teacher nodded to Decadence and – with Suffer still muttering to himself in his corner – the band erupted. The Exorcist began by attacking his snare and bass drum with the least sophisticated, but loudest, rhythm imaginable. Decadence and Bolverk then joined in with a barrage of distorted, tuned-down riffs that lifted the pace to a raucous gallop.

Distracted by all that noise nobody noticed over in his corner Suffer had removed his jeans and tatty T-shirt and was standing in his underwear.

Twenty seconds into the band's first song, he ran over to the microphone and began screaming into it.

As has been the case every time he has appeared on a stage since, the moment he arrived at the microphone Suffer assaulted all senses of his audience. You are already familiar with the sound he can strangle out of his throat and the stench he conjures up from the deepest of sewers; I can assure you that the ensemble was no less repulsive at that inaugural gig as it was four years later at Oslo.

His attack at the school was full frontal. Almost-naked, Suffer is a confusion of lumps, scars and crevices. His dry and brittle skin is made up of a patchwork of pallid smears, vivid crimson weals and liver spots of every hue between yellow and brown. Gorse-tipped boils festoon all regions of this terrain whilst inexplicable craters pit the topography like the no-mans-land between the trenches of Flanders.

So you can probably imagine the horror visited upon that room of Kragerø parents when the near naked and visibly aroused Suffer began screaming into his microphone.

Ten seconds after he started, the power was cut and three of the teachers bundled him off the stage. By the time the crowd's distain had reached its crescendo, he had been suspended again.

Mrs Suhm was absolutely furious. I had never seen her so angry. That very night she berated the headmaster and had to be physically restrained by those same three teachers that had earlier removed Suffer from the hall. The following day letters were written to the school, our local member of parliament and one to the Secretary-General of the United Nations.

She was not angry that Suffer had exposed so much of

himself. She was incandescent with rage that The Exorcist's performance had been cut short.

Thankfully, the band's thirty second performance had been filmed and went online that very night. It quickly became something of an internet phenomenon, even featuring on a late-night Dutch TV show the following week. The performance itself might have been cut short, but the fallout from it was going to last.

With just one catastrophic performance under its belt, Baphomet's Agony had taken its first step towards stardom.

And, ultimately, annihilation.

25

Bolverk and I arrived backstage in the green room of our life-defining Bergen gig to find a relaxed Decadence sitting on his own and running through chords on his unplugged electric guitar. He had lit some candles and the air was thick with the fragrant but slightly abrasive aroma of expensive marijuana.

The guitarist had already applied his corpsepaint, so his face conveyed a theatrically deathly pallor through white make-up and artificially accentuated cheekbones. When you see a band fully corpsepainted in full flight on stage, hammering at their instruments and beckoning up Lucifer from the depths of hell, it can look menacing and cool. However, out of context it is, quite frankly, daft. If you ever have to watch corpsepainted band members doing their own roadying, saying "one, two" into a microphone, or sniffing the milk before they pour it into their coffees, that cool menace will quickly evaporate.

"Praise be to Od– " Bolverk began, but it was cut short when, without looking up from his fret board, Decadence waved a joint over his head. "Ahhh, Bolverk would like that very much."

He reached for the drugs.

"Watch yourself," Decadence said. "It's as strong as you'll ever have it."

Bolverk snorted at the suggestion there could ever be a substance about which he would need to take care. Over the next ten minutes he devoured two joints in quick succession and in silence. The uncharacteristic fervor with which he propelled himself towards oblivion did not go unnoticed.

"Edvard, seriously, be careful with that stuff," Decadence repeated. "You're never at your best stoned and we need you to be at the top of your game for this show."

"You leave Bolverk to worry about that," Bolverk grunted. "Now throw him one of those beers."

Decadence tossed him a beer. Bolverk caught it, mumbled a half-hearted "Skaal" at us and then snapped the bottle top off with his teeth. Before any of the lively fizz could escape, he had poured two thirds of the bottle down his throat.

Leaving them to it, I went to check out the venue.

The support were due to start in thirty minutes and Baphomet's Agony were supposed to be on stage about forty-five minutes after that. I therefore expected just a handful of the most eager fans to have congregated in and around the venue. The band's fanbase included a lot of über-cool, decadent Satanists who would no doubt arrive fashionably late, en-masse and in a blaze of choreographed sex and violence like a scene by Hieronymus Bosch with tattoos. But then there were the other fans who were decidedly not cool, sexy or prone to choreography – the anxious and socially awkward teenagers who rarely ventured out from their bedrooms. A lot of those kids weren't well practiced in the art of the dramatic entrance and were so unused to leaving the sanctuary of their parental home they had no idea whatsoever how long it would take them to make the journey to whatever venue it was that the band was playing.

So, with an hour to go before the boys were to take the stage, I expected to see just a small gaggle of those earnest fans who would have been studying train timetables for weeks and who would have planned their journeys meticulously to ensure they didn't miss anything. What I saw instead was a heaving crowd, standing room only at the bar, and a queue snaking out of the venue and down the road.

If that wasn't enough, on my little tour of the venue I discovered touts! Yes, that's right, we actually had fuckers buying and selling Baphomet's Agony tickets at well over the face value. The variety and sheer volume of people that had been attracted to the Bergen show, without us using a single piece of conventional advertising, filled me with pride.

My name is Marta, Queen of Satanists, I thought to myself as I stared out across those legions of black metal fans. *Look on my works ye Mighty, and despair!*

I saw a lot of parents that night – a lot of middle-aged women looking uncomfortable in old jeans they had dug out from the back of a wardrobe and which were vivid with the styling of a bygone age. They accompanied their teenage children either to protect them or in a well-intentioned attempt to understand them. In either case they were doomed to fail.

The rest were boisterous kids staving off their boredom with clumsy flirting and affectionate acts of violence. With a single sweep of his hand, one of the teenagers launched a thousand paper-flyers off a ledge and into the air: filling the room with yet more words extolling the virtues of shitty clubs with shitty toilets playing shitty music.

There were also some familiar faces. The Wheelchair Goth sat at the balcony like a ghost-train waxwork waiting patiently for small kids to frighten. Popcorn Lady wandered around propositioning anyone she could find, much to the horror of the mothers accompanying their teenage sons. The Ginger Christian was on the stage busying himself with cables, pedals and tape while checking out the girls in the audience. In a remarkably short space of time, he had gone from devout, God-fearing redneck to sex-crazed, Satanic pleasure-seeker and roadie. It must have been a severe blow to the Christian Rockers from whom we had kidnapped and corrupted him.

And of course, my favorite two journalists stood dutifully at the bar categorizing and judging everyone that stumbled across their gaze. I wandered over to hear what pearls of wisdom they had to offer.

"I could go for a cute looking hentai-chick like that one," said Sigurd, pointing the rim of his beer bottle at Popcorn Lady.

"I did a feature on girls like that once," replied Od, "they're called kawaisa."

"What about her?" asked Sigurd, nodding towards a small, carefully made-up girl with neat dreadlocks tied up behind her head. "What would you call her?"

"A crust-punk," said Od. "But not a very convincing one and certainly not my type."

The balance of power had shifted in Od's favor since I had last heard them speak together. Sigurd's presence at the gig of a band that he had so recently panned probably put him on the back foot, although he would have no doubt been able to justify his presence there by reference to the support act. The fact that Od had sex in front of Sigurd at the last Baphomet's Agony show, or *at all* come to that, probably also helped alter the dynamic between them to Od's advantage.

"What about the one she's talking to with the neon extensions weaved into her dreads?" Sigurd asked.

"A cybergoth," Od replied. "Now I could definitely go for a bit of that!"

So, memories may differ on what precisely happened next, but my recollection is that Od saw me first.

"On your own tonight beautiful?"

"No," I said.

"Well, let us keep you company until your friends come back."

Sigurd pretended to decipher the logo on my T-shirt.

"It says stop staring at my tits," I told him.

"I wasn't looking at…I was looking at…I was trying…"

"It's a vintage Darkthrone, Sigurd," Od said. "I could see that from across the room."

"Of course I know that!" Sigurd spat the words out, visibly

offended by the thought that he didn't. "I was trying to see which version of the logo it was so I can figure out the precise date it would have been sold!"

"Oh Sigurd!" I said as I stroked his arm. "Don't you know that Darkthrone haven't changed their logo since they adopted it in 1991?"

He held his breath and his face reddened as he weighed-up the pros of cons of appearing ignorant about that obscure piece of black metal history.

"Okay. I admit. I was staring at your tits."

Such a cock-sucking prick! But business is business so I leaned in to whisper my next words.

"Well, say some nice things about my band and perhaps you'll get a better look the next time round."

Leaving him with that thought I spun around them both and returned backstage, just as Péjé Swartz from Satan's Spawn started making his way through the crowd. *This is it*, I thought. Everything is ready. What could go wrong?

26

Back in the green room I discovered very little had changed since I had left it. Decadence was still strumming his guitar and Bolverk was still sucking hash into his lungs, although at least somebody had applied corpsepaint to his face to get him ready.

There are aspects of hanging out with a band that are cool and dangerous and there are aspects that are depressing and tedious. After a gig there are groupies, sex and drugs; everyone blows smoke up the bands' collective ass and there is a festival energy. But before a show, green rooms are among the worst places to be on earth. You might have the odd *(or "Od", ha!)* journalist stop by, or a record company prick might look at the band as you would fish in an aquarium, but otherwise it's just the band being morose and apprehensive in an industrial space with exposed masonry, concrete floors and cheap furniture. Oh, and mirrors. Fucking mirrors everywhere.

If it's possible, that night in Bergen the green room was even more dull than usual. Bolverk was being all silent and weird, Decadence had lost himself in some sort of pseudo-mystical-creative trance, The Exorcist wasn't there, and I hadn't seen Suffer since earlier in the day when he had punched me in the womb on the occasion of our parting.

But, as was always the case with Baphomet's Agony, those sometimes long periods of tiresomeness were punctuated with twists of sudden violence. And tonight was no different.

Something heavy was hurled against the door. Then again. Its wooden frame groaned as it split and a short man flew into the room four feet off the ground and at some velocity. He crashed against the opposite wall and collapsed in a heap on the carpet.

"FUCK!" The word was shrieked at a terrifying pitch and volume as Suffer stalked into the room. He looked round with wild, dangerous eyes. Spying the crates of beer bottles close to Decadence, he sprang over to them and began hurling them around the room with both hands. We all ducked and covered our heads as they exploded in arcs of green shrapnel and froths of beer. That none of the bottles hit us was down to luck rather than design.

When he had exhausted the crate he stood still, panting heavily, fists clenched by his side. To one side, Bolverk let out a small puff of white smoke, as much an exclamation of surprise as relief. While Decadence lowered his arms cautiously.

"You alright, Suffer?"

"No, I'm not fucking alright!" He kicked the groaning man he'd just flung into the room ahead of him. I recognized him as one of our devoted and unpaid roadies. "Go on, tell them. *Tell them!*"

The man curled into a ball to avoid more punishment as he spoke. "We waited in the van outside The Exorcist's flat. We were there for thirty minutes, but nobody showed. When we called, his mum told them he was sick and wasn't coming."

Decadence rolled his eyes. "For fuck's sake."

"Then we can't play," Bolverk said, searching for another joint. "Not without drums. Right Marta?"

I didn't get to respond before Suffer screamed across us all.

"Bullshit! I can play the drums. That prick is fucking useless anyway and I will do a much better job of it."

"We need you to do your thing at the front of the stage," I said calmly.

"How the fuck can any of us do anything without drums you stupid whore-bitch-cunt."

"I've got a drum-machine set up that's been programmed and is ready to go," Decadence said. "I figured this day would come. It'll be fine. I can set each track off with pedals."

"Since when have we had a drum-machine?" Suffer spat.

"Since about a month ago."

"Fuck you Snorre!" Suffer looked as though he was going to leap at Decadence and rip his face off, but then his face turned pale and his eyes rolled skyward. He collapsed, holding his head tightly in his hands, while full body-twitches convulsed his thin, malnourished frame.

None of us moved to help him. We'd all seen this before.

Suffer was afflicted by a neurological disorder that occasionally locked his brain into spasm. It's difficult for the likes of you or me to appreciate the true horror of those moments and Suffer has certainly never shared his experiences with me. But from what I have read it's not unlike the sensation of your brain suddenly swelling beyond its normal size and being constrained in its expansion by your skull.

The twitching passed but Suffer remained on the floor mauling at the skin on his bald head as if to prise it apart. After a few more seconds, that too passed, and he sighed and crawled back to his feet.

"I wrote the drum parts for every song," he groaned. "I listened to that fuckwit Peter screw them up for this long but I'm not going to let you replace them with a machine now I've finally got the chance to put it all right."

That was yet another of the strange things about Suffer: he cared nothing for anyone or anything, not even himself, but in the band he had seemingly found something positive, something in which he could take pride.

"It's just not possible Ailo," Decadence said. "Even if we had the time, without Peter we don't have the right gear with us to mic-up the drum-kit. And we're due on in ten minutes. You've barely got time to change."

Suffer shook with fury. Then he glanced at Bolverk who sat voraciously imbuing his system with yet more chemically-enhanced marijuana. Suffer walked over to him and swung his fist back. When Bolverk removed the joint from his lips,

Suffer hooked his fist round and into the bassist's face with all the force he could muster. Bolverk's face absorbed most of the blow but there was enough force left to rock him gently backwards in his chair, almost in slow-motion, and topple him onto the floor.

He lay there for a moment, in exactly the same position he was in when upright, before exhaling a large cloud of smoke from out of his lungs with a long and contented sigh.

27

The most important gig of the band's existence went both better and worse than expected.

For a start, there was no dramatic entrance that night and the anti-climax for the audience was palpable. They were expecting earthquakes, whirlwinds, the Holy Trinity copulating with farmyard animals on stage, and then each of them exploding as they gave birth to a band member. Instead, Decadence led Bolverk and Suffer on stage like he was taking his pet monkeys to the vet.

While Suffer sang, it was Bolverk who usually fronted the band. But there was no banter from him tonight. He was heroically, monumentally wasted. Suffer had tried to argue we shouldn't even let him on, but his absence would have made the lack of a drummer that much more obvious. Plus there was the symmetry to think about. No, don't laugh. Feng shui does have a part to play in black metal.

As people saw the shambles on stage, there was a palpable buzz of disappointment rising from the crowd like wasps from a disturbed nest. Decadence quickly leant into his microphone.

"Baphomet's Agony welcomes all the sinners, blasphemers, gluttons, perverts, criminals and deviants of Bergen. May we all burn in Hell!"

Then Suffer pierced the air with an inhuman wail and the excruciatingly high pitch he achieved caused the first four feet of the crowd to physically shrink-back from the stage like the backwash from a wave. Decadence depressed a pedal on the floor and a thunderclap burst out of the PA system. And at the climax of the peal, the drum machine was triggered and a double bass-drum roll combined with an impossibly fast snare-drum attack set the backdrop to the razor-abrasive riff Decadence drilled out of his guitar.

Battle had commenced.

Despite being so stoned he could barely see, Bolverk still managed to find some semblance of his groove. His familiarity with each song was clearly so intimate that, even with the novelty of the drum-machine taking The Exorcist's place, he fell in time with admirable skill. Meanwhile Suffer was on fire. I mean that literally: he doused his T-shirt in lighter fluid, ignited it and then dived into the crowd. If the audience had been disappointed by the pedestrian arrival of the band on stage, that had all changed by the time he'd turned himself into a petrol bomb.

Over the next thirty minutes, what little remained of Suffer's T-shirt ripped off to reveal his undulating chest riddled with dozens of vivid scars and bruises whose numbers swelled over the course of his insane performance as he flung himself around and off the stage with abandon. When he wasn't singing, and occasionally when he was, he would ping sprite-like from one side of the stage to the other. More than once Bolverk proved to be an annoying obstacle and rather than walk around him he scrambled over him to get where he needed to be. Suffer actually delivered a large part of one song squatting on the bassist's head like a gargoyle before leaping off of it and into the crowd again.

Those in the audience that were not already transfixed by the bizarre antics of Suffer were almost certainly looking at Decadence now. His guitar-playing was ferocious that night, choking out brutal riffs from a guitar that had never been designed for the extensive abuse he subjected it to. Songs would begin and end with a cacophony of distortion, while he shot through the middle with slow, doom-laden and bass-heavy riffs, plunging the crowd into chaos.

The endearing ineptitude of The Exorcist's drums had always given the band's songs an earthy pulse. But the machine that took his place that night ripped out that soft, warm heart and replaced it with rhythms that were harsh and mechanical. The effect was to take the music out of a dark and sinister forest and relocate it to an industrial hell that crunched iron, spat molten steel and pumped noxious fumes into the atmosphere.

I am biased. I wouldn't have put Baphomet's Agony together if I had thought The Exorcist would be replaced by a drum machine. But even I had to admit the sound the band created in Bergen that night was better than anything they had done before.

The crowd reacted accordingly. The mosh pit which initially seemed like it might not even appear, soon grew until it covered the entire hall, the bars and the toilets. Even the staff behind the bar were barging each other and hurling beer around.

Funnily enough, my point of focus as I watched it all unfold was Sigurd's left eye. At first I watched it as it bobbed up-and-down. Then I watched it spin as he was hoisted up into the air and flipped over the heads of the crowd. I watched it narrow in anger when he was kicked in the thigh and then I watched it widen with delight when his assailant toppled over and had his head stamped upon. I watched it glaze over with opportunistic lust as he surreptitiously cupped a breast of the crust-punk he'd eyed-up at the bar earlier in the evening, and then finally I watched it being punched by the cybergoth and bade it a fond farewell as the skin around it bruised into a vivid plum and closed over it.

I learned later that Bolverk witnessed these scenes through a curious filter. There came a point during the show when, as far as he was concerned, he ceased to be on stage in Bergen and instead found himself on the stark coastline of his ancestral Norse homeland at the time of Ragnarök. The sky overhead was a vortex of black clouds stirred into a violent storm. He looked down to his hands and he didn't see a bass guitar, he saw his mighty hammer Mjöllnir which was aglow and humming in anticipation of the brutal exercise it was poised to enjoy with its master.

Beneath him, and stretched out across the entire panorama, a sea of famine-ravished human warriors thrashed around in an odious melee. Those at the front tried in vain to drag him down into their seething stew of repugnant mortal flesh. He knew that even he, the most formidable of Odin's warrior sons, stood no chance of winning this battle. There were many thousands of the repulsive blackened creatures, angry mortals ravaged by the winter of Fimbulvetr, disfigured from hunger and cold, and driven to madness by a thousand days of darkness.

"No matter," he thought to himself, hoisting his hammer above his head with both hands. "If Þórr is to perish this night he will make sure that he diminishes the numbers of Miðgarðr by no insignificant measure!"

By the time Bolverk had finished marauding across the auditorium, seventeen people needed hospital treatment, his bass guitar had been reduced to an unrecognizable lump of splintered wood, blood and hair, and, most importantly, Péjé Swartz from Satan's Spawn had instructed his lawyers to prepare a contract.

Despite everything, the name Baphomet's Agony had just attained legendary status on Norway's black metal scene and we were poised to bring our evil to the world.

I wished Peter could have been there to see it.

28

I have been asked many times what it was like to be loved by Decadence. For some of the more obsessive fans, my relationships are part of Baphomet's Agony folklore.

It was a question normally asked by foolish girls who were besotted by Decadence, but who could have just as easily chosen an American film star or Korean boy band to fantasize about. The difference being that neither the American film star nor the Korean boy band would have had a facility on their website to enable fans to book online for their virginities to be taken.

For the record, he got over the whole blubbing mess he started out as and became a great lover. Did I talk about that already? I can't remember. But he'd want you to know that and I suppose I've said enough bad things about him already to grant him this acknowledgement, at least.

Before he degenerated into a cock-sucking prick (which was, I suppose, my fault) Snorre was as attentive as I needed him to be and he gave me the space I so often insisted upon. Given I was someone for whom love was not at all normal, he was a damn near-perfect boyfriend.

Something happens to you when you are loved by someone very beautiful, like he was. You become empowered, albeit an ever-darkening force that propels you forward. Fame does a similar thing – pumps you full of confidence while quietly eating away at your soul. I certainly felt that chemical rush of adrenalin and those cocaine highs when Snorre and I were lovers. Those of you of a romantic bent might say that I was just witness to the power of love, but even back then it wasn't really his love from which I drew my strength. I have always fed on darker meats. I took my nourishment from my domination of a physically superior human being and from the jealousy I saw in others.

He and I were together for two years, from sixteen years old through to the end of school when we were eighteen. During that period, Snorre evolved into Decadence while I…I sort of increasingly retreated into myself. I should have been content in what we had, but I was not. In fact, it was the idea that I should be content which scared me. I could see the possibilities of what lay ahead, the idea of a strange kind of happiness with him on offer, and it made me anxious.

To distract myself, I threw myself into my obsession with the devastation of world order.

In the transition from child to adult, I had been looking more closely at the world around me. Seeing the shadows beneath the veneer. I was surrounded by clean and safe prosperity, but I saw it all through darkening cataracts, so I could only make out filth, danger and famine. Although cataracts make for a poor metaphor, I think. It implies my vision was distorted, when I wasn't misinterpreting my environment, I was simply better able to see the truth laying behind the lies out there.

Take Norway. We are evidence, if ever it was needed, that at its core the human species is base and hateful. We have massive natural resources, a strong economy and a well-educated population. We have mobile phones, healthcare and peace prizes. But does that mean my generation are all docile, contented and fair people? Are we grateful for our lot? Read the papers, look around the room at a Baphomet's Agony show, stroll through the aisles of my subterranean shop, consider again the story I have been telling you. If you give a nation everything it could want, if you strive to make your children wealthy and safe, why does this band and its fans exist?

It's all about human nature. If you relieve a man of every need to struggle you expose his true self. Here in Norway that true self is black metal. Our country is like a skillfully cultivated field in which care and love has been lavished on the land to create a panorama of delicate flora and fauna. Black metal is the indigenous weed that will inevitably grow between the imported flowers, choke them to death and give truth to the lie.

We can't be the only country either. I'm sure the same can be said for so many others too. It's the nature of the society we've created in our western world. Our hygiene and self-satisfied luxury is a freshly cleaned façade, one that disguises our true selves lingering in the cracks between the clean, white tiles.

As soon as I realized this, I began to spend more and more of my time among the bacteria festering around the edges where detergent can't reach. Bacteria like Suffer.

While I began my odyssey into the mire, Decadence began to fulfil his potential. He grew in confidence, he discovered his style, his cool. It was always going to happen, I suppose, but freed from the self-imposed restraints of his mother, made part of a band that was quickly becoming the most important cultural phenomena in Kragerø, and shot full of self-assurance from his sexual awakening, Decadence turned into the most fashionable, charismatic and engaging teenager in town.

Bolverk, The Exorcist and I found ourselves swept along in the slipstream of his nitrous-powered ascendency into popularity. When we arrived at a bar or a party you could sense the eyes of the room had been trained on the door, awaiting his arrival. There could be no party until Decadence and his crew arrived.

Bolverk flourished under the intense heat of those lights. His puerile humor and childish obsession with Vikings, which had until then seen him relegated to the status of class clown, suddenly became eccentric wit and profound pagan spirituality. He became everyone's favorite sage and raconteur. The

Exorcist and I fared less well in those greenhouse conditions. We weren't used to crowds of people, small conversation, and the hysterical enjoyment our peers seemed to derive from weak anecdotes and bad jokes after just a few drinks. What's more, many of the girls who gravitated to Decadence on those occasions displayed their resentment towards me openly.

"Magda is it?"

"It's Marta, Rebecca. We've been at school together for the past eleven years."

"Of course, I'm sorry Marta, I didn't recognize you for a moment there. You've filled out since we last spoke."

While I didn't enjoy that sort of environment, I soon realized how important it was to attend those events, monitor everyone's behavior, gather information and then use all of that to my and the band's financial advantage. For example, it was in watching other men looking at Decadence that it dawned on me how overtly gay all heavy metal can be perceived to be. It must have occurred to you before, no? All the leather, straps, and muscles? Do you know any woman turned on by that stuff? Of course not. It's a specially crafted plumage designed solely to attract mates of the same taste and gender.

So it was that those great masses of man-meat would gaze upon the band (but Decadence in particular) as if they were rare butterflies recently arrived upon a vase of delicate flowers. Their eyes would glaze over. Then, in a primitive courting ritual, they would proceed to attract the band's attention by getting riotously drunk and fighting each other.

It was while watching such things unfold before me that I put the finishing touches to the band's look and began to form a business plan for their career and the shop in my head. That was how, in time, I eventually learned how to derive some satisfaction from my exploitation of those otherwise painful social occasions.

The Exorcist, however, never found anything in those events from which to derive joy. He attended them dutifully, kept close to Bolverk or me and just bided his time until I told him he was allowed to go home.

Suffer went to just one of those high school parties. It was the night we think he killed Rebecca's grandmother and burnt down her house. You have just met Rebecca and I'm sure you'll agree with me she had it coming (although whether her grandmother did I cannot say), but you probably appreciate now why Suffer didn't get invited to many parties.

29

The Exorcist's no-show at the Bergen gig was a surprise. The fact the band still managed a glorious thirty minute performance was staggering. And Bolverk's drug-fueled Viking apocalypse took everyone unawares. But the most astonishing thing to me was that it was all allowed to happen without being sabotaged by Oslo Iron.

All the information gleaned through my Satanic spies and my silent stalking of sociopathic networks pointed towards Oslo Iron launching a violent crusade against us at the Bergen gig.

We did have a small problem with half a dozen Christians that night, who had been handing out "missing persons" flyers filled with photographs of the Ginger Christian. But when their missing-presumed-dead-and-now-Satanic brother appeared out of the back of a truck, waved at them in his Baphomet's Agony T-shirt, and then helped roll Bolverk's bass cabs through the stage door, it all got a bit ugly and they began hurling abuse at everyone. That didn't last long though. I hand-picked four of Bolverk's more terrifying pagans, who proceeded to run the Christians out of the venue (and then may or may not have kicked the shit out of them in the alley outside).

But Oslo Iron were strangely absent. That they hadn't attacked us worried me.

"Black Metal 2.0", "Nu-Black Metal" or "Porno-Satanists": that's what Oslo Iron and its nostalgia-powered supporters called us. Their numbers longed for the good old days when

Black Metal bands and their exclusively male fan base sat around in darkened rooms smoking cigarettes all day, beat up the occasional gay to relieve their pent-up homosexuality and dragged coffins through the snow. They resented the fact our younger generation spent more time fucking than fishing.

The more popular Baphomet's Agony became, the angrier Oslo Iron got. Their anger had been contained until the Oslo gig, but then Suffer's attack and the knowledge that we were being eyed by a record company *really* pissed them off.

After Bergen, all of that changed.

Within hours of Bolverk's rampaging climax, I'd had multiple messages and missed calls on my phone from Péjé Swartz, practically dictating a Satan's Spawn recording contract down the phone and begging me to accept it.

This was it, the deal we had worked towards. The gateway to the destruction of the world. And yet I was still the band's manager and wasn't going to commit them to anything without taking some rudimentary legal advice. So I found myself a rudimentary lawyer. One in London, who knew fuck-all about the music industry (in fact I've come to learn he knows fuck-all about all sorts of things) but that suited me fine. I could read the contract and I knew what commercial terms I wanted, I just needed some comfort that there were no nasty little legal traps hidden in the Latin. Which, by the way, there were. So it was only after a substantial re-write of the contract that I let Péjé send the signature copy over and I signed it on behalf of the band.

By that point I suspect I could have demanded 100% royalties on all exploitation of the recordings in all media. Just its name being occasionally mentioned in the same sentence as Baphomet's Agony would have been sufficient incentive for Satan Spawn to sign us. That alone would boost Satan Spawn's credibility within a massive and expanding youth sub-culture and etch its name into the DNA of the burgeoning black metal universe the band and I were in the process of creating.

Almost simultaneously as I hit "send" on the email attaching the signed contract, there was an explosion of Satan's Spawn/Baphomet's Agony cyber-publicity. Pop-ups proliferated across screens like acne and viral marketing campaigns spread like syphilis through a seminary. News of our contract-signing reached Oslo Iron quickly and by all accounts the rage with which it was met would have struck fear into the black heart of Satan himself.

All of this happened within a week of the Bergen gig. Being so busy sorting it out, I had seen little to nothing of the band. Decadence I'd encountered once or twice at the shop and I'd been sending updates by text to The Exorcist and Bolverk but had heard nothing from either of them. Every time I tried to see The Exorcist his mother would shoo me away and Bolverk lived too far out for me to bother stopping by. Of course, Suffer didn't own a phone (or anything really other than the rags on his back), so I had no way of contacting him without paying him a visit which I just didn't have the time – or inclination – to do.

However, after a week, I decided we needed a band conference so I demanded Bolverk's and The Exorcist's presence at the shop on the Saturday. Suffer rarely attended any meetings or rehearsals but I still thought it wise to send a nervous messenger to drag him out of his swamp.

When he eventually turned up, late, Bolverk was no happier than he had been the week before.

"It's not evident to him why you needed Bolverk to come all the way into town. Why couldn't you just call him or send him a text?"

"I *have* been sending you texts, you great big prick!"

Bolverk checked his phone to find a crack running through the screen and it refusing to turn on. "Oh," he said.

"Let's set aside the fact you haven't checked your phone for a week after the biggest gig of your life," I said. "You need to show your face around town anyway. You're quite the celebrity now, after that crescendo of violence. Who would have thought it's you and not Snorre or Ailo that the kids of Norway are celebrating as the personification of the country's moral decline!"

He grunted. "Have you heard from the police?"

"No, and I bet you haven't either. The band is at the forefront of the biggest thing to hit youth culture in our lifetime. As far as those kids are concerned, even the ones you crunched your bass into, you are their Gods. They won't have reported you and nobody else who was at the gig would have done either."

"Bolverk doesn't want to be anyone's God."

Decadence was sitting silently in the background and raised an eyebrow at this point. "I'm looking forward to acquiring godlike status," he said. "To be honest with you, that's the main reason that I was keen for us to get a record deal. That and the prospect of fucking girls beyond this shithole of a town."

I gave him a look and then gestured to the door. "It doesn't look like The Exorcist or Suffer are going to show up then. No surprises there with Suffer, but what's up with Peter do you think? Bolverk, have you heard from him recently?"

Bolverk shrugged, which I took to mean no.

"Fine," I said. "Let's go drag him out of his pit."

30

That party I mentioned earlier – the only one that Suffer was ever invited to – took place one Saturday night in the spacious home of Rebecca's family. This was midway through Suffer's suspension prompted by his crazed antics during the band's gig at the school's annual musical extravaganza.

Pretty much every kid in Kragerø knew of Suffer, but between his suspensions and truancy very few had actually seen him. You would never know that from the way people spoke about him though. According to the numerous messages left by the online video clip of the band's inaugural gig, hundreds of the coolest kids had witnessed the performance. Yet I can only recall a few dozen of the more solemn musical-types being there with assorted parents and grandparents.

Anyway, that Saturday night the band and I arrived together at Rebecca's house where the party was in full swing. As usual, Decadence drew in the eyes of all of the girls and a handful of the more macho boys, while Bolverk was sequestered by an earnest group of metalheads newly converted to the trend that was quickly sweeping across Kragerø. The Exorcist and I tried to blend into the background as best we could, a feat that I achieved with much more ease than the six foot seven yeti that accompanied me.

From the off, Suffer behaved strangely. He positioned himself in the middle of the room, with his hands by his side and turned in a slow circle quietly muttering. It was such a disconcerting sight that even after ten minutes none of the party could conduct anything close to a normal conversation without constantly being drawn back to his bizarre pirouette.

Eventually he stopped and stood motionless in the middle of the room, staring at an ornate crucifix that hung high up on the wall. This, at least, was less distracting for the party and after a few minutes everyone had kind of got used to him being there and a good-natured hum of conversation and laughter was restored.

The Exorcist didn't like Suffer but it was not in his nature to be unpleasant or openly hostile towards anyone, so he always remained tolerant and polite despite the cruel and obscene offence Suffer directed back at him. That night in Rebecca's living room The Exorcist was even more uncomfortable than he was usually in that sort of environment. He kept looking over towards Suffer and twitching. Eventually he could contain his kindness no longer. He poured a small plastic cup half full of beer and before I could stop him he was approaching Suffer with his peace offering held out in front of him. All eyes in the room were suddenly pulled away from their conversations and fixed on The Exorcist.

Suffer continued to stare up towards the crucifix, oblivious of the giant bearing gifts. The Exorcist bent his head down and round so that it would appear directly within Suffer's line of focus and yet still Suffer paid him no heed. It was only when The Exorcist placed his free hand softly on his shoulder that Suffer snapped out of his reverie with a jolt, flinching violently from the gentle physical contact.

The far-away look of calm that had descended onto Suffer's features in the preceding ten minutes vanished in an instant and he slapped the cup out of The Exorcist's hand, stepped in towards him so that his face was less than a centimeter from the drummer's chest and stared up into the underside of The Exorcist's jaw. A conversation vacuum sucked all sound out of the room as Suffer peeled the skin back off his eyes until two thirds of each eyeball popped proud of its socket.

"There is only one thing I will ever take from you, you contemptible shit, and you had better pray to your God that I don't take it any time soon."

He spat his words loud enough for the whole room to hear while jabbing a finger into The Exorcist's chest for emphasis.

Not even the commercial heavy metal soundtrack Rebecca had chosen to pipe into the living room was loud enough to mask the silence Suffer had brought down upon the party. He stepped away from The Exorcist and looked around the room with contempt. Everyone took care to avert their eyes and once Suffer had surveyed the masses he spat generously onto the carpet before fleeing the room with a sudden haste.

The Exorcist stood motionless, his fingers still curled around a cup that was no longer there. He looked towards me with a terrified smile I knew so well. He wasn't scared because of the cryptic threat that had just been made against him, he was scared because he didn't know what he should do next. I tilted my head in a gesture that beckoned him over and, like a lumbering but obedient wolfhound, he loped back to me.

31

Many would have you believe that Norway is cold, bleak and ice-strewn. Black metal documentaries certainly portray it as a grim country, perpetually shrouded in darkness, made up of harsh countryside and concrete-slab towns. Don't believe their propaganda. Of course it gets dark at night and cold in the winter, but down here in the south of the country the summers are warm, the days can be long, and, on a day like the one when Decadence, Bolverk and I walked in silence from the shop to The Exorcist's flat, the midday sun fills the air with a light you will not see anywhere else in the world. It's almost as if the atmosphere is suddenly filled with microscopic mirror-sided particles that bounce the sun's rays off each other and apply a glossy, opaque, soft-porn sheen to everything in your field of vision.

We arrived in Kragerø harbor as the last of the fishing boats was pulling up to unload its cargo. Bolverk waved to three men standing on the deck of one of the larger vessels: colleagues from his previous life. Both he and they smiled artificially as they waved but none were able to fully mask the acute envy they felt for the other.

Decadence pressed the buzzer of The Exorcist's flat. After a short while the familiar strains of Mrs Suhm's voice crackled through the electronic fuzz.

"Hello. Who is that?"

"Hello Mrs Suhm," I said. "It's me, Marta. I'm here with Snorre and Edvard. We've come to see Peter."

"Hello Marta, hello boys. I'm afraid Peter is still a bit under the weather."

"We'd like to see him nevertheless."

There was a short pause of crackle and fizz over the intercom.

"Alright then," Mrs Suhm answered eventually. "Perhaps it will cheer him up to see you."

The fuzz disappeared and we waited for the familiar click as the door latch was released. It didn't come but the fuzz returned.

"Marta?"

"Yes Mrs Suhm."

"Ailo isn't with you, is he?"

"No Mrs Suhm. It's just me, Snorre and Edvard."

"Alright then. Up you come."

The door clicked open and we commenced our long, hot climb up four flights to the two-bedroom flat. By the time we reached it, Bolverk, leading the way in his leathers, looked decidedly uncomfortable.

"What's that smell?" he asked, stopping short in front of Decadence so that they almost collided.

"All I can smell is you," Decadence replied. "With your fat ass in my face and your body odor up my nose you've got a kind of monopoly over my senses right now."

"How can you not smell it?" Bolverk insisted. "It's a sort of musty, earthy smell with a bit of sweetness to it. Like an old orange-peel lying in damp mud."

"Is it a good smell or a bad smell?"

"It's alright. Bolverk could get to like it given time."

"Then stop worrying about it. It's probably someone's lunch."

We continued along the landing and Decadence rapped on The Exorcist's door with a knuckle. It triggered the muffled sound of slippers shuffling over carpet before the door opened three inches and the kind old face of The Exorcist's mother peered out over a brass chain. Once she was sure just

Decadence, Bolverk and I were there she smiled at us, released the chain and beckoned us inside.

As we crossed the threshold Bolverk tugged on my arm.

"Tell me you can't smell it now?" he whispered.

I yanked my arm back without answering.

"You sit down there while I finish making some coffee." Mrs Suhm walked off into the kitchen where the coffee machine was completing the final movement of its overture. I sat on the sofa amidst the chintz of the small living room, lodged between two of Norway's most infamous champions of black metal.

"How was your jig the other night in Bergen?" Mrs Suhm asked from the kitchen as she extracted the carafe.

"It went very well Mrs Suhm," I said. "Although we missed Peter of course."

"Yes, that was the first day he took to his bed, poor boy." By then she had arrived in the living room with a tray. "Now, did you see my niece Margunn there? I told her to go along and say hello. You wouldn't have missed her if she was there because she has a very distinctive voice: she stutters whenever she starts a sentence with a vowel. You would have thought she would keep quiet with an affliction like that, but you can't shut the girl up."

"I don't recall hearing anyone like that Mrs Suhm. But it *was* very loud."

"Oh, perhaps she didn't go then. She normally has choir practice on a Tuesday night, but I told her to bring the choir to the theatre with her to sing along with the boys. That would have been as good a practice as any wouldn't it?"

"I'm sure that it would have been Mrs Suhm. Perhaps we'll get them all along to the next gig."

"Yes, that would be lovely." Without any obvious purpose in mind Mrs Suhm shuffled the carafe, plates, cups and fruit cake around her tray, before saying, "Now, don't expect Peter to be very talkative. He's still very much off-color. Could you get the door for me please Edvard."

Bolverk jumped up from the sofa and led the four of us towards The Exorcist's room. Mrs Suhm insisted Decadence and I follow Bolverk, while she brought up the rear.

I have to admit, by then the strange aroma that had troubled Bolverk earlier was becoming quite powerful. It was a familiar smell to me. A troubling one. It sent a shiver down my spine.

Bolverk hesitated before the door and Decadence had to give him a poke in the back to make him proceed.

Almost as soon as he entered the room Bolverk turned around wide-eyed and tried to leave, but Decadence gave him an almighty shove, with me not far behind.

Peter's corpse lay on pristine bed clothes. He wore green shorts and an immaculately ironed white T-Shirt adorned with the head of a Viking above the words, "Norway: The Land Of The Vikings". The handle of a knife stuck out of the middle of Peter's forehead. All but a sliver of the blade was buried beneath his skull.

Mrs Suhm took a cup of coffee and a saucer from a small table at the side of the bed and handed them to Bolverk.

"Hold that for a minute will you Edvard. I'm not sure Peter has touched that you know, but it's cold now so I'd better give him a fresh cup. All hell would break loose if he didn't get his hot cup of coffee in the morning!"

A minute of near silence followed as The Exorcist's mother poured four cups of coffee from the carafe and then added milk. The noise of the crockery shaking in Bolverk's hand all but drowned-out the gentle sound of liquid splashing into china cups.

"Don't stand on ceremony there children. Sit yourselves down."

Decadence and I looked at each other, then made our way to the only two chairs in the room. Mine was close by so I could just drop into it, which I did, while trying my best to avoid staring into the decaying face of the man who had been my best friend. Decadence had to pirouette around Bolverk to reach the other one. It left Bolverk with no option but to sit uncomfortably on the bed next to our friend Peter's clean and decomposing remains.

Mr Suhm fussed around her dead son's body, gently placing the back of her frail hand against the dry skin of its cheek to make sure that its temperature hadn't risen.

It hadn't.

She used the handle of the knife to lift Peter's head so she could pull out the pillow and his neck made a sound like snapping twigs. Bolverk, Decadence and I flinched. The face remained inclined forward as if he were concentrating very hard on his navel as his mother fluffed the pillow, then replaced it. Satisfied the corpse was as comfortable as possible, she sat on the bed next to Bolverk and took up the cold white hand of her dead son in her own.

"He's been terribly down over the last few days you know." She spoke conspiratorially to us to ensure that the carcass next to her didn't hear. She was patting his hand softly and on the third or fourth pat a fingernail was dislodged and fell into her lap. "I think that he's upset to have missed your recital the other night."

Silence.

"Well, I'm sure you'll have more fun without me here, so I'll leave you four to chat together. Don't forget that there's a nice bit of cake there I made fresh this morning and do let me know if you need any more coffee."

Mrs Suhm left the room and shut the door behind her.

"Fucking hell." Decadence spoke the words flatly as he reached over from where he sat to cut himself a large slice of cake. "This is insane. Have either of you got a camera on your phone? I'm all out of power. Not slept in my house since the night before the last Black Mass so I've not had a chance to charge my phone in over a week. I wonder if that little shop on the corner sells those little disposable cameras?"

"Snorre," Bolverk said, his shoulders tensed, his eyes wild, as though holding back an entire thunderstorm by himself. "Peter's dead body is sitting there with a fucking knife sticking out of his face. How can you sit there eating cake and contemplating a photo shoot?"

Still chewing his cake Decadence leaned over the bed to examine the weapon.

"Marta, have a look. Hasn't Ailo got a knife like this one?"

I didn't leave my chair. I couldn't. I didn't want to get any closer than I already was. What was happening?

"I don't know," I said.

"It's a very pretty knife. It's got amazing floral carvings across the entire hilt. That looks like mistletoe creeping up towards the blade."

Nobody else shared his enthusiasm for the craftsmanship of the weapon.

"I tell you, it's a damn sharp knife that can pierce a human skull," Decadence continued. "I've tried to do it on that skeleton we took from the cemetery at Fantoft, but I've never managed to get very far with any of my knives."

He pulled a few stands of hair from under the head of the corpse, making me wince, then pulled them taught between his fingers and ran them into the small part of the blade that remained exposed. The knife cut the hair with only a minimum amount of pressure being applied.

"Look at that!"

He was clearly impressed and leaned round to show Bolverk and I the small bundle of hair he had separated from the corpse. He looked back at the knife in awe, then pointed to the handle.

"Holy fuck, I think she's actually been polishing it."

"Be serious for a moment will you Snorre!" Bolverk stood up and began pacing the floor. "Peter's dead. *Dead!* Somebody murdered him. What are we going to do?"

"You're probably right," Decadence said. "I've never heard of someone committing suicide like that."

"Who would have done it?" Bolverk asked.

"Now let's see…" Decadence looked up at the ceiling and tapped at that immaculately formed jaw-bone of his. "How many psychopaths do we know? And, of them, which has never wanted Peter in the band?"

"Suffer is crazy, true, but he's smart enough to know he'd never get away with this?" I said.

"Maybe. But when he gets into a rage, I'm not convinced he thinks through the long-term consequences of his actions. But perhaps it wasn't Ailo? Perhaps it was Peter's mother. Maybe she sent Peter to ask his father what his plans are for the weekend?"

Decadence laughed at the perceived cleverness of his little joke.

"What do you think Marta? What do you reckon the afterlife has in store for the Suhm boys this Saturday night?"

"I suspect they'll be fucking your mother like everyone else."

His laughter ceased abruptly as if its power had been cut off at the mains.

Bolverk pulled gently at his hair with his hands, unable to stop staring at Peter. He seemed in pain. "This… this is all going to be discovered before long. There's that stench of rotting flesh the neighbors are going to ask questions about sooner or later."

Decadence reached over The Exorcist's body to open a window. "If Suffer did this then we've got to think long and hard about the future of the band. Record sales will go through the roof in the short term, but where will it leave us? Let's ponder this for the next day or so, maybe speak with Suffer, and then decide what to do. If in the meantime all of this gets blown open so to speak, then so be it and we'll just have to deal with it as best we can."

Both Decadence and Bolverk stared at me, seeking approval for the suggested course of action. I sat stock still and stared at my hands.

"Earth to Marta," Decadence said, reaching over towards me to stroke my hair. "Any sign of life out there?"

"Fuck off Snorre." I slapped his hand away.

"What about her?" Bolverk nodded through the wall in the direction of the living room.

"What about her?" Decadence said. "She's not going to tell anyone that he's dead. As far as she's concerned he's just suffering from a bit of a migraine."

"She's a fragile old woman, Snorre," I said. "Maintaining the fiction her husband is still alive has worn her down and driven her crazy but this…" I gestured towards Peter's corpse without looking at it, "…This is too much for her to cope with. She won't last out the week."

"Not my problem." Decadence stood up and cut himself another piece of cake. "Anyway, anyone that can live their entire life believing that an all-powerful megalomaniac hippie has lived up on a cloud for all eternity should have no difficulty convincing herself that a couple of aspirin and a good night's sleep are all that this dead fuckwit needs to get him back up on his feet."

I threw my untouched, still warm coffee in his face.

"Jesus Marta! I've only just washed my hair!"

Decadence opened the drawer of a nearby chest and pulled out a clean black T-shirt.

Meatloaf: *Bat out of hell*. The Exorcist never did manage to get his head around black metal.

The T-shirt had been meticulously ironed by Mrs Suhm so that there were no folds to obscure any of the action depicted on the front. The edges and creases were as crisp as an envelope. Decadence wiped his face with it and then tossed it back into the drawer.

"Come on, let's get out of here." Decadence stood, found a mirror and teased some stray dampened locks from his cheeks. "It's bad enough that I now stink of coffee, I don't want the smell of putrefying flesh to get into my hair as well."

We filed out of the bedroom and Decadence made straight for the door out of the flat. Bolverk and I ignored him and walked through to the kitchen with Bolverk carrying the tray of plates and cups. With a reluctant groan Decadence turned around and followed us.

"Thanks for the coffee and cake Mrs Suhm," I said, as Bolverk placed the tray on a surface in the kitchen. "We'll be on our way now."

"I heard you kids laughing in there. Was he telling jokes again?"

"No Mrs S. He wasn't really on sparkling form today." Decadence spoke before Bolverk or I could answer. "He must have something on his mind."

I glared at him with a look that promised violence if he made light of events again.

Mrs Suhm opened the refrigerator and removed a package wrapped in silver foil. She handed the package to me and then slid her arms into those of Decadence and Bolverk and walked the three of us towards a cabinet in the living room.

"That's a little something in case you get hungry tonight on your little adventure."

"What are we doing tonight?" Decadence asked.

"You're burning down that awful church in Dønnisal. We'll see if Peter feels up for it later on, but I suspect you may have to do it without him."

"Christ!" Decadence said. "I'd completely forgotten we were supposed to do that tonight!"

Mrs Suhm removed her arm from that of Decadence, took a second packet from the cabinet and handed it to him.

"I'd be grateful if you didn't take The Lord's name in vain in my house, Snorre."

"I'm sorry Mrs Suhm," I said on his behalf.

"That's all right. Now, there's some paraffin wax and candles in there. You can use the candles as fuses that you can put into the wax. That should enable you to get nice little blazes going at all the key points around the nave. Father Larsen has blessed the candles so that should help."

"I… um… thank you, Mrs Suhm?" I took the package from her. "But I'm not sure we're still going church-burning tonight, what with… well, with everything that's happened this week."

Mrs Suhm looked across to Bolverk and Decadence to contradict me but they both nodded in agreement.

For the first time since we had arrived at the flat her mask cracked and I saw the face of a tired old widow who had loved her late son dearly and whose efforts to maintain the fiction of his life was already draining hers away.

Her suddenly frail hands, which had previously gripped the arm of Decadence and Bolverk with a rock-like permanence, groped to find the arms of the two men as if she were having trouble seeing them. Once she found them, she held them in a pathetic grip.

"You must go." She pleaded in a soft, weak voice that in all my years in her company I had never heard before. "Nothing has changed this week, nothing. Don't even think it. Just go on with your lives as usual. That's the only way. If you have faith in The Lord then He will provide. Regardless of how things appear, He will provide. He might test us along the way but if your faith is strong He will reward you."

Her arms began to shake and she slumped into her chair.

"I'm not much longer for this world," she continued. "That's fine by me. Old Mr Suhm has been waiting for me long enough now. But it's important to me that I leave this world nice and quietly with Peter happy and well."

Her damp eyes looked straight into mine. "Please Marta. Just carry on as usual. I just need a few more days. I outlived my husband and that's sorrow enough for one woman's lifetime."

Bolverk and I had known The Exorcist and his mother all our lives. That she still prepared three servings at mealtimes went some way to explaining how Bolverk had managed to reach the size that he was. The most startling thing we heard that day was her admission that The Exorcist's father was dead.

To my knowledge nobody else in Kragerø was aware that she had ever accepted that truth.

I looked down to the kind old face of Mrs Suhm. Her steel-blue eyes were damp and flickering with doubt. She was blameless in all of this. She was never supposed to get hurt. But then again, she wasn't the first to suffer for the greater good and she won't be last.

Other thoughts raced through my mind now. What of the band? Death had robbed us of my friend, but also the drummer of a record-label-signing group. Would the contract still stand without him? Or would the news lift us into the stratosphere, make us infamous, even more desired? Black metal thrived on death and murder and all things evil. Could this be the final push we needed to achieve our goal of destroying the world with our music?

I walked over to her chair, knelt on the floor and took her hands in my own.

"We shall burn down the church, Mrs Suhm," I said. "I will give you a call tonight to see if Peter feels up to it. And, if he doesn't, we shall do it in his honor."

She seemed to take nourishment from my words. She breathed in deeply through her nose, raised herself up and visibly inflated until the ageless matriarch, as eternal as the fjords themselves, stood before us again.

"Good," she said. "And thank you, Marta. Thank you for what you have done."

"You're welcome," I said.

32

It was almost two years ago to the day that we found, furnished and filled our subterranean shop. Prior to that I had been pondering how I could turn the band's appeal into hard cash and the inconsistent nature of their performances and recordings meant that ticket and record sales were not going to make us rich any time soon. A shop filled with overpriced junk seemed as good a way as any to supplement our income.

It was a fun summer that the four of us: Decadence, The Exorcist, Bolverk and I, spent renovating the empty catacombs we had identified a few years earlier. The moment our compulsory education came to an end we began working for fifteen hours a day to create our lair. We labored to an exclusively black metal soundtrack under the harsh heat and light of generator-powered spotlights.

It was a blazing northern summer that year and the only way we could cope with the heat was to avoid daylight and work through the night. Even then, the heat was so intense down in the cellars that within minutes of arriving all four of us would have to strip down to our underwear. We'd then blend a creamy paste of sweat and dust onto our skins as we collapsed walls, swept floors, sawed wood and hammered nails, before emerging at sunrise like herons from an oil slick – blackened ghouls covered in a glossy layer of grime that shone in the sunlight like seal skin. We would walk, half naked, through the back streets of the town, down the cobbled hill to the bay where the crisp seawater would wash us clean.

During Kragerø's hottest summer on record we hardly ever saw the daylight. While our peers browned in the sun the four of us slept through the day and then toiled all night underground, leaching all pigment from our skin and taking on a pallor that would have been death-like had our alabaster hide not been stretched over healthy teenage muscle and sinew that was continually being toned by hard physical labor.

If I had any puppy-fat, I lost it that summer. Teenage curves were hammered flat and each morning as I emerged from the sea I felt like an increasingly mature woman drying off on the quiet pebble beach. As well as the grime, my adolescence was also being washed away those summer mornings.

It took us nine weeks of hard work to clear, clean, fit-out and fill the shop with stock. While we were all very proud of what we had done I think that as the summer wore on we each felt a pang of sadness that our long nights of hot and humid intimacy were coming to an end. It was like the sorrow of arrival. The melancholy of achievement.

Bolverk and The Exorcist especially seemed to resent the swift progress we were making and their work-rate declined exponentially the closer we came to completion. Towards the end they would arrive late, take long breaks together and even take the occasional night off, leaving Decadence and I to put the finishing touches to the shop on our own.

Whilst he complained about the absences of his bandmates and joked about what they might be up to together, I suspect Decadence cherished the nights he and I spent alone there.

There is something about his stubbornness, his determination, which I always found compelling; far more than his looks. I first saw a hint of it in the way that he immersed himself in the most unfashionable and politically incorrect realms of death metal. At the time, there seemed not to exist a label, magazine or blog on death metal that Decadence did not subscribe to. Then, in the intensity of his vendetta against The Exorcist, I watched as his passion was blackened by pain and loss. It then revealed itself in the enthusiasm with which he embraced our love affair and Baphomet's Agony, and then within the heat and noise of our underground lair I saw it again in the concentrated and methodical way he went about his physical labor. That single-minded passion, that ambition, triggered a primeval urge within me to mate with him, to fuse our flesh and our genes.

Decadence and I achieved a perfect sexual understanding that summer. Under the spotlights, with all that black metal ringing in our ears, I found myself in regular need of his cock. And at the same time he developed a sensitivity to my needs that was almost psychic. Every time I felt my lust begin to fizz and shiver beneath my stomach, he would appear behind me to maul at my sweat-dampened breast and bite down on my soot-soaked neck. The interval between my arousal and my penetration was seconds rather than minutes. Our sex was swift and furious against walls or over counters and boxes. With my back to him was always best, when I could feel his desire but didn't have to endure the love in his eyes.

I've mentioned before that I couldn't love in return. Perhaps that's true. Perhaps not. Thinking back, I sometimes wonder if great swathes of my mind, body and soul fell in love with Decadence that summer. On another plane of existence, that blissful summer could have been the beginning of a beautiful life he and I would spend together, perhaps leading to marriage and children.

But it wasn't to be. In fact, I *needed* it not to be. Despite all those feelings of lust that looked like they were fading into love, there remained and still remains a significant part of me I keep locked-up tight and secure. Nobody gets to see it and even back then Decadence wasn't an exception. I have a black hole that centers and defines me. It creates its own gravity. Pulls at truth and emotions, twists them, distorts them and then destroys them. I let that core drag me away from Decadence in the end. I hadn't come all that way to allow those softer emotions to get the better of the *true* me. True me killed Mrs Lant and would go on to do a lot worse, as you will hear if you can bear to stick with me. Even as I was ostensibly succumbing to the charms of Decadence, my dark core was plotting his demise. In fact, when I look back, I can see that my black heart was always in control. It made it appear to everyone (myself included at times) that I was softening to Decadence, but in fact, I was just luring him to a higher peak from which to dash him on the rocks below.

33

Our grand opening was a big deal for the youth of Kragerø. We stole a dozen crates of expensive wine from the cellars of the town's most exclusive restaurant and a few well-placed comments from the key influencers were sufficient to draw in nearly a hundred kids from the area.

Our doors opened one Friday night at midnight, and by 4am we had run out of stock and my pockets were so full of cash I was forced to tuck my T-shirt into my jeans and shove cash down my front. Even then 100 Krone notes were spilling out of my bra.

Fortunately for our turnover (but less so for our customers) the pattern of behavior our clientele displayed was predictable and exploitable. Newcomers arrived in the shop wide-eyed and cash-rich, spent two-thirds of their stash on stock and then spent the final third getting drunk at the bar. That was when they were at their most vulnerable, which is where Decadence came in, wandering the floor, mingling with the crowd, being charming, handsome and endearingly self-conscious.

"How many copies of this album did you buy?" Bolverk asked, raising a black gatefold adorned with images of hatred and surmounted by an indecipherable logo.

"Just the one." I held open a plastic bag designed to fit the sleeve close like a prophylactic.

As Bolverk slid the album into the bag it made a satisfying sound like oiled wheels along a well-made runner. A light wind rushed out of the bag and rippled its open edge like a burst of static. "No, Bolverk asked you how many did you have when you started?"

"Just the one." I closed my eyes and savored the scent of the warm air, tinged with solvents, that wafted out of the bag.

Bolverk frowned as he took the cash from an eager outstretched hand, pulled open the front of my T-shirt and dutifully dropped the notes down my cleavage.

"But that's the third one that Bolverk has sold tonight!"

At that point Decadence arrived from the bar laden with bags we had only recently filled for our now-drunk customers. He lowered them gently on the counter and I carefully unsheathed the albums from their bags and laid them in a pile. Decadence did likewise and we soon had a neat pile of albums, of T-shirts and hoodies emancipated from their new owners.

"Oh no!" Bolverk said. "That's not right!"

"Are you growing a conscience where your balls used to be?"

"You're stealing from our friends!"

"They're not my friends," I said, as Decadence and I began re-stocking the racks with our booty. "Anyway, it's just the principle of market forces reduced to its most basic form. You remember all that crap we learned in economics? We've just found a neat way of turning the supply and demand principle into an endless loop that will keep churning out profits until your friends sober up! Which reminds me: you need to go steal some more booze."

I pulled a 100 Krone note from my T-shirt and waved it under his nose.

"Go on. You've been good up until now so you can get yourself some sweets too."

Bolverk shuffled uncomfortably. "It's theft Marta, that's what it is. Bolverk didn't spend his entire fucking summer slaving to create this place so you and Decadence could fleece people in the name of some great capitalist experiment!"

Decadence stepped forward and placed an arm around each

of our shoulders. "Let's calm down. What we have here is the beginning of something radical. We are going to change the world, claw back power, and give Norway something new to believe in. But we need to make a living too and right now the gain we get from recycling stock far outweighs the hardship we're causing these rich kids."

He paused and looked around the shop. New arrivals had to walk through the shop to get to the bar and all of them were delighted to find their path strewn with counterfeit Chinese-made band merchandise, albums and CDs crammed full of ear-bleeding cruelty, and three shelves of aliens, robots and orcs cast in lead. Metalheads love aliens, robots and orcs that have been cast in lead. They fluttered from aisle to aisle like anti-moths, instinctively drawn to the darkness we had on offer.

"Look at them Edvard!" Decadence said. "When they spend their money here they're not really bothered about increasing their material possessions. They're buying into a movement that we're building for them. If that means that we have to front-load their subscription with a bit of creative stock taking nobody is going to begrudge us that."

"Fantastic," said Bolverk without emotion. He snatched the 100 Krone note I still held in my hand, then walked to the stairs.

"Do hurry back Edvard!" I shouted after him. "The shit is beginning to back up in the men's toilet and somebody needs to get in there and chop it all up so it can squeeze down the drain. You can pretend you're a Viking demi-God hacking his way through an army of malicious Christian turd-monsters!"

I was screaming by the time he left and wasn't entirely sure he'd come back.

We turned over the same stock four or five times for ninety-six hours straight – working in shifts. By then we had made over 100,000 Krone which was enough seed capital for the business to become legitimate, or at least partially legitimate.

Bolverk did come back. He wasn't happy with his shifts and

he insisted that The Exorcist work the same shifts as him in future so he didn't have to speak to me. Plus he wanted the two of them to take the same time off together. But at least he turned up to work. For a self-proclaimed Viking warrior "born into the wrong age" as he liked to put it, Bolverk was capable of petty grudges and mood swings that would embarrass a pre-menstrual drama queen with a hormone imbalance and a drug habit.

The Exorcist didn't have much of an opinion about any of this and was just happy someone else was making decisions for him, and that he could spend his time with Bolverk and help me. He didn't like the friction that soured the air between Bolverk and me, but he had seen us have worse fights. I once stabbed Bolverk in the head with a pencil. The wood and graphite snapped before his skull did but he still needed a tetanus jab.

After our initial ninety-six-hour marathon we shut the shop for three days while we slept and re-stocked and then on the following Friday, a week after we launched, we had a party. It was a great party. Looking back at it, it was the most important party we ever hosted and if I had my time again I wouldn't have it any other way.

34

The Exorcist was dead.

Bolverk, Decadence and I walked back to the shop in silence. I imagine we were all thinking about the consequences of the discovery we'd just made. Although, if the murderer were among us, they would have already known. Presumably they had thought through the consequences long before.

The streets around the shop were strangely quiet and it was then I remembered a political rally was taking place in Oslo. I had meant to attend because it had good potential for escalating into all-out riot. Officially the march and peaceful occupation of a municipal building had a green agenda, but I knew for a fact it was going to be hijacked by anarchists and Satanists who planned to set fire to buildings while they had orgies inside. I knew that because it was my idea to do the hijacking and my Satanic emissaries had been dispatched by coach earlier in the day. However, band commitments had kept me in Kragerø so the best I could do was to apologize the night before for the fact that Baphomet's Agony would not be leading the charge and then hand out free T-shirts to those on the coach so the TV footage would broadcast the band logo all over the world.

When we eventually reached the shop, Bolverk, Decadence and I were in such a quiet and contemplative mood we forgot to switch the shop's PA system on. So we heard the Ginger Christian thundering down the street, bellowing in panic, before we saw him crashing down the staircase.

"Up on the hill." His words came out in gasps and in English so we had to concentrate hard to understand him. He'd clearly been running for a while. "Hundreds of them. With sticks and bats and knives and chains."

A strange light-headedness came over me. I think it was caused by the blood draining down into my gut.

None of needed to ask who he was talking about. *Oslo Iron* were inevitable.

"They're heading this way and even the police are scared of taking them on. They fill up both sides of the road!"

I opened my phone.

"We'll just hide out in the Crypt," Decadence said. "We'll be fine."

"What makes you think that a mob is going to respect your privacy just because you hang a 'do not disturb' sign on the door?" I asked as I began scanning my favored feeds.

"We'll lock the big iron door."

"Ha!" said Bolverk. "Don't you remember the time Peter tripped on the curb and crashed open that door with his head?"

I didn't like hearing Bolverk mention his name. He hadn't been spoken of since we left his flat and Bolverk had just breached what I had assumed was an unspoken rule. If none of us spoke his name none of us need think about him and what one of us might have done to him.

Fucking Bolverk.

My phone had started to receive calls and messages. The vibrations of each one hitting my inbox was creating a monotonous drone. I ignored them all and focused on the feeds from the locals. "He's right" I said. "That door is all style and no substance. It's got about as much integrity as you have."

There were a lot of posts about the Oslo rally and lots of the Satanists were lamenting the fact that Baphomet's Agony weren't there. Shit. I guess on reflection my public disclosure of us having to remain at home to attend to business was a massive mistake. I had effectively broadcast to the world, Oslo Iron included, that our entire fan base would decamp to the nation's capital leaving just the band and a few of the less adventurous stragglers to remain in Kragerø.

Photos of the approaching mob had already been posted. I turned my phone to show Bolverk and Decadence what fate befell us. The streets of Kragerø were clogged with embittered men headed towards us with violence and bloodshed writ large across their tired old eyes. As the Ginger Christian had attested, many of them were armed and some of those that weren't carried Nazi flags.

"We won't stand a chance if we stay down here," I advised the others. "Our only hope is to make a run for it. Come on!"

I gathered up my stuff and I was about to dart up the stairs when Bolverk swept across my path and blocked me.

"We're not running from anyone."

"Edvard, you've seen the photos – that shit's happening in real time!"

"She's right Edvard," Decadence added. "There's over a hundred of them. If we stay down here they'll smoke us out like badgers."

"We're not going to stay down here."

"Then why are you blocking our path?"

Already I could hear the sound of boots scampering across cobbles as the few customers smoking on the street saw or heard of the advancing mob and fled.

"Because you're not armed."

There was an eerie calmness about Bolverk I had only ever seen in the moments before he went on stage.

"What do you expect us to do?"

Bolverk puffed out his massive chest, "We're going to stand firm, face our enemies and fight them like men."

"But we'll die," Decadence said.

The heavy flesh of Bolverk's genes had fashioned clumsily into a face rippled with a pure and beautiful joy. His small eyes – dropped in among the folds as an afterthought – twinkled as he struggled to contain the smile that was fighting to crease the grim facade he had fabricated.

"Well, there's no shame in that!"

35

If the launch of the shop was an epiphany for the burgeoning black metal sub-culture that had been festering beneath Kragerø's picture-postcard veneer, our launch party was a Satanic trial, crucifixion and resurrection condensed into eight hours.

Suffer kept his distance from us throughout that summer but when I asked him to perform with the band he agreed. I say he agreed, what I mean is that I stood on the threshold of the squalid gravedigger's hut he haunted – at the time I didn't even know if he lived there, it was just where we usually found him – and when I asked him to perform he responded by hurling a brick out of the gloom.

It must have been a "yes" though, because the next day he turned up in the shop ready to perform.

While we had spent our summer building the shop, Suffer had spent it taking positive steps to accelerate his degeneration. I had never known him to be pleasant-smelling; at his most hygienic the closest Suffer got to a bath was when he would stroll naked along the private industrial beaches out to the east of the town in the early hours of the morning and let the arctic spray coat him in a film of chemical waste. But as the band began to generate a groundswell of popular support he took it upon himself to become the personification of repulsiveness. Mainly by taking to wearing the clothes of the newly deceased and buried, who he then dug up to strip of their attire.

So, like a repugnant fanfare announcing his arrival, his eye-watering reek preceded Suffer down the stairs to the shop. Despite the fact that the faces of the crowd had already been set to revulsion before they even saw the source of the stench, they still managed to twist themselves into further and unexpected convulsions of fear and loathing at the sight that befell them when he arrived within their midst.

I don't think that Suffer had ventured out into the open much that summer. He must have just lived off whatever unfortunate mammals and insects had scuttled within his reach. He was more gaunt than I remembered and his skin was stretched so tight around his face that his eye sockets had been pulled back creating a dark space around each of his eyes. His skin was thin with a complexion the hue of an empty tin trough. This pallor made his red sores seem angrier and his yellow pustules more toxic.

In the months since we had last seen him he had acquired a limp which made him look even more like a zombie as he shuffled through the crowd that cautiously made space for him to pass. But there was another something new in his repulsiveness, something hinted at before but never, until then, given free reign over his behavior.

Suffer had discovered his cock.

He was a small man, which meant that in a room in which women stood he would have had to lift his chin in order for his gaze to fall on their faces. But then again, most men that stood a full head taller than Suffer managed to affect a default outlook on the world that never saw their gaze lift above a woman's neck. If all that Suffer had done was stare at the tits of the girls at the party his behavior would have been unworthy of comment. What Suffer did was far creepier than that.

To begin with he would fix upon a target, stand one or two meters away, and stare at her groin. He wore his tattered jeans without a belt or buttons and displaying no discernible shame. And he indicated no preference in his lechery: tall, short, fat, thin; he cared not. The only criteria he seemed to care about were gender and proximity.

I was certainly not spared his attentions. In fact, I was standing with The Exorcist at one point that opening night when the drummer grabbed my shoulders and lifted me bodily up and round in a one hundred and eighty degree arc. As I landed, I saw Suffer had been kneeling on the floor precisely behind where I had been stood.

"What are you doing?" The Exorcist asked him.

Suffer muttered something as if he were vomiting dust. Then he was on The Exorcist's chest with their faces close together and with an arm hooked round the larger man's neck.

"I was smelling her shit!"

He spat out a laugh and then jumped down and scuttled back across the floor like a cockroach in search of a darkened crevice.

We had told everyone that Baphomet's Agony was going to perform during the party and right up until that moment, things were going to plan. But The Exorcist had had enough.

"I don't want to be in a band with him anymore," he said. "I don't want to have anything to do with him. He's evil and he makes me sick."

I rubbed his arm. "Peter, you play drums in a black metal band. You're supposed to be evil and you're supposed to make people sick. That's your job. Ailo just happens to be much better at his job than you are."

"He had his nose pressed up your ass, Marta! How can you defend him?"

"It's my ass, Peter, and it's not like you've noticed it before. If you care so much about it now, I'm afraid you're going to have to confront Snorre before you complain about Ailo."

By then The Exorcist was eighteen years old, fully bearded and stood at six foot seven. Yet he was still capable of giving a convincing impression of a five year-old child that had just been declined a puppy for Christmas. He dropped his head and quietly absorbed the blow I had deliberately dealt him.

"I just can't bear the thought of him thinking bad thoughts about you."

"The thought of him thinking bad thoughts?" I poked him gently in the ribs as I teased him. "That's a hell of a lot of thinking for you Peter. It's more than three times the amount of thinking that you can normally cope with. You're going to have some sort of brain hemorrhage if you keep this up."

He fought to contain a smile but the power of deception was absent from his skill-set, so his hang-dog look was shattered by that smile which, in turn, was broken by a giggle.

I laid a hand upon the center of his broad chest. There was a space there and for as long as I can remember my hand had fit it perfectly. Throughout our lives it was as if my hand and that space between his ribs had been carefully engineered counterparts. As my fingers slot into place he felt soft yet strong, yielding yet eternal; he felt like a warm wall.

"I'm not asking you to like Ailo or to be his friend," I said. "I just need you to hit a drum every now-and-again to create something approaching a rhythm to supplement his screaming."

He placed one of his massive hands over mine and I had one of those King Kong moments that had become so familiar to me over the years.

A breath hesitated on its way out of my chest but I checked myself and that other Marta reasserted herself. *It's a bit late for that you fucker.*

"You're on in ten minutes," I said, pushing him away.

The band had jammed very little over the summer and Suffer had not even spoken to the rest of them for nearly four months. But, as usual, it all came together that night in a terrifying, chaotic and just about coherent way. The drums, guitar and vocals were like three suspicious travelers from different parts of the globe that had met in a bar but shared no common language and had no real desire to communicate with each other. Bolverk's bass lines brought them all together like a cynical bartender that gets them all drunk and provokes them into a brawl.

For those that have plotted the development of Decadence and his guitar style (and believe me, there are many of them) this was an unsettling period that split his devotees. On the one hand you had those who loved all the rapid chord crunching, finger-tapping, arpeggios and string-wailing. It was certainly a masterclass in technical virtuosity. On the other hand there are those, like me, who tired quickly of all that shit, who missed the amateur shoddiness of his earlier style and who preferred the more tortured brutality of what would eventually follow.

I knew precisely what had gone wrong with Decadence during this period of the band's story: he was happy. Nothing good can come of happiness. Contentedness makes fertile soil for complacency and the banal. Decadence had planted himself within a lush field of satisfaction and was reaping a rich crop of wank.

It was all my fault. I was giving him something that looked a lot like what he needed and this made him feel joyful and secure. He needed love and having got used to the invisible love of his mother he interpreted my ill-disguised hostility as an ineloquent attempt to express my feelings. It was an easy mistake to make, particularly when my open and public humiliation of him was punctuated by our very agreeable sex.

He was wrong of course. He and I were not taking nourishing draughts from some deep pool of love. I could not allow myself to gorge on such tonics. Instead, the happier he became, the more I grew mean and malicious. His mother's death had changed him for the better, but I had foolishly given him some hope of a life content. It was time to put an end to that too.

Even at this period of their development, Baphomet's Agony still had the propensity to create mayhem whenever they performed. I was therefore keen for their shop-opening gig to end before the crowd had been whipped up into anything approaching a violent frenzy. I had 100,000 Krone of stock and a heap of stolen furnishings to protect.

So as soon as someone rushed the stage – probably to stage-dive but who could really tell – I cut the power to the band and threw up the lights.

"Um, thanks folks," Bolverk growled into the microphone, side-eyeing me. "That's the last you'll probably be seeing from us so savor the memory."

It was an odd comment. At first I thought it was a joke, then I realized Bolverk didn't really make jokes.

"What was that all about?" I asked afterwards.

"It was about Bolverk and Peter leaving the band."

"*What*?" The word fell from my mouth; clumsy like food dropped from a fork.

"Hah! Bolverk has rendered Marta speechless. Who would have thought it possible?"

"Peter?" I looked towards The Exorcist. "What's going on?"

The Exorcist tried to feign nonchalance but in attempting a casual shrug he dropped a cymbal on his foot.

I turned back to Bolverk, who sat down on the lip of the stage, lit a cigarette and pulled me down next to him.

"There's a trawler leaving Hammerfest on Monday morning and heading north for a two month trip. Peter and Bolverk are going to be on it. They're going to be fishermen Marta. It's in their blood, there's no point in denying it."

"But the band? And you've got a shift in here on Monday!"

Bolverk took a slow and deliberate drag on his cigarette.

"Regrettably, it's Bolverk rather than Marta that will determine Bolverk's fate and Bolverk's decided that he's going to be fishing on Monday."

I glanced at Peter, who was rubbing his foot. "What's this really about?"

"It's about being fishermen, Marta."

"No, really. Come on, Edvard. What the fuck?"

"Eloquently put Marta, Bolverk too asked that same question. 'Bolverk, what the fuck?' he said. And do you know what Bolverk said in reply? He said 'The fuck is not following your dream. The fuck is pretending to be a rock star when you are in fact something much more dangerous, much more exciting: when you are, in fact, a Viking!' Wise words don't you think? He's a smart guy that Bolverk."

"A Viking? Oh for Christ's sake, Edvard, you are not a Viking. There are no Vikings. There haven't been any Vikings for a thousand years! You're a portly bassist in a black metal group. Why can't you just get over the whole fucking Viking thing?"

"Bolverk is a Viking in here!" He slammed a fist into his chest with such force that glasses on a table on the other side of the room trembled.

"Okay, well what if you are? I hate to break it to you, but Norwegian fishermen don't sail in longboats anymore and those trawlers that set out from Hammerfest tend not to conquer many new lands. Anyway, even if you *did* think that fit your Viking dream, and I can find another bassist – hey, maybe I'll take it up myself! – you need to leave Peter here." I was working myself up into a rage at the idea he might be taken from me. He wasn't mine, but that didn't mean I wanted him to be off with anyone else.

"Peter!" I stood and yelled. "You get down here right now!"

The Exorcist shuffled down the stage, avoiding eye-contact with anyone, and stepped off the lip as you or I would a shallow kerb. He sat down next to Bolverk in the space I had just vacated.

"Look me in the eye," I said, "and tell me you're going off to be a fisherman with Edvard."

The Exorcist said nothing.

"See?" I said triumphantly to Bolverk. "He's staying here. Conversation over. Edvard, you're free to fuck off whenever you choose. Don't forget to bring us back a souvenir will you."

The Exorcist spoke softly, keeping his face to the floor.

"I'm going with him Marta."

His comment left a distinct shadow of sound after it had passed, like the echo of a gunshot.

"Say that again."

"I said I'm going with him."

I swung my arm back and hooked it round into his jaw with all my strength. His face didn't move the tiniest fraction but the pain in my hand was explosive. It felt like the bones in all of my fingers had fragmented into dust.

"I told you to look me in the eye!"

"Stop your bullying Marta!" Bolverk said. "You treat him like a child! He's a grown man capable of making his own decisions."

"No, he's not. I know what's best for him and packing him off on a boat to die like his father is not it. Leave him here!"

"Marta, what's the big deal?" Decadence interjected. "What's it to you what he does? Let him go! More often than not he gives back in change more than he's handed in the first place so profits from the shop will shoot up once he's gone. And he can't drum for shit. It's time for you both to move on. If he trips over his laces and falls into the sea then a dodgy set of genes will have been taken out of the pool and all of mankind will benefit. It's win-win as far as I can see."

I gave nothing away. But inside me a switch was flicked and then fused shut in a crackle of static and spark. I had tolerated Decadence's hatred of Peter so far, tried to understand it, but now it irritated me.

To the side, Suffer drew closer to the group. He had not really spoken to any of us that night but the ugly conflict at the foot of the stage had drawn him in like a mercenary to a war zone. A plan formed in my mind. Like all of my plans, it was malicious and horrible and perfect.

I turned to Decadence, feigning need.

"Will *you* ever abandon me, Snorre?"

Decadence literally swelled with joy that I had asked him

such a question. That I seemingly cared if he went away. He looked like a man dying of thirst in the desert who had just seen a mirage.

"Never Marta. Never. I swear it!"

"Do you love me Snorre?"

Some profound change must have occurred at a chemical level within his bloodstream because he continued to grow in stature, light radiating from his face. A sweet and pure elation almost lifted him clear off the ground.

"Yes!" he said, breathless and relieved, finally, to have an opportunity to give voice to his devotion. "Yes, I love you with everything that I have. With every cell in me. With every moment of my history and my future!"

I lifted my face to his and as his mouth descended upon mine I saw in his eyes, for the briefest of moments, the possibility of a simple life full of love and security. Despite my impure intentions, I was surprised by how tempting it was. I let myself linger in his kiss – a kiss so deep and complex and sweet and intense, it would surely season the bitterness of his tears to come.

Locked in this loving embrace I reached out with my right hand to where I knew, from his stench, Suffer was stood. I found his arm, ran my fingers down it and pushed my hand beneath his waistband that was crisp from layers of dried residue.

I let Decadence break the embrace and then slowly, never taking my eyes off him, I stepped backwards to reveal the full, horrific tableau to him. However, so complete was his immersion within love and devotion that all he could see was my smiling face. He failed completely to see what had struck the others dumb.

With my gaze fixed upon Decadence I stepped aside from him, slid my hand out of Suffer's pants and took his small, calloused paw in my own. I unbuttoned my jeans, pulled them down and pulled aside the crotch of my panties. I then lowered myself to the beer-soaked floor.

On some level Decadence must have been processing what he was seeing but the transition from joy to disgust was not an instant one. I suspect the gap between the elation and humiliation I gifted him that night was too great to cross within the timeframe allowed. Even as I pulled Suffer down to the floor and then inside me, Decadence looked on in a haze of sublime contentment.

While inside me Suffer had one of his brain-freezes. His eyes rolled so far back into his head that his iris vanished. Paradoxically, I remember thinking that without his iris Suffer looked more human than he did normally.

The freeze lasted just a moment. With his cock softening within me Suffer shook himself out of his near-coma and slapped me hard across the face. Then, without another word, he stood, walked up the stairs and out onto the street.

The realization of what had just happened began to dawn on Decadence as I stood and pulled up my jeans. He was trying to make sense of it, but it wasn't easy. And then those eyes, those beautiful eyes, changed indescribably. It was the same change that occurred when his mother died. And that made me smile.

The perfection of my disgrace was utterly beautiful.

36

Popcorn Lady, Decadence and I walked up the stairs of the shop with Bolverk and the Ginger Christian carrying the Wheelchair Goth. Once out on the street Decadence and I stood nervously in the middle of the road, holding our weapons of choice and awaiting the hordes of Oslo Iron. Popcorn Lady chatted away amiably while the Wheelchair Goth turned his head from side to side very slowly and blinked lugubriously.

Ever the Viking, Bolverk was as excited for violence as a child is for Christmas morning. Our impending doom was apparently the catalyst he needed to blast away the despair he clearly felt from Peter's death.

With his helmet askew on his head he was bouncing between us and whispering instructions and motivational sound bites. To Decadence he said, "Remember this is a battle of hearts and minds. It will be won and lost before the first blow hits home. An army fears what it doesn't understand so disorientation and surprise are our key weapons. If Bolverk had that pretty face of yours he'd be maiming right now as we speak: deep slashes into the cheeks. The pain will focus your rage and your self-sacrifice will strike fear deep into their hearts."

Decadence didn't look convinced. He eyed me looking for a way out of this mess, but I gave him nothing back. No change there.

In the time that had elapsed since I let Suffer desecrate me on the floor of the Crypt Decadence had transformed from a sulky, grief-stricken adolescent into the cynical hedonist whose career you have been following over these pages. A long weekend of drugs and whores in Hamburg with his father helped but I'm pretty confident that the bulk of his transformation was down to me and my expert manipulation.

No applause? You fuckers have no appreciation of art.

Anyway, Decadence, the cynical hedonist you have come to love, was peculiarly absent that morning. The version stood next to me was altogether more anxious. I wish the same could be said of his bandmate.

Bolverk turned to me next. "Pick out the largest and most ferocious of them and go after him first. Dispose of him quickly and then move on. Your strength with ebb over time so you want to make the most of that initial burst of adrenalin. Don't allow yourself a moment of rest until at least dozen have fallen at your hand."

I nodded and raised the giant, two foot long pink dildo I was carrying in salute. It still had a smear of the Ginger Christian's blood.

To Popcorn Lady: "Be ruthless and show no mercy. If they hit you absent-mindedly in the face you stab them in the heart with all your might, rip down to the stomach like this; and then tear out their entrails like so. Wear them as a scarf if you choose but if you have the stomach for it you should devour them so as to harness their life force."

To the Wheelchair Goth: "Don't just focus on the man in front of you. Plan your moves three, four, five steps in advance. As you kick the first of them think how you can use your momentum to follow through with your fist on the second and your blade into the third."

In return for that wise advice Bolverk received another epic blink.

To the Ginger Christian: "You keep close to Bolverk. His axe will strike each of them just once so if they fall with any strength left in them you must finish them off. Point your head down like this and furrow your brow so as to keep the blood from running into your eyes."

Decadence continued to be less than enthusiastic about our all-but-certain-certain death as the mob gathered on the street before us. He had no quips to mock our predicament. He, like me, was just plain scared. He brandished a curious wooden club out of which a dozen viscous spikes protruded irregularly like the teeth of a shark (remarkably, we sold dozens of those clubs every week) but I could see that there was little strength in his grip.

The mob was ugly. Over a hundred strong, these were men for whom their best years were behind them and many of them had that mid-life-crisis look about them. I'm confident a good few of them had only been allowed out by their wives for a couple of hours before being required back at home to do their share of the childcare. Their leathers ill-contained the additional kilos they had gained since they had purchased them some thirty or forty years ago.

Yet there were others, less awkward, more dangerous, in among their number. A small contingent of nasty, small-minded fascists who had devoted most of their lives to black metal thuggery and had decided to tag along to whatever was about to happen now.

Their leader was well known to me by reputation. A charming individual, this Grand Prick of Cock-Suckery (and Neo-Nazism), who went by the name The Sultan of Hades or, more often, just The Sultan. As a vocal anti-Islamist his choice of name was not without its irony.

It was he who pushed himself to the front of the mob and took charge.

"False metal impostors!" he said. "Are you ready to suffer the consequences of your crimes against true black metal and the injuries your rabid *Suffer* inflicted upon us in Oslo?"

"Fuck off," I said. I had never meant it more.

The Sultan seemed annoyed to be talked to by a woman.

"Can't you keep your bitch on a leash?" he said to Decadence and Bolverk.

"If you can't cope with her tongue," Bolverk replied, "you've come ill-equipped for Bolverk's axe."

With that, he raised his weapon over his head and lunged into no-man's land.

Have you ever seen a crowd flinch? It was quite something to see. To a man, every one of the hundred plus black-metal soldiers drew back a meter. As a synchronized dance move it would have done the most exacting of choreographers proud. It was accompanied by the beautiful sound of a battalion of black leather boots scraping sharply over the surface of the road.

With its head faced upward Bolverk slowed and gently lowered his axe onto the road, leaned on it and let out a resounding laugh. "Priceless! Bolverk shall enjoy making blood eagles of you all."

Oslo Iron outnumbered Baphomet's Agony by at least twenty-to-one. And, worse, I could see that a lot of our enemy were on something. I could tell from the dilation of their pupils: small-pricked guys with pin-prick eyes. The drugs made them edgy and unpredictable. Already glass bottles were being hurled in our direction – poorly – and shattering on the road around us. But mixed in with the knives and clubs these dickwipes held in their sweaty palms, I could see there were some pistols, and yet it still came as a shock when a shot rang out over the sound of Bolverk's laughter.

Wheelchair Goth raised his bored and sullen gaze from the ground in front of him and settled his tired eyes on each of us in turn. After an eternity he followed our collective stare towards his shin where thick blood had begun to ooze like treacle from a wound hidden beneath the distressed black denim.

"Guns?" Bolverk boomed. "Have you no shame you wretched cowards! This is Norway, not L.A. Here in Norway we fight like men! Like Vikings! Isn't that what Oslo Iron is supposed to stand for? For the sanctity of pure Satanic Norwegian black metal? Guns have no place here."

Staggeringly, in a Satanic street fight between one hundred drug-crazed anarchists and the most depraved heavy metal band on the planet, Bolverk had managed to find some moral high ground to climb onto. I was almost proud of him.

The Sultan was snookered. Running like a spine through all black metal (right the way down to its asshole where Oslo Iron had located itself) was the nobility of Norway's pre-Christian heritage. Mixed into that was violence, misanthropy and the mild hero worship of a handful of seminal bands, but anything vaguely foreign or exotic was anathema. Bolverk had called them out on this and there was no conceivable way they could back down.

"Holster your pistols," The Sultan said to his forces as Baphomet's Agony won the first point against Oslo Iron. Although it didn't mean we weren't going to die.

Bolverk stood beside me and I could sense that he was primed and ready to launch into the fray. I knew Decadence wouldn't be of any use, yet to my surprise he still stood on the other side of me, unwilling to run. Not without me, at least. Despite everything I had put him through, he remained by my side and now that I looked at him he took my hand in his. Instinctively, I squeezed my fingers around his as he maneuvered me backwards so he was between me and the mob.

Surprisingly, I let him.

"You can't keep her safe from us, lady-boy," The Sultan said, laughing. "We came here to kill you and that's what we're going to do, guns or no guns. You're trying to change black metal. You're turning it into some sort of trend, making it fashionable, cool, profitable. Black metal is not about money, glamour and sex, it's about hardship, isolation and despair."

"Nothing to do with the fact that the youth of Norway have chosen us over you?" I said over Decadence's shoulder. We were going to die, so I might as well get my digs in. "That you're no longer relevant to them? To anyone, really?"

The Sultan visibly reddened. "Enough! No more delaying. If you have any last words, now is the time to voice them."

"I'm going to shove my dildo up your ass!" I yelled.

The Sultan snapped. He began the charge towards us. His mob quickly followed, although once they caught up with him he slowed enough so he was no longer at the forefront of the stampede.

"Ásatrú!" Bolverk yelled and commenced a charge that far surpassed that of the mob in its ferocity. The Ginger Christian wasn't far behind him.

I didn't follow. Instead I took a breath and dropped the dildo. A wave of peace and calm washed over me and I was reminded of the one time that I took heroin. I didn't want to inject that shit in Suffer's filthy hut, but he'd sat on my chest with his back to my face and pinned my arms to the floor with his knees. My fear of Suffer, my shortness of breath, the pain in my arms, even the stench of Suffer's squalor, it had all been washed away as the dirty brown sludge flushed through my system, replacing my blood with muck and slovenly ecstasy. It was like that.

I had intended to fight, but now the moment was here I found greater solace in accepting my fate. And those few seconds that the mob charged towards me were quite simply beautiful. It was the closest that I ever came to pure peace.

37

In my daze, I watched Bolverk and the Ginger Christian cut through Oslo Iron like two fingers dragged through soup. The middle-aged arseholes and their fascist mates fell under and away from our blood-hungry lunatics, until they had run straight through the entire crowd. They emerged on the other side before they lost any of their momentum.

Of course, what that meant for Decadence, The Wheelchair Goth, Popcorn Lady and me was we now faced the enemy on our own. Our vanguard was on the opposite side of the enemy from where we were stood and I suddenly found myself within a few meters of The Sultan.

Ridiculously, like the rest of his crowd, he'd turned his back to me and was concentrating on what Bolverk and the Ginger Christian were going to do next.

I was so close to The Sultan I could smell his fear. It was a strange thing to admit, but I was accustomed to the smells of men and I knew how to categorize them. I had grown up around sweetness of The Exorcist and the pungency of Bolverk. I had then advanced to the more fragrant Decadence and more recently had subjected myself to the putrid reek of Suffer.

I knew the smell that men gave off when they were working, when they slept, when they were happy, when they were horny and when they were angry. The smell of a Baphomet's Agony crowd was my favorite combination of man smells. It was a heady and wonderful blend of scents: an intoxicating mixture of sweat, alcohol and spunk.

The smell that Oslo Iron gave off was similar, but different. The aroma of sweat-infused leather was there, as was the earthy tang of rarely washed hair. But rather than the musk of pure sexual excitement that hung over the crowd at a Baphomet's Agony show, and more diluted in the shop, these guys gave off a stench of desperation. They smelled like a fruit on the cusp of decay: lurid in its eagerness to prove that it was still ripe even as its skin wrinkled and the rot began to gnaw its way to the surface.

This close to the Sultan I could see the sharpened edge of his machete. I could see two small nicks taken out of the blade that shone black within the otherwise polished steel; I could even see a fine hair that adhered like a magnet to its surface and swayed in a light breeze. I could see his fingers twitching on the hilt of his weapon and the skin on his hand prickling with excited anxiety. I could hear a faint rasp in his breathing.

It's difficult to describe but I found that I was both terrified and fearless simultaneously. Physically, I was gripped with fear: my blood ran so cold through me that it felt as if it had frozen and any movement risked snapping my veins. But mentally I had resigned myself to my death and I even felt defiant in its presence – my body and my mind were adopting contradictory positions faced with identical circumstances.

With Oslo Iron still focused on Bolverk and the Ginger Christian, I turned just as a new crowd of young, banner-waving, blood-thirsty thugs turned a corner behind us. This new crowd was marginally bigger in size than the existing crowd of old, banner-waving, blood-thirsty thugs ahead of us and they still wore leather and denim – the uniform of a metal militia – but these kids' clothes were not exclusively black. There was color in there, and badges, and where the Oslo Iron hordes carried themselves with a weary despondency, these kids bounced around across the road with vim and vigor.

Christians!

I learned afterwards that they too had been monitoring the Baphomet's Agony chatrooms and had discovered, just as Oslo Iron had, that we were going to be vulnerable to attack during the Oslo riots. Close to one hundred and fifty of the worst dressed teenagers you could ever imagine had therefore descended on Kragerø with the intention of fucking us up. They'd even brought tar and feathers. What the fuck? Where do you even get that shit from?

Anyway, they arrived to take us down, but what they hadn't bargained for was finding an altogether worse group of humans already confronting us to do the same thing.

Having turned the corner and seen the mass of Oslo Iron, the Christians stopped in their tracks. Oslo Iron found themselves positioned between the Christians on one side, and Bolverk and the Ginger Christian on the other. Everyone remained frozen to the spot in perhaps the most bizarre three-way Mexican standoff ever seen.

It took Bolverk to kick things off.

"Fuck this," he said, and then charged at Oslo Iron with the Ginger Christian not far behind him. Oslo Iron retreated towards the Christians who interpreted their retreat as an attack at which point, they mounted their own counter-attack.

The ensuing battle was reported quite widely across Norway and a lot of Northern Europe. It even troubled some of the news reports in the US. Two Satanists and a Christian died. I watched the Christian die: someone planted an axe in the crown of his head. Like a puppet with its strings cut he just collapsed to the floor in a muddle of limbs with blood squirting out from his skull like fizzy pop from a hole in a shook-up can. It didn't look like a real death at all. Surely a real death would have involved a bit of a struggle, some wailing and a dramatic swoon in the finale? Surely nineteen or twenty years of living couldn't just be extinguished in the blink of an eye like that? But there you go; it turns out death is one of those things that just happens to some people in the split-second they're looking the other way.

In all the craziness the bags of feathers were breached and their soft white contents filled the air. The effect was surreal. The scene unfolded before us like a medieval battle depicted within a snow globe. The feathers somehow made all the violence look picturesque and charming, like a brutal insurrection mashed-up with a boarding school pillow fight.

Of course, the arrival of the Christians took all the fun out of proceedings for Bolverk. There was nothing noble or romantic for him about fighting against Satanists alongside Christians or fighting against Christians alongside Satanists. He was crestfallen. He never even entered the mêlée. When he saw the battle unfold he simply stopped, cast his axe aside and shuffled over to join us out of harm's way in mourning.

"That was Bolverk's one great chance to show his mettle," he said. "To prove to the world that he was a splendid Viking."

"Poor Edvard," I said, doing my best to hug him but barely able to cover half of his circumference with my arms. "Don't worry. I'll find you another way to die."

The Wheelchair Goth seemed not the least bit concerned that he had been shot. But he was bleeding, so while everyone else was still fighting I directed Popcorn Lady towards the hospital and suggested she take him there quickly before all the other casualties began to arrive in their droves.

Sadly, that was the last we ever saw of the Ginger Christian. I guess he joined his old friends and went back home after his misadventures with us. Probably a good thing.

"Come on boys," I said to Bolverk and Decadence. "We don't want to be here when the police arrive. We've got a church to burn tonight."

"Without Peter?" Bolverk asked. I winced again and this time even Decadence looked surprised that his name had been mentioned.

I nodded firmly at both. "We'll do it in his honor. Now go get some sleep and we'll all meet up again in the Dønnisal churchyard at midnight. Dress for arson."

To be fair, they had no idea what they were walking into and no amount of sleep could have prepared them for what was to come next.

38

It was under a gibbous moon that Decadence and I sat on the edge of the churchyard at Dønnisal.

I had only briefly considered asking Bolverk to bring me there on his bike. In the state of self-pity I had left him in earlier that afternoon, following the revelation about The Exorcist and then his own failure to die a Viking death, my chances of arriving in one piece did not look good. Instead, I swallowed my pride and rode in the Decadence Love Truck.

The band had a panel van that we used to transport equipment here and there but, in addition, Decadence had a pimped-out van he used during his nocturnal burglaries and fuck-adventures. It was a black Mercedes with tinted windows, leather upholstery, mirrored ceilings and a bed in the back. Decadence tended not to wash his sheets very often so the familiar yet mildly repulsive smell of his sex-sweat hung heavy in the cab like a porno air-freshener.

Midnight was approaching in the van on the way up there, but even this far south summer nights in Norway never darkened beyond a benign twilight. Flies could still be seen buzzing between the tombstones and both the sun and moon cast their eerie shadows over any structure that stood on or in the ground.

Decadence pointed at the V-shaped silhouettes cast by the graves: "It looks like they have their legs spread," he whispered, barely suppressing a child-like giggle. "They must have heard I was coming."

The quip was about the full extent of our interaction so far that night. We hadn't discussed The Exorcist's death since leaving his mother's apartment. I doubt that Decadence cared much and I wondered if that had made him the prime suspect in the others' eyes. He had made no attempt to disguise his contempt for The Exorcist and had spoken openly about the revenge he would one day wreak on him for brain-fucking his mother's skull with a guitar head (he didn't actually use the phrase "brain-fuck" – that's my embellishment). He was the one with obvious motive.

We sat there in the churchyard waiting quietly. As veterans of numerous nocturnal raids we both knew churches and churchyards attracted visitors at odd times of the night, so it was always a good idea to wait patiently for up to an hour before assuming there was nobody about.

The churchyard at Dønnisal was a large one and at both ends of it were war memorials. The one at the south celebrated those who died fighting the British during the Napoleonic wars while the one in the north remembered those that died fighting alongside the British during World War Two. A Christian church constructed from the timbers of a pagan temple suffered little embarrassment sitting comfortably between those two contradictory monoliths.

Decadence and I were sat close to the older monument in the south. In the weird light of the night both the sun and the moon cast eerie shadows between the tombstones; schizoid outlines that swayed on a non-existent breeze. The ominous movement gave the masonry an organic quality that clearly unsettled Decadence, so as the monument's shadow crept towards us he moved away so as to avoid falling under its province.

He settled in a new spot some six feet away from me and for the next ten minutes he kept an eye on the sinister shadow. We could both see it was imperceptibly creeping towards him, which was to be expected. However, what caused hair-prickling to sweep down through my body and the color to drain from his face was the sound that the shadow seemed to make as it did so. The first time I heard it I thought that I was either mistaken or it was a coincidence that the sound of crunching undergrowth and the upsetting of dry earth accompanied its movement.

Decadence and I exchanged a glance. I shook my head as if to dismiss the significance of what we had both just noticed. But the second time it happened there could be no mistake. It was now evident the creep of the shadow was being accompanied by crunching dead grass and twigs.

As the pace of the shadow's movement increased, so the sounds became louder. Decadence found himself pressed up against a hedge and unable to retreat any further. I somehow knew if the shadow touched him he would be lost forever, but we were both frozen, unable to move.

Mrs Suhm had spoken of the "evil" that infested the churchyard here. "The souls of the Pagan dead clamoring for entry into the Kingdom of God but forever denied peace because of their sinful beliefs," she had said.

My mother had her own stories about the Dønnisal churchyard. She maintained when the frost thawed across the rest of the town it would always remain the longest here. She believed the temple and the church that superseded it sat at the intersection of ley-lines that transmitted mystical powers to any structure built upon it. However, the Christian elders who converted the temple into a church strove to suppress those ancient powers because they were inconsistent with Christian doctrine. In so doing, the priests drove the powers deep into the earth where, during the ensuing generations, they had brooded and turned malicious.

I had always had little time for these silly ghost stories but sat there in the dark with a visibly evil and very audible shadow stealing towards Decadence, my doubt and cynicism were being quickly dissolved and supplanted with a primeval fear.

Crunch.

Munch.

Chomp.

The shadow was churning the earth like an invisible, supernatural plough, dredging up a stench that reeked with a thousand years of decay. It continued towards Decadence. Would one human life satisfy its hunger? Or would that just whet its appetite? It was now clear the sound could not just be that of a single spirit: a horde of demonical spirits must have been trapped within the shadow which was by then racing towards him. He began the process of a scream but the message from his brain to his mouth was seemingly being frustrated by the same curse that had ensnared the spirits. His mouth opened but only the smallest sound emerged.

Before the scream could develop any real sound the mutilated form of a demon burst from the shadow and crashed onto the grass in front of Decadence. It tumbled as if it had just been spat violently out of the earth before settling on all fours in a crouching position. It was blackened, shriveled and stank like a tropical killing field. Still crouched it contorted like the charred corpse of a deformed hound. Decadence began a wail but before he could generate sufficient volume to attract any attention the demon pounced and knocked him backwards. A clammy paw was placed over his mouth to muffle his scream.

"Shut the fuck up you feeble-minded cretin!"

The familiar contempt of Suffer's voice hissed through the night air and broke the curse.

"Ailo?"

Both Decadence and I whispered his name with a feeling of relief mingled with a new anxiety.

"What the hell are you doing here?" Decadence added.

"Why shouldn't I be here?" Suffer said as he stood up. "You're here to burn this dump down and I want to be part of it."

"But how did you know?"

"Edvard told me. Stocky cunt, bad beard, Viking complex. Remember?"

"Did he come round to your hut to tell you?"

"Yes. But I didn't let him in," said Suffer. "I let him get close enough to shout his message to meet you here."

I was confused. "It's uncharacteristically obedient of you to do as you're told, Suffer."

"Shut up bitch!" he spat back. "I'm not here because he told me to come. I'm here because he assured me if I came you would help me burn down this shit-filled monument to wank. I haven't burnt down a church in weeks."

"So do you know about Peter?" Decadence asked as he stood up.

"I know that he's a weak-willed shit. He lives with his imbecile mother. He can't drum and he drove his thick-skulled father to kill himself. What more is there to know?"

"Peter has been murdered."

I paid close attention to Suffer to see how he reacted to that news.

"Good."

Suffer took it as you might a report there was to be no rain at the weekend. He continued to dust the grass and dirt from his clothes without looking up. Even Decadence seemed surprised.

"Good? How can you say that?"

"Don't tell me you've started giving a shit about that fucking moron! He's always been holding us back. The Bergen gig should have put that well beyond doubt. It was the best show we've ever done so this news of his death is the best I've heard all year."

Decadence went through a series of poorly executed facial contortions in which the scales visibly dropped from his eyes.

"So you did it," he whispered. "Shitting hell."

"No, I did not. Though I'm envious of whoever did. I might have hated him, but quite honestly I hate you more than

anyone that's ever lived and yet here you are, still breathing."
Suffer began to cross the churchyard, but as he left us he threw
Decadence a look. "Anyhow, I've not got half the motive that
you have."

I raised an eyebrow as Decadence looked at me with a
theatrical expression of innocence. His face flushed, he ran
after Suffer.

"Ailo! Hey! Wait, what the hell did you mean by that?"

"By what, you motherless prick. That you had motive? Fuck
off. Everyone knows you wanted to kill him. I'm just surprised
it took you this long!"

I was following at a slower pace, listening and wondering
with interest where this was going. On the face of it, the band
seemed to be falling apart. The Exorcist dead. Bolverk spiraling
into a hole of depression. Now Decadence was playing with
fire by getting in Suffer's face, risking a beating. Or worse.

"Drum machines, keyboards and sequencers," Suffer said.
"That's what you want the band to play over. Real drums have
no role in your simplistic little scheme. You have been trying to
sideline Peter since you started the band. Don't get me wrong,
as I just said, I hate the cunt too and I couldn't give a fuck if
you played drums, guitar or just scratched your balls behind
me, as long as you never try to sideline me."

Suffer continued walking towards the church and we
followed.

"I'm pleased Peter's dead," he continued. "But it always
made no real difference to me whether he lived or died.
You're the one who wanted revenge for the death of your
frigid mother, you're the one that wanted rid of drums, you're
the one who craves the publicity a death can bring a band
like ours. And you're the one who subscribes to an infantile
pseudo-religious morality that allows you to do anything that
furthers your own cause."

I decided to stoke the flames.

"I think you've been busted, Snorre!" I said, giving

Decadence a tilt of my head and a teasing grin. "How long do you think a pretty-boy like you is going to be able to preserve the integrity of his arse in prison? I suspect we're not talking weeks or days here, I reckon it will be about an hour and a half before you're split right the way through."

"Fuck off, I didn't do it!"

Suffer stopped again. This time his huge, lifeless eyes homed-in on me.

In all the time that I knew Suffer he rarely looked me in the eye. That didn't bother me in the slightest. Looking into his eyes there was always the risk that you might catch a glimpse of his soul and, trust me, that is something that you do not want to dwell upon.

Right now though I couldn't help but squirm and wilt under his perverted gaze. He spoke in a low hiss.

"Don't pretend you haven't got your own plans and aspirations, bitch."

"I never said I hadn't," I replied, maintaining what I hoped was a nonchalant smile.

"I know you've done a deal with that suit from the record label to carve yourself out a nice little career in 'artist management' once the band has outlived its usefulness. And if that happens sooner rather than later then you'll not lose any sleep."

I admit, I was surprised by that. Not the accusation, but that he'd known of those conversations I'd had with Péjé Swartz.

He licked his lips. "Yeah, you think I didn't know? You're such a fucking arrogant bitch. You don't realize that you're as transparent as piss and anyone with eyes can see the way that your tiny little mind works."

Suffer turned and carried on towards the church.

Decadence shot a look across at me. He didn't seem to be too concerned about the accusation. Instead, he opened his jacket to reveal an iron crowbar nestled under his armpit. He nodded towards Suffer.

"If you're so confident that it was one of us then you've got to be worried that you'll be next," he shouted to the vocalist.

"Not really," Suffer shouted back. He'd reached the walls of the church and turned to face us again. "Main reason being you're a fucking coward, Snorre, and you haven't got the guts to insult me let alone kill me. Marta, of course, would kill me in a heartbeat if she had the opportunity, but she knows far better than you how easy it would be for me to overcome you both."

Suffer paused to allow the significance of his veiled threat to sink in before he continued.

"But, as usual, you weren't listening to me just now: I never said that either of you did it. I just said that both of you stand to gain by Peter's death. I know precisely who killed Peter and it wasn't either of you."

Interesting.

"Who was it then?" I asked.

Suffer ignored the question, turned away from us and began looking for a way to get into the church.

Decadence waited a while before following up. "Ailo, come on, fucking out with it! Who killed Peter?"

Eventually Suffer stopped at the wall of the vestry underneath a small window that was positioned about four meters from the ground. "Ask yourselves which one of the band isn't here now."

"Edvard?" Decadence answered in disbelief. "No fucking way. Edvard was closer to Peter than anyone alive. Why on earth would he kill Peter?"

"Edvard and Peter are lovers. They have been their entire lives and in his deranged-pagan mind the only way Edvard could redeem himself before Odin and secure safe passage to Valhalla was to sacrifice his lover."

"Bullshit. That's ridiculous. It doesn't make any sense."

But of course it did. And I'd known all along, though I still felt a sting at the thought of the pair of them together.

Suffer sneered. "Perhaps you're right. Perhaps I just made it up to cover my own tracks?" He then walked up to Decadence and kicked him straight in the groin. Decadence expelled the entire capacity of his lungs in one high pressure burst and fell to his knees, while Suffer reached into his jacket and wrenched out the crowbar.

"Did you really think that you could hide this from me?"

Skipping backwards he rolled the iron bar back and forth with his wrist to ascertain the balance of its swing. A few swipes were all that he needed to master the weapon. Decadence remained on his knees, cradling his balls.

With a leer of cunning and malice on a face twisting headlong into violence Suffer ran at Decadence with the crowbar raised above his head.

39

So what do you really know about Edvard Kittelsen? Bolverk looms large from these pages as he did from the streets and basements of Kragerø, but ask yourself what you really know about him. Might he be gay? Would you be shocked to discover that he was?

As is often the case with people that create outlandish public personas, the real Bolverk was quite a shy and sensitive creature. The Paganism and the third person bullshit: that was just a big (and successful) smokescreen. I'm convinced he erected those eccentricities to create a barrier between the real Edvard and the rest of the world. Of course, he would never admit that, certainly not to me. I was definitely on the other side of the barricades from him. But there was someone you know who was allowed through those fortifications.

If you ever caught Bolverk and The Exorcist speaking out of earshot from anyone else, or you saw their text messages, you wouldn't have seen or heard anything sentimental or emotional. But you would have heard Bolverk speak in the first person.

"I'm on my way over."

"Let me know what you think."

"I'll see what I can do."

The rest of the world saw and spoke to a character, a comic strip Viking superhero even Bolverk referred to as a distinct character from himself. The Exorcist was the only person the real Bolverk ever spoke to.

I was there when the other, the public-facing, Bolverk was born.

His parents were forced into a marriage by their respective parents when his mother's pregnancy became too obvious to disguise. But, according to my mother, they were a bad match. They were emotionally distant by the time Bolverk was born and they were divorced a week before his first birthday.

His father left Kragerø and headed north where he married again and carved himself a relatively successful career as an Arctic fisherman. He fought for custody of the infant Bolverk but he lost and the legal battle soured what little goodwill remained between him and his ex-wife. Thereafter, Bolverk's mother enforced the custody and access principles imposed by the Court with iron-fisted rigidity. Bolverk's father was entitled to visit his son in Kragerø one weekend a month, and three weeks a year he was allowed to take Bolverk away.

However, there was no flexibility permitted, so if Bolverk's father was fishing during one of the allocated week holidays there was no prospect of the holiday being postponed: it was immediately forfeit. Bolverk's father had to travel thousands of kilometers south to see his son on his allocated weekends or school holidays and if he arrived early he had to wait outside the apartment block. If he arrived even seconds late he was denied access. Many were the sad weekends that Bolverk's father arrived late and then spent two days getting drunk in the Kragerø bars with his fisherman buddies while Bolverk was prohibited from leaving the flat in case he should chance upon his father in the street.

When Bolverk was about twelve years old his father and his step-mother divorced. It had been a condition of the custody order imposed by the Court that Bolverk's father provide a secure and conventional family environment for Bolverk whenever he left Kragerø. This second divorce gave Bolverk's mother the excuse she always wanted to put an end to those week-long excursions that Bolverk had come to cherish. The bitterness and resentment this provoked between Bolverk's parents was so intense that the Kragerø weekends that followed the decision became incendiary.

Bolverk's father was a stout and passionate man, much like his son. On one occasion, one Saturday morning, his first ex-wife provoked him into such a fury he smashed his fist down onto her breakfast, disintegrating both the plate and the table. This gave Bolverk's mother a much-cherished excuse to rush back to the Courts to demand a further erosion of her ex-husband's access rights. The weekend trips were cut back to four a year, with supervision from his mother at all times, and he was only allowed telephone contact once a month.

It was during one of those telephone conversations that Bolverk first removed himself emotionally from the physical (and by then substantial) space he occupied in the real world and retreated into fantasy.

It was his fourteenth birthday, a short time after The Exorcist and I lost our fathers. It was the year his father bought him his Viking helmet and a quite beautiful, illustrated copy of Snorri Sturluson's *Prose Edda*: the definitive compilation of Norse Mythology. The helmet was a true Viking helmet, not the horned nonsense of cartoons. It was conical, fashioned from wood and leather and reinforced at the edges with dull brass.

The Exorcist and I were in Bolverk's flat when the phone rang. We only heard his mother's half of the conversation.

"Hello, who is it?"

"Who is 'me'?"

"If I knew I wouldn't ask would I."

"Oh, it's you."

"What makes you think that you're the only person that calls me?"

"Is who here?"

"Why don't you speak to me like a normal human being

rather than trying to engage me in your stupid guessing games?"

"He's not here."

Bolverk, The Exorcist and I traded glances.

"I mean what I just said. He's not here."

"I have no idea. He must be out with his friends."

"Is that Dad?" Bolverk asked. "Put him on!"

She ignored him.

"No, it was nothing. Just the TV."

"Well, I'm telling you he's not here!"

"I am here!" Bolverk said, confused.

"No, you are *not*!" his mother said through clenched teeth with her hand held over the mouthpiece on the receiver.

"No, no, I told you it's not," she said, returning her attention to the phone and walking into a bedroom. She slammed the door closed behind her, but the thinness of the walls and the volume of her voice meant that her seclusion in another room had little impact on our ability to eavesdrop.

"He went out over an hour ago."

"No, he didn't!" Bolverk called.

"Well perhaps he didn't care that you were going to call."

"He does care! Dad! He does care!" Bolverk screamed at the closed door.

"It's just the TV."

"Look. He's fourteen years old now and he's getting as tired of you as I am."

"No, he's not!" Bolverk insisted, almost in tears now.

"You know he threw that crappy old book and that tatty hat of yours straight in the bin without even taking the wrapping paper off."

"He didn't! He's wearing the helmet now, Dad!"

"I opened them after he had gone out, that's how I know wise-ass. The truth is he has never enjoyed your visits, your holidays or your calls."

"Yes, he has!"

"He tolerated it all for your sake, but it's time you accepted what you should have accepted thirteen years ago – you have no role to play in his life. You never have."

Bolverk by now was reduced to a confused, blubbering wreck in an authentic Viking helmet.

"Well, I'm sorry but only yesterday he told me that he has never loved you."

"No, he didn't," Bolverk whimpered.

"Yes, well, I'm sorry to break it to you but life can be shit like that sometimes."

"And you can fuck off too!"

Bolverk never saw or heard from his father again and that was the last time I ever heard him refer to himself in the first person. He sort of accepted his mother's logic that there was another Bolverk that threw his father's presents in the bin and then went out with his friends. He maintained that fiction for the rest of his life.

When his mother slammed the phone down, she shut Bolverk's father out of his life forever, but she also shut out from the world at large a confused little boy. He coped with this estrangement as us fragile humans often do by erecting barriers and creating a subterfuge: an avatar as large in personality as he was in physical proportions, a magical Viking demigod from a world of fantasy and mythology who seemed, unwittingly, to have got lost in time and stumbled into Kragerø at the turn of the twenty-first century.

But, despite all of this sadness, he had something that I didn't have. He had Peter. And despite all that bullshit Viking *ragr* homophobia, Peter had him. There I have said it. I have said what neither Edvard, Peter nor I have ever admitted out loud to anyone else.

What Edvard had was something I wanted desperately. Something I would kill for.

40

I quote: "If you accuse a Viking of being ragr he has every right to kill you to disprove your allegation so just be careful what you say to me on this subject."

Bolverk's interpretation of the pagan Viking faith had, unsurprisingly, a primitive view of homosexuality. He was not alone in holding those beliefs within the Norwegian black metal community, as we've discussed. With that in mind, and with Bolverk and The Exorcist finally getting some "them" time on the trawler during those weeks after they left me bruised and defiled on the beer and grime soaked floor of the Crypt, picture this scene that I have imagined so often that it's become more real to me than many of my true memories.

There you are, stood with The Exorcist at the bow of the ship. It's a quiet, secluded space, hidden away from prying eyes where the two of you have often sought sanctuary from the rest of the crew. As ever, The Exorcist is by your side.

He is strong.

He is loyal.

He is beautiful.

You close your eyes and his arms are around you. His mouth is locked to yours, soothed by the sweetness of his tongue. All your anxieties, everyone and everything in the world dissolve from your consciousness. And you are left with an overwhelming sensation of order and tranquility.

It feels sensational doesn't it?

Then some cock-sucking prick discovers you. Now imagine

you have the strength and Viking worldview of Bolverk. What would *you* do next?

Look, I guess we'll never *really* know what happened to that trawlerman that never came back from Bolverk's and The Exorcist's little fisherman adventure. What we do know is that Bolverk and The Exorcist eventually made their way sheepishly back home to Kragerø after a cursory police investigation. At which point we carried on where we left off with Baphomet's Agony *and nobody asked any questions*. Why would we?

And that, you'll be pleased to know, kind of brings you up to speed on how we arrived where we did on that night in Oslo when I started this story. As Suffer suggested, everyone in the band had a reason to kill the Exorcist. But I can tell from the uncomfortable way that you are looking at me that you know by now who really did it.

I think we're ready to head back to the churchyard at Dønnisal now.

41

So where have we got to?

Pan across the murky, midnight churchyard. There's just enough light to make out three characters by the wall of the building.

Decadence is knelt on the grass, Suffer's kick to his testicles still dominating his senses. He had his head down and his eyes shut tight. Which meant that he couldn't see Suffer bounding towards him with the crowbar held over his head.

What did I feel as Suffer charged towards the injured and defenseless Decadence? That's another well observed question. Terror: yes, of course it is terrifying to witness anyone look death in the eye. But at the mixing desk of my emotions, the sound engineer had scaled back the terror and had brought all sorts of other sensations much higher up into the mix. There was definitely a lot of excitement in there but, surprisingly, sex was making its presence felt within the production. It often does in my moments of horror. My terror, excitement and shock had all congregated in my abdomen and I felt an intense orgasmic spasm weaken my legs.

What Suffer might have in store for me also crossed my mind. There seemed little chance that he would allow me to live should I witness the imminent murder. For the second time in twenty-four hours I teetered on the brink of certain death, but whereas the first time it happened I felt a morbid resignation, the second time I felt a strong excitement. My descent into depravity seemed to be accelerating.

He didn't kill him though. Instead, when he arrived at a point about a meter from where Decadence crouched in anguish, Suffer leapt off the ground, used his victim's shoulders as a springboard, and launched himself up to the vestry window.

For a short while he hung on to the ledge of the window with one hand, looking like an oversized black squirrel. With the tendons and sinew of his left arm almost glowing with tension and effort he deftly prised open the antique window with the crowbar in his right hand. In another display of superhuman strength, he then appeared to flex the fingers on his left hand and fire himself up into the air again so he could wriggle through the opening like the proverbial rodent in a drainpipe.

A few moments later the wooden door to the church swung open and Suffer walked back out into the night. He threw the crowbar onto the grass near to where Decadence now lay face-down.

"I'll look after this," Suffer said, as he ripped off the black backpack that Decadence had slung over his shoulders. "And you'd better get up of your ass soon and help me or I'll bury you right there."

Suffer walked back into the church and Decadence lay face down for a few minutes longer. I could see he was savoring the cool grass on his face while waiting for the pain to subside.

I left him on the grass and made my way after Suffer.

During the day, when they are full of light and people, I have always found churches unbearable. That's not to say I come out in hives, babble or froth at the mouth when I approach one. It's just I find all the pomp and solemnity soul destroying. Isn't it strange the way that even with their massive high ceilings churches feel stifling inside? In my subterranean catacombs I feel comfortable and I breathe freely, but on those few occasions that I was dragged to church by Mrs Suhm I felt continually anxious the ceiling would fall in on me and my breath came in short gasps.

Alone at night, however, with its congregation safely tucked up in their beds, a church becomes a completely different proposition. Shrouded in darkness and bathed in silence, a church lets down its guard. At night you can see mice and other vermin scuttling between the pews, you can hear the beams creak and the smell of damp, cold and urine is no longer disguised by incense.

To whom did the urine once belong? God knows – literally. The rats maybe, the mad old women that attend every mass in the schedule, the infants that piss in the Baptismal Font. I like to think that the priests get so caught up in their devotional prayer that around the time of the Communion they lose all their faculties and stream piss down their legs: hence their need to stand behind an Altar and wear long flowing robes.

At night the forces of nature conspire to strip a church of its carefully crafted awe and majesty and replace these elements with decrepitude and vulnerability. At night you see the building laid bare and exposed for what it is: an empty stage upon which a daily theatre is acted out for the populace. A prop in a two-thousand year-old pantomime.

Tonight it took a while for my eyes to adjust to this particular stage. The curious light of the Norwegian night struggled to penetrate the stained-glass windows and only succeeded in creating a hazy twilight within.

I sensed movement on a scale larger than a rodent quite close to the font and focused my attention there. After a short while a small, trembling flame illuminated Suffer's face. The flickering light seemed nervous about revealing such a scene and did so with trepidation. If it had any choice, I suspect it would have chosen not to.

The flame came from a candle. Then another was lit. Then another. Three candles on a huge and ancient looking candelabra, before he moved to light them on a second. By the time the last candle had been lit, the light was sufficient to show us that Suffer had shed his clothes.

"Why are you naked?" I asked.

Suffer ignored my question.

Decadence appeared at my shoulder. "Why the fuck is he naked?"

"We don't know yet," I said.

Suffer walked towards us with the lit candelabras, one in each hand. His naked and malnourished body was equal parts pitiable and terrifying and each time I saw it there was something new and disgusting about it. That night I noticed how dirt appeared to have been deliberately smeared into wounds on his chest caused by the repeated lash of a whip.

He handed Decadence one of the candelabras. "If we're going to do this at all, we're going to do it properly. Church-burning is a deeply symbolic ritual and should be a travesty of the normal principles of church attendance. These aisles are used to a congregation dressed in its conventional finery so tonight we're going to turn that on its head."

He fixed us both with his disconcerting stare – a stare that manages to burn into your soul while at the same time remaining cold and distant.

"Strip."

Despite the groinal abuse just inflicted upon him by Suffer, Decadence didn't need to be asked twice. I guess there was something about the gothic image of three naked Satanists laying waste to a church by candlelight that appealed to him. Almost before Suffer spoke the word Decadence had put his candelabrum down and was beginning the long and tortuous process of peeling himself out of his jeans.

I, on the other hand, had my reservations.

"I'm not getting undressed in front of you two."

"Come on Marta," Decadence said. "You've got nothing that we've not seen before."

In point of fact, I'm not sure Decadence was right there. He and I had certainly seen each other naked and I had seen Suffer naked. However, while Suffer and I had engaged in our brutal intercourse on numerous occasions, I don't recall us ever being naked together. That's just not what we did.

"I wasn't asking," Suffer said to me in a flat monotone. "It was an order."

"I don't care. You two get your kicks howsoever you choose but don't involve me in your perverted fantasies."

Suffer closed his eyes and I watched a convulsion of pain ripple across his face like a stone thrown in a pond. Then he jabbed his candelabra into my face.

I shrieked in pain as a candle extinguished itself on my chin.

Decadence was still pulling down his jeans so his movement was restricted, but he managed to lurch between Suffer and me. It was a successful maneuver in the sense that I was protected from Suffer's wrath, but Decadence paid a price as the base of the candelabra caught his head a glancing blow. I suspect it was only his long, freshly washed and conditioned hair that saved him from a skull injury. Still, the force of the blow was enough to knock him to the ground again.

Suffer loomed over Decadence with the candelabrum raised over his head. This time I didn't think there was anything other than murder in his mind.

"Stop!" I yelled. "Enough Suffer! I'll strip. Just back the fuck up will you?"

Suffer remained motionless with the candelabrum still raised over his head. The church seemed full with the sound of heavy breathing and pounding hearts.

I quickly pulled my t-shirt over my head, threw it down and began unbuttoning my jeans. When I got down to my underwear Suffer took a step back and I paused.

"All of it." he said quietly.

I sighed and began to unclasp my bra. Decadence rolled onto his side and looked up at me.

Once fully naked I felt deeply uncomfortable with their eyes on me. These were the only two men in my life I had fucked and yet I still felt the need to cross my legs, fold my right arm across my breasts and cover myself with my left hand. Both Suffer and Decadence just watched me.

After about ten seconds I got bored.

"Oh, for Christ's sake!" I said as I uncrossed my legs and let my arms fall to my sides.

Lying naked on the cold stone floor of a church, with a lump forming on his head, because a psychopath had almost killed him, Decadence still managed to grow a hard-on.

Men.

Suffer walked off and Decadence smiled up at me. There was lust in that smile but there was something much warmer and softer there too. He held his hand up to me, so I took it and pulled him up off the floor.

"Thank you for getting in the way," I said quietly as I turned to move away.

Decadence kept hold of my hand and pulled me back to him. We stood very close. The tip of his penis brushed against my bare belly and my nipples pressed against the muscles on his stomach. He placed his hands on my shoulders and looked down at me kindly. I took the shaft of his cock in my hand.

"Don't push your luck," I said and squeezed with such force he yelped like a kicked dog.

I released him and took a look around the church.

It was a beautiful building. The woodwork showed such great craftsmanship and had the feel of ancient timbers fashioned for an entirely different place. That's not an easy thing to do. Timbers have their strengths but they have their weaknesses too and the task of finding new uses for old wood, while maintaining the integrity of the new structure, is no mean feat. The parallels between what those craftsmen had achieved and what I was trying to do with Baphomet's Agony lifted my spirits some.

Before I felt a dig of guilt for what I was about to do to that beautiful work.

Guilt is a terrible thing. It's the most important tool of any religion or authority because once you permit a single cell of guilt to enter your body then, by subtle manipulation, those skilled in the oldest and darkest of arts can work that guilt up remotely until it becomes a device capable of giving them absolute control over every aspect of your being.

I had always assumed that by setting in motion the killing of Mrs Lant I had successfully eradicated all guilt from my body. It was, therefore, with no pleasant nostalgia I welcomed it back.

I shook myself and made a concerted effort to focus on the job at hand to suppress this dangerous weakness.

"Ailo!" I called out. "What do you want us to do?"

Suffer was up on the floor of the chancel, squatting with the backpack open in front of him. He had pulled out the contents and was deep in thought. Perhaps that's why he ignored my question; but I suspect not.

Mrs Suhm had given us everything we could possibly need to burn down this place, including paraffin wax and candles. The candles were of the blue and pink striped variety that decorate children's birthday cakes more often than they ignite places of worship. Suffer began dividing the paraffin wax and candles into two piles while muttering expletives to some unseen adversary.

"Who are you talking to?" Decadence asked as he joined him on the chancel.

"Fuck off."

I have to admit it: until that night I hadn't realized just how magnificent Decadence looked naked. The two years that had passed since I'd last seen his body in all its glory had been exceedingly kind to him. What had been a perfectly pleasant adolescent frame had been overhauled entirely and replaced by a complex network of muscle and sinew over which soft and flawless skin had been lovingly stretched. How he managed to achieve that definition around his pectorals and abdominals I do not know: as far as I am aware he never did any exercise. It must have been entirely down to his vigorous sex life.

Stood tall and upright next to the squat form of Suffer, and with both of them naked, the contrast between Decadence and Suffer could not have been starker. Watching them from the pews I could just imagine how Michelangelo's David would look like displayed alongside a garden gnome.

Decadence wandered into the chancel behind Suffer and approached something that was just out of my line of sight on the altar.

Fascinating patterns were thrown across his features. I knew well the face Decadence pulled when he saw something that turned him on, as for a time it was an expression over which I had exclusive rights. I also knew the glassy sheen that would overlay his eyes when I told him how much money we were making.

His face up on that altar was the love-child of those two parents. When he looked up from his discovery and searched for me in the gloom, I saw a face filled with such joy for a moment I wondered if he had discovered God.

In a way he had.

He beckoned me up to join him and rather than ogle over me as I strode naked towards him he looked back down at what he had found.

An antique Bible lay open on the surface of the altar. Decadence carefully removed its Perspex cover and laid it to one side. Even in the dull light of the candelabrum the ancient and brightly illustrated pages shone oddly iridescent within their gilt-wood cover that served as a frame.

On the page that was visible a sumptuously robed scribe in a golden mitre, joyous in his labor, was depicted in one corner. In his crouch over a desk the figure formed a capital "G". This thing was hundreds of years old, yet the ink was of such quality, and had been applied so thickly, that the words stood out proud from the page and still appeared wet. If you tilted the book you would have feared the ink running down the page.

The detail in the artwork was incredible. Inked around the edge of each page were intricate depictions of plants, animals and glyphs. Decadence turned a page and the heavy papyrus made a sound like a diamond-tipped sword cleaving glass. The next page, and each one that followed, contained ever more wondrous art and calligraphy. I had no idea what words those letters formed, but such was their beauty I would have enthusiastically endorsed any message they conveyed.

Like Decadence before me, I quickly lost myself among those exquisite pages.

"Lutheran pile of crap."

Suffer's contemptuous growl upset my reverie with such shocking force I actually flinched.

"What is?"

"That Frederik II edition you're both drooling over."

I looked at Decadence in confusion before turning back to Suffer.

"Since when did you become an expert on religious literature?"

Suffer had now finished poking the small, thin candles into the conical piles of paraffin wax around the altar, so that each little tor was surmounted with its own jolly little spire.

"I study the King James Version daily."

"Fuck off!" Decadence said laughing. "No you don't."

Suffer carried two handfuls of incendiaries towards us. He didn't look as though he was joking. Decadence quickly shut up.

"You study the Bible?" I asked.

Suffer's massive, empty eyes bore down on me. I felt like a train hurtling towards a tunnel into hell.

"Yes," he replied. "In order to fulfil my potential I need to fully understand His message."

"A message from whom precisely?"

"God."

I held out my hands so that Suffer could drop the crude pyrotechnics into them. Decadence did the same.

"You believe in God?"

"Of course."

I suddenly realized it had never occurred to Decadence or me to probe Suffer on his ideological beliefs. We had just assumed. It seemed obvious, right? You've heard this story, so you know what I'm talking about. He was the fucking Anti-Christ: the son of Satan born of man. What more was there to know?

By now Suffer had picked up his incendiaries and was making his way towards the grand carved pulpit. Suddenly though he dropped them, fell to his knees and grabbed his head between his hands. For thirty seconds or more he knelt, shaking, gripping his head tight. Then, as if nothing had happened, he tidied up what he had dropped, stood up and continued walking.

Decadence and I exchanged a glance that was equal parts childish amusement and unbridled fear. We began placing our paraffin piles on the wooden pews.

"So what's this *message* you mentioned?" Decadence asked, trying to sound casual. "You are the most hateful person I have ever heard speak of. If this is a message from God, is it that you must hate the world and also hate Him?"

"No, I don't hate Him. I love Him."

It was so strange to hear Suffer use the word "love". I had no idea he had a place for that word in his emotional vocabulary. I knew he could hate, I knew he enjoyed ridicule and I knew he valued fear and suffering. But to learn he could love? It was like suddenly discovering the decrepit one-room bedsit in which you had always lived had a swimming pool on the roof.

I was confused. "You love Him, but you set yourself up in opposition to Him?"

Suffer lit the first of his party candles from the flame of his candelabrum. The tiny candle flame looked puny and insignificant next to the eternal majesty of the carefully worked oak and you could almost hear the church beams above laugh at the threat posed by Mrs Suhm's paraffin towers.

"There is no disagreement between us, if that's what you're trying to get at. If you need to understand it in nice simple terms, you could say He and I have come to a special understanding."

The three of us stopped our work and watched the candle burn down slowly. Suffer had pushed the candle deep into the paraffin wax so we didn't have long to wait before the small flame arrived at the wax and created a flash and pop like one of those old-fashioned photographers. He then reached into the backpack and pulled out a small tube of washing-up liquid Mrs Suhm had emptied and carefully filled with spirits. I could just picture her filling the thing with a funnel, taking meticulous care not to spill anything on her kitchen worktop.

Suffer squirted the spirits around the base of the pulpit and the flame leapt from the paraffin wax and immediately took hold.

"OK then, let me ask my earlier question again," I said as Decadence and I resumed our work. "The God that you have an understanding with: is He the same one who sent His son to earth two thousand years ago? The same one the good people of Dønnisal come here to worship on a Sunday?"

"Yes."

Decadence shook his head. "Look, I don't understand –"

"Silence!" Suffer shouted at him with such brutal command even the quickly fanning flames obeyed him and hushed their crackle and fizz. "I know where you're going with this Snorre. You're going to tell me an externalized God is a fiction, that God, Christ and Satan are just devices used through the ages to subjugate the masses. I have heard it all before. You're a boring, predictable wanker. Argghh!"

Suffer grabbed the edge of a pew to steady himself through another brain spasm. He massaged his temple to ease the pain, then continued.

"I know how your limited mind works, Snorre. If I had it my way, you would have died many years ago, preferably at my own hands. I only tolerate your existence because you unwittingly assist me to do what I need to do."

The fire at the pulpit had taken hold quickly and the whole thing was now ablaze. Flames were licking up into the air and the ancient oak beams directly above the pulpit were beginning to blacken. I could both feel and smell the heat crisping the fine hairs on my arm.

Our time here was running out.

"What is it you need to do?" I asked. "What is the understanding you have with God? And what's his message?"

Suffer turned to me. "I've been in your band for four years. All this time, you've not given a shit for what anyone else thinks or feels. Why is it you're suddenly interested in what makes me tick?"

"Humor me."

Suffer turned his back on me and continued with his work igniting the incendiaries Decadence and I had left on the pews.

"There is of course only one true God," he said, lifting his voice to be heard over the growing fire. "That is the one true God that created the world and everything in it. In other circumstances I would have been happy living in His love. But I was never included within it. No surprises there. I was left outside that community in pretty much the same way I've been left out of every other community I have ever chanced upon."

He spoke in a calm voice, devoid of anger, bitterness, pain or any of his usual vitriol. His tone was new and more unnerving than any I had ever heard from him before.

"There was a purpose behind God's decision though. He had a mission in mind for me. Kindness, love and beauty cannot exist in a world that doesn't know evil, hatred and pain. That is where I come in. I create the darkness out of which the light can shine."

As he spoke his speech was punctuated by the pop and sparkle of the paraffin wax igniting. There was almost a rhythm to it.

Decadence's voice seemed weak in comparison. Yet still he asked his questions, trying to make sense of all this.

"So your acts of violence on others and your self-abuse are done deliberately in order to put God and the wonders of His creation into sharper contrast?"

By now small fires were spreading across those pews and wooden fixtures that Suffer had doused in spirits.

"For a Godless fucking imbecile, you've summarized it quite well," Suffer said. "Yes, I beat, maim, rape and kill for the glory of the one and all-powerful God. I do these things so others don't have to."

"But... why?" Decadence asked. "Why you?"

"Because if I can isolate as much evil as possible within me then there's less need for anyone else to be evil. This is my purpose. I am the Satanic Messiah. The Anti-Christ."

As the fires began to suck all sound out of the room Decadence and I had to remain close to Suffer in order to still hear him. A new and dynamic light was gradually filling the church and the crackle and spit of the flames provided a pleasing ambient soundtrack to our arson.

"And the band?" I asked.

Suffer's brain attacks were coming thick and fast now, as though he was reaching the crescendo of his diabolical existence, the zenith of his meaning. He lowered himself to the floor, closed his eyes tight and sat in silence for a moment as the pain passed through him.

"The band provides me with a way of expressing my pain and hatred to a wider audience," he said finally. "It is an irrelevant and replaceable vessel that I fill with my shit and then hurl at the world. You of all people should understand that, Marta. It's why you set it up, after all. You feel the same as me, don't deny it. The band is a weapon for corruption. For destruction. Nothing more and nothing less."

I raised an eyebrow, but said nothing.

Meanwhile, Decadence had no snappy line or statistic he could throw at Suffer to defeat his skewed logic. Though he felt obliged to at least try.

"How can you believe in a loving God when children around the world starve to death every day?"

"You're full of fucking shit!" Suffer had to shriek to overcome the increasingly loud sound of the flames. "Have you ever had an original thought in all your life? Don't trot out your bullshit clichés to me. I know all about your puerile version of Satanism. It's just a justification for capitalism and greed dreamt up by salesmen and designed to offer soundbites instead of salvation." He stalked towards Decadence now, a naked gargoyle among the flames of hell. "Why bother learning ancient wisdom through careful study of the Bible when you can condense an alternative manifesto into a pocket-sized paperback and stamp it with a flash logo? As an excuse for masturbation those ideas work admirably. As a world religion providing structure, hope and purpose to the planet they're sorely lacking."

I attempted to draw some of his ire. "What does your God think of you, Suffer? Does he accept you perform a necessary supporting role?"

"He needs His Satan."

"But you're only twenty years old. If that's true, how did He cope before you arrived on the scene?"

"You're asking sensible questions. I've clearly been fucking some sense into you."

Suffer twisted his nasty little face into a smile, but even this seemed to cause him great physical anguish and he swooned a little before steeling himself against the pain.

"Our civilization has been in decline for centuries and our morals have all but vanished. Our society has tolerated the spread of filth. How do we recover from this when without Satan you can't put God in any context? This has happened before and He has intervened in different ways. The first time it happened at Sodom when God Himself got involved. Then it happened again during the Roman Empire and He sent His son. This time He has sent me to finish the job."

"Finish the job?"

"Yes! We are fast approaching the end, and when it comes I will be there, dancing on the ashes of the unrepentant. I am the goat upon whom the guilt of the world is heaped on The Day of Atonement."

Suffer's eyes rolled back in his head again until the pupils had all but vanished. He collapsed to the floor before us. We were near the back of the church now, creating small flames along the way. Parts of the building that had until then been enveloped in darkness were now revealing their secrets. For the first time I became aware of a small sword with a bejeweled hilt displayed in a case on the south wall.

I looked from that to Suffer. The epic scale of his delusion had surprised even me, but along with this phenomenal insanity the frequency of his attacks was increasing at a terrifying rate. That would make him more dangerous.

Decadence saw me looking at the sword and with a nod from me he acted. A fire extinguisher sat on the floor by the door and he strolled over to it, weighed it in his hands, and then crashed it into the glass case that housed the sword. On the third attempt the glass shattered and fell to the floor. The sword was attached to the back of the case by two simple hooks and Decadence had no difficulty lifting it out.

Christianity loves its swords. Saintly effigies invariably feature a sword or a dagger of some sort. That symbol of violence and brutality is frequently intertwined with more traditional images of doves and fish with the deliberate intention of lacing the Christian message with the threat of a painful death to anyone that sets themselves up in opposition.

It was a beautiful thing, that Dønnisal sword. The long silver blade shone white even in the gloom of the church and Latin text covered the blade in such a tiny font that the best part of an entire Gospel was legible on its two sides. The golden hilt was formed of a coiled snake wrapped around an ornate girder into which a large ruby and emerald had been set.

Decadence smiled down at the sword. It was so perfectly weighted that the tip of the blade barely appeared to move at all as he tossed it from hand to hand; it just swung like a pendulum.

Eventually he looked back at me and then Suffer.

With the noise and intensity of the fire taking hold, I couldn't tell if the creature was alive. I still approached his prone form cautiously though, because I'm not stupid.

Up close I could see he wasn't breathing and from what I could see of his complexion, if blood had ever pumped around his face, it had all long since departed. I nervously moved my outstretched hand towards his neck so I could establish a pulse... or lack thereof.

The instant my fingers touched him he lurched forward, his forehead crashing into my face. I felt my lip split like a crushed grape. My mouth filled with blood and vision blurred but I could still make out Suffer's naked form crouched over me, fists clenched and eyes ablaze with fury.

With him kneeling between my thighs and Decadence stood close by, that little tableau would have closely resembled that fateful scene earlier in my story when Suffer first defiled me in front of the cuckolded Decadence. Thankfully, this time Decadence found his voice.

"Whoa! Suffer, it's just Marta. She was just checking on you, man. We thought we'd lost you there for a minute."

Suffer remained panting heavily, his fists still curled tight, ready to pulverize my face.

"Speak to me," Decadence continued. "Where had we got to? You have been sent to Earth by God to fuck it up so He can rescue the righteous. Is that it? Okay, great. Now where does Marta fit in to your plan then? Did Satan ever have a consort?"

Suffer's fists unclenched as he snapped back to reality and stood up.

"She performs no divine or prophesied role. She is irrelevant."

"Thanks," I said.

"Don't pretend to be offended! You are a whore, Marta. A jezebel. You are just one of the many tools I use to debase and degrade myself for the greater glory of God."

Decadence frowned pathetically. "Don't tell me you don't enjoy having sex with Marta!"

I laughed coldly. "Believe me, Snorre. Pleasure of any type is the last thing either of us expect when Suffer and I subject ourselves to sex."

"So why do you do it then?"

That voice, the one that Decadence used to ask the question, was one I had not heard in many years. It was soft, cracked and sincere, and entirely unlike the smug, self-satisfied sneer he had adopted since that night he declared his love for me, immediately before Suffer fucked me on the floor.

Decadence had never asked me why I left him for Suffer and despite everything unravelling as I thought it might, I was entirely unprepared for the question stood there naked in a burning church.

I could do nothing but ignore him.

"Do you do it just to hurt me?" he persisted.

Suffer spat out a laugh and then flinched as a bolt of pain shot through him.

"As usual you have placed yourself at the center of a world in which, in truth, you inhabit the periphery," he said to Decadence. "She doesn't care about you and nothing that she has ever done has been done to hurt you. You've been hurt of course, but that's just collateral damage, a bit of friendly fire. You were never on her mind when you were together and you certainly weren't her focus when she left you."

In a way he was right: I never cared much for Decadence

when we were together and he was never my target. But in a way he was wrong too because I had set out to hurt him. To change him. To ensure he couldn't change me.

Why else would I have killed his mother?

Decadence looked at us both in puzzlement. I kept my eyes down.

"I don't understand," Decadence said, a little boy lost.

"That's because you're a self-obsessed prick," Suffer said. "Take a step back and stop forcing yourself center stage in her life. Ask yourself who she was trying to help when she set up the band. Ask yourself who it was that she set out to make jealous when she began fucking you. Ask yourself who else was going to be upset when she abandoned you for me. Ask yourself why she was thrown into a deep, dark spiral when she had it confirmed where Edvard had been parking his dick all these years."

"Peter?" Decadence said in disbelief. He picked me up and grabbed my shoulders. "*Peter?*"

"Yes," I said.

That's my secret. That's why all of this happened. That's why I am who I am and why I turned everything to shit.

42

Had you figured out I was madly in love with The Exorcist? I suspect you had.

It's a funny thing, love. I can see the point of it. I understand how affection encourages loyalty and I can see how two animals loyal to one another stand a better chance of raising an infant that will survive and go on itself to breed.

But when love goes wrong, when one's love goes unrequited... well, fuck. The consequences can be far reaching. Or, in my case, apocalyptic. If love played its part in bringing the world into existence, I know that love will certainly bring about its downfall.

At least that's my plan.

Don't try to guess where my feelings towards The Exorcist came from. God knows I've tried. I know that he was an idiot, a simple child-like creature, the butt of all jokes and the most unlikely soulmate for an ambitious, cut-throat bitch like me. But he was *my* idiot. Deep within me I had locked away a box of title deeds that granted us absolute dominion over each other. Any circumstance that prevented us from being together was an affront to natural justice and I would lie, steal, fuck and kill to protect what was mine.

Similarly, there's no point asking me when my love for The Exorcist started. I have no idea. It was always there. I cannot recall a moment in my life when it was not at the forefront of my mind and influencing my every thought and decision. It is like a hereditary memory, a genetic predisposition. It is a more dominant influence on my lifestyle and personality than my membership of the human species.

When I was a child, I personified my love for The Exorcist. It was such a massive part of my world that I felt it justified a distinct identity.

I named her *Hel* after Loki's monstrous daughter. In Norse mythology, Hel presided over an underworld populated by those that had died of sickness and old age. She was relatively normal looking from the waist up but below the waist she was all decaying green mulch.

I never really had many people I could confide in when growing up. I had my parents (briefly, before I had just one of them), I had The Exorcist and Bolverk, and I had my love for The Exorcist – Hel. Unsurprisingly, given the alternatives, it was Hel to whom I turned to in my delicate and private moments. It was she to whom I confided my secrets and it was she who corrupted me and turned me into the heartless fiend that you are learning about.

I didn't like Hel much. Unsurprisingly, she was malicious and mercurial. Most significantly, Hel was insanely jealous. She would chastise me whenever I spent the briefest moment doing anything other than loving The Exorcist. She was jealous even of The Exorcist himself. It might sound ridiculous, but she resented it when I spent time with him because time spent in his presence was time I wasn't spending thinking about him. Which led to me treating him horribly, as you've seen.

Love is irrational and capricious, and Hel took that part of her role very seriously. She never had any issues with Bolverk initially. Which is insane when you realize it was Bolverk who was the greatest barrier between me and The Exorcist. But somehow while both she and I knew from very early on that Bolverk and The Exorcist had a more complex and physical relationship than met the eye, she didn't care about that and was more suspicious of The Exorcist than she was of Bolverk. It was almost as if she needed there to be space between me and The Exorcist.

Ha. You should see the looks on your faces as you scribble this shit down! You weren't expecting any of this were you? No, I bet you weren't. It'll make for good headlines, I suspect. Or at least it would have done.

What do I mean by that? Please don't fucking interrupt. Let me finish talking.

Over the years, Hel became increasingly distant from me and the world at large. Her methods of manipulating everyone around her became darker. What little excitement and joy she and I shared in our youth became lost in a complex web of sadistic plotting designed to harvest pain and suffering on which she could feed. There were many occasions where I felt my own desires and happiness were being subjugated to progress her sinister agenda.

If you think about it, this is all her fault.

If you look at everything through my perverted love prism it all sort of makes sense in a fucked-up kind of way. From day one, I suspected Decadence hated The Exorcist. But when he ended up blaming The Exorcist for his own mother's death – when I was behind it all along – Decadence became a threat. That's why I started fucking him.

Does it make sense? To Hel it did.

The Exorcist and I shared a quite special relationship throughout our lives. I suspect he loved me. But not as a lover, more like a brother.

It pains me to tell you that.

"I love you like a sister."

Fuck, can you imagine? That's probably the most devastating sentence a girl can hear uttered from the lips of her beloved. The Exorcist never said it to me, but I know it's how he felt. He cared about me deeply, he worried over me, he was protective and he was jealous of my lovers. Hel knew that and grew delighted she could both distract and seek control over Decadence while exacting revenge over The Exorcist.

Around the same time, I began thinking how I could create

a livelihood for both The Exorcist and myself that would sustain us into adulthood, while simultaneously binding us together more tightly. Baphomet's Agony achieved that and additionally appeased the ever-twisted, increasingly evil Hel because of the unsettling nature of the music we produced.

Stirring the vile Suffer into the mix was a natural development and, at the time, seemed a great way to advance the fortunes of the band. By then my love for The Exorcist had got twisted up into Baphomet's Agony and the two had become sort of interchangeable; in my mind at least.

Of course I was never attracted to Suffer. He repulsed me upon our first meeting as he did everyone and my repulsion has grown significantly as I got to learn more of him over the years.

So why did I hook up with him?

Get your perverted-love prism out and revisit my carnal desecration that night on the floor of the Crypt. Witnessed again through that love-fucked kaleidoscope, does it make any more sense? Probably not, but can you at least see that there was a weird, vindictive logic behind what I did?

The Exorcist had just revealed that he was leaving the band for a life of sea and (I knew) Bolverk. My head was spinning, my brain was being pulled in different directions by rage and despair. And Hel was screaming at me to do something. When I couldn't, she took charge and seized upon the most disgusting spectacle her warped imagination could conjure.

"Fuck him!" she shrieked into my inner ear. "Fuck the deranged and diseased freak! Endanger yourself, defile yourself, infect yourself. Then Peter will know. Then they'll all know!"

On the face of it she was encouraging me to reveal to The Exorcist what horrors were likely to befall me if he was no longer around to protect me. It wasn't really about Decadence at all. The truth was she wanted me to punish The Exorcist, to send him off to sea racked with guilt and shame and with that scene of animal horror etched indelibly into his brain like a cerebral tattoo.

It was good advice. The Exorcist set off on that trawler with a heavy heart and I'm pretty confident had The Exorcist not been worrying about my welfare he wouldn't have pressed Bolverk so forcefully to return to Kragerø when their misadventure was done. Bolverk was a proud man and I know it would have required a great deal of persuasion on the part of The Exorcist to coax him back home to face us all as a failed fisherman.

Once they were back in Kragerø you might have expected me to break off with Suffer and make a play for The Exorcist, but that assumes my love for him occupies the same space as your conventional love. The same love depicted by Hollywood and in books. Sadly, your love is nothing like my Hel. My Hel is the sullen girl with black lipstick and facial piercings who doesn't have any friends and certainly doesn't get invited to sleepovers with the popular girls at school.

When The Exorcist returned she barely allowed me to speak to him. Instead, she encouraged me to heap further guilt and pain upon him. So instead of welcoming The Exorcist back with open arms like the prodigal son that he was, I was required instead to crawl into Suffer's lair and invite him to ruin me further.

Suffer never asked me why I allowed myself to be degraded by him or why I kept going back for more. I don't think he cared, but I suspect he always knew the true reason. That's one of the (many) terrifying things about Suffer: he is as smart as hell and sees through to the truth of things faster than anyone I have ever known. Although we never spoke of it, I'm confident he always knew about my feelings for The Exorcist and exploited it mercilessly. Had Hel been a human being, I suspect she and Suffer would have got on famously.

Any other questions for me? Any more loose ends for me to tidy up before we head back into our burning church? Perhaps you're curious how I felt about The Exorcist's death. Sure, let's explore that a little because it is quite interesting.

I felt a gaping loss. A chasm opening up in front, behind and on all sides of me. But that catastrophic loss lasted just a moment, before it was replaced by a magnificent sense of freedom.

With The Exorcist dead I was released from my confinement. Part of me vanished in a sulphureous puff leaving an empty space and a bitter smell in her wake. Along with the freedom, it wasn't quite elation I felt. But the mere absence of that burdensome presence brought with it a welcome calm. That noise in my head, those constant demands on my time, emotions and energies that I had lived with for millennia had suddenly gone. It was as if I had been released from the realms of the sick and infirm and finally permitted to walk amongst the living.

I was free to pursue the record contract, to take our evil to the masses, to not be distracted. Nothing could stand in my way.

Oh, but before we head back to that church, I can see you're thinking about Decadence and where he fits into all this? Did I really hate him as much as I've suggested?

If you have learned nothing else from our little chat you should have learned that, for me at least, there's no real difference between love and hate, just as there is no real difference between good and bad, or ugly and beautiful. One is a head and one is a tail but they both belong to the same snake. And when the snake bites down on its own tail, like the Jormungand of Norse myth, all distinction is lost.

There were moments, a few of them, as you've heard, when Hel was caught napping and I felt a momentary warmth and affection towards Decadence. That summer we spent building the shop and the Crypt, when we faced off to Oslo Iron, even in the aisle of Dønnisal church when he intervened to protect me from Suffer... each time, an alternative future suggested itself to me. In those fleeting visions, I caught a glimpse of a world destined to be happier than any that I could have hoped to share with The Exorcist. It was a life of shared ambition, tastes and interests which compared favorably to the life of care, guidance and constant explanation that The Exorcist had offered me. Of course, Hel never allowed any of those thoughts to gain traction. She would re-assert herself and chase away any competing emotions like protective mother. Nobody has ever been able to compete with her.

What was that? Please repeat what you just said.

"I make Hel sound like a real person"?

But aren't I?

43

I was hot as Hell in the church. Nearly everything made of wood was now on fire. Flames were crawling up and across the beams above us, giving the impression the roof was held up by an infernal latticework. The fire was now surely visible from outside. I figured we only had a few minutes to collect our possessions, get the priceless Bible, and flee.

I might have explained my love of The Exorcist to you, but I gave Decadence no such comfort. While he absorbed the gut-punch of information I'd just admitted – trying to realign his understanding of the world around it – I left him standing at the back of the church, while Suffer and I finished off our fire-starting. Suffer was now in high spirits and he went for some time without any visible pain tremors. I have no doubt his glee over Decadence's shock had something to do with it.

The south wall, where Decadence stood in contemplation, was the furthest from the large window beyond the chancel. Above him, a gallery of portraits looked down as if passing judgment over the naked Satanist before them. From the attire of these men (unsurprisingly, there were no women sat upon this jury), I guessed it was a rogue's gallery of Dønnisal's vicars through the ages.

The roaring light from the fires seemed to animate these characters; the light and shadow jostling together on their features gave a semblance of movement in their ordinarily static expression. It was beautifully eerie.

Decadence was staring at them when I finished my work and returned to him.

"Such a shame," he said.

"If we'd seen them earlier we might have had time to get at least some of them into the van," I offered.

"That's not what I meant."

I remained silent.

"Does doing all this ever make you feel bad, Marta?"

"No, Snorre," I lied. "You know how I feel about guilt. I've evolved it away."

"Remorse then? I'm not sad we don't get to own this stuff, but I kind of feel bad that we're destroying it. These paintings are beautiful and we're removing them from the world. Doesn't it make you feel terrible that we're diminishing society's stock of beauty?"

"You are the worst Satanist ever," I said, only half-joking. "Burning down this church is an act of violence. It's a massive statement. It's the unrestricted exercise of my will in total disregard for the law and conventional morality of a society I am no part of. That empowers me! Yes, I do like these pictures and they are admittedly beautiful. But their beauty is an energy that can never be erased. By destroying them, I'm just converting that energy into something else. I'm converting an energy of craftsmanship and beauty into an energy of hatred and despair – my hatred and despair towards everyone else, and theirs for me."

"Christ. Burning down a church in the middle of the night is not a particularly eloquent way of expressing your frustration!"

"Bull*shit* it isn't. No words could articulate my rage more eloquently than what we're doing now, Snorre. Anyway, don't pretend that your motivations are any more righteous and noble than mine. You're as crammed full of hatred as I am."

Decadence turned towards me and stared hard. There was no leering, his gaze didn't stray down to my tits or my ass, he just fixed the side of my face with those crystal sapphire eyes.

I felt uncomfortable under that stare. In all our interactions I always held the power. But, on that occasion, he caught me off-guard. I couldn't bring myself to turn to him while his eyes bore down on me. I was off-balance and he was in control.

"Why do you think I do this?" Decadence asked.

"Do what?" I asked petulantly, knowing precisely what he meant.

"Everything. The band, the sex, the drugs, and this."

"If you want the truth, I think it's because you're a childish misogynist. You're the product of some fucked-up parenting. But then, aren't we all?"

"No," he said softly. "You're wrong, Marta. I do it because I love you."

I hesitated. The glimpse of that other life flickered in the flames of his eyes.

"You get high and fuck girls by the busload because you love me?"

"Yes."

It was ridiculous. But I knew it was true. The heat from his stare was so intense I had to take a step away from him, towards the fire, to cool down.

"I watched you invite that freak Suffer to push you down on the floor," he said. "And watched him defile you. It scrambled my brain. I spent weeks trying to make sense of it, only to realize that you needed to keep pushing down into sickness and depravity in order to come through to the other side. There you would find a wholesomeness and nobility in amongst the filth. Do you remember when you first heard black metal? It sounded insane, didn't it?"

I nodded.

"Insane and horrific," he continued. "Those were my first thoughts too. It was the sound of pain and anger and hatred and despair and hopelessness and loss. It was unbearable to listen to in anything but small doses. But eventually, after time, you grew to take larger doses. And soon it took hold of you and made you realize music which didn't shroud your soul in darkness just isn't worth listening to. You began to crave ever-more inaccessible, abrasive and disgusting music.

"It dawned on me that when you sacrificed yourself to Suffer, that was you being black metal. And if you were going on that journey into Hell, I wanted to come with you."

He paused and I continued to stare at him.

"I do this because I figured it's what you wanted me to do, Marta. I thought it would bring us closer together." The expression on his beautiful, soot-smeared face crumpled in the way I feared the church was about to do around us. "But I was wrong, wasn't I?"

"Yes," I said.

Decadence's head dropped to stare at the floor. Despite myself, I took his hand in mine, stepped into his chest, and pulled him down into a kiss. It was a soft and tender kiss. Not a kiss calculated to achieve any aim or further any of my plots or schemes. It was a kiss intended to convey my affection and pity.

I would later realize it was the most honest and meaningful kiss of my life.

"I'm sorry," I said, and meant it.

At that moment a crack like the loudest and longest thunderbolt you have ever heard racked the smoke-filled air of the church. A gaping hole was torn into the east-most quarter of the roof and what were once tiles began to rain to the floor. As the roof was rent asunder, small segments caved in sequence and the sound of its destruction built to a slow crescendo as it all fell in slow motion.

A wave of smoke and dust swept towards Decadence and I. He swung me round, turned his back to it and pulled me in to his naked chest. I gripped him tightly, my fingernails penetrating deep into the flesh of his back and his ass.

The ash stung my arms and I was reminded of a childhood holiday, a harsh wind blowing unexpectedly across a fine sand beach.

For a full minute we remained locked in that strange clench. But then the influx of night air fed the flames and the ferocity of the fire grew significantly around us. We parted, sweating, covered in sweat and dust.

Decadence pointed me towards where Suffer was hunched along the aisle.

He had found the prayer books and was ripping them apart in a wide-eyed frenzy of unintelligible oaths, as if each tear was inflicting a sharp physical pain on a mortal enemy. The collapse of the roof seemed to have passed him by unnoticed. Squat on his haunches with a thick layer of grey ash covering him, he looked even more like a gargoyle than he did normally.

Decadence looked around, then led me towards the altar.

"We've got to get out of here. The police and fire brigade will be here soon."

"I'm going to get the Bible. Marta, you collect our clothes and we'll go."

The noise of crashing timber over the crackle and spit of the fire made it difficult for us to hear each other, but I still managed to catch Suffer's comment in the background.

"You're not taking that Bible anywhere!"

I was closer to the altar than Suffer, and Decadence was even closer. Yet, in the blink of an eye, Suffer had suddenly scuttled on all-fours ahead of us, before springing into the air and landing softly onto the altar.

He spun and faced us.

"Fuck off!" he screeched and swung an open hand wildly at Decadence, fingers bent round like a claw. Decadence only just ducked the blow.

Decadence looked across at me, his pale skin glowing in the firelight, clearly caught in two minds. Nobody wanted to take on Suffer, but the vocalist was about to destroy one of the few treasures left in the flaming church.

It was at that moment I noticed the other treasure in Decadence's hand.

The short, bejeweled sword we'd found earlier.

I have thought back to that moment many times since. When our eyes next met, what did Decadence see in mine? Did he see the encouragement from me for what he should do next? Or was his decision to raise the sword and point it towards Suffer entirely his own?

To be honest with you, I don't know the answer.

Suffer watched, delighted, as the sword was raised against him. The polished silver blade shimmered with the heat from the fire.

"Finally!" he said, his round eyes twinkling with excitement. "But I should warn you against what you are doing. There are three ways that this can end. I could back down but, knowing me as you do, we all know I would find an opportunity at some point in the future to take my revenge. You'd be watching your back forever. Wouldn't that be fun?" He laughed. "Alternatively, I could call your bluff and you would have to back down in humiliating fashion. It's safe to assume I would still exact a fearsome revenge on you anyway for having dared to confront me. Which leaves us with the final, and probably your only viable, option. You're going to have to kill me now."

The smile on his face displayed a level of pleasure I had never seen in him before.

"Are you man enough to kill me, Snorre?" he continued. "If the tables were turned, I would kill you in a heartbeat. I've done it before. Have you?"

I looked across at Decadence. I expected to see fear and doubt reflected across those fine features. But they weren't there. He looked at me, strangely relaxed and confident. I smiled. He said nothing.

"Why the delay?" There was a hint of frustration in Suffer's voice now. "Let's get on with it!"

It was by then uncomfortably, impossibly hot. Even the stone floor beneath our bare feet was like a stove-top. I had to hop from foot-to-foot to avoid burning my soles.

Decadence remained serene and impassive.

"Go on, do it. *Do it!*" Suffer implored. "Prove to us and to yourself that you're not the weak, pathetic coward everyone believes you to be."

A bolt of pain must have shot through Suffer in that exact moment, as he tilted forward over the Bible, only saving himself from a tumble by clutching the altar tightly.

The balance of power was shifting. Decadence still didn't speak a word, even as Suffer seemed to regain some control of himself.

"Stab me you dismal piece of shit!" he yelled.

Hysteria had begun to infect his speech. The rictus grin was still there but it was no longer a smile of happiness. Pleasure might have initially turned up the corners of his mouth but something else now kept them there.

"Stab me, Snorre!"

Decadence looked to me again. I made no movement, gave him no physical indication of what I wanted, other than meeting his gaze. It was enough.

He stepped forward towards Suffer.

"Stab me!"

Another step.

"Please God – STAB ME!"

Have you ever watched one of those little insects skim across a pond? They don't float, they use the surface tension on the water to stay dry. If you look closely, you can see tiny indentations on the water's surface where the bug manages to distribute just the right amount of weight to each of its feet. If you ever try to replicate that yourself, with your finger, you find that for a brief moment you can feel that surface tension yourself. A skin on the water yields for a fraction of a second before breaking and engulfing your finger.

When you slowly push a sharpened blade into the soft part of a human being something similar happens. On initial contact with the skin you make just a smooth hollow. You have to increase the pressure considerably before the soft hide will yield to the cold metal of your blade. That's assuming, of course, you don't thrust your blade straight into bone, in which case it's entirely different.

Once the surface tension on Suffer's stomach had been broken, the shaft of that ancient blade slid into his flesh with almost no resistance.

Decadence, Suffer and I stood transfixed by the blade sliding into Suffer's stomach. It took us all by surprise, although the last to notice appeared to be Suffer's circulatory system. An age passed before it figured out what had happened, established what the protocol was, and then gushed his thick blood out over the sword.

Decadence looked down at the hilt in his fingers – now decorated in a rich dark treacle – as if it were a complicated new piece of music technology he was learning to master. He looked into Suffer's face with a kindly expression that seemed to say, "Am I doing this right?"

Suffer answered his unspoken question with a bewildered look of approval so Decadence pulled the blade out slowly and then plunged it back in a few inches to one side of his first incision.

This time Decadence smiled at Suffer. "Isn't this great!" he seemed to be saying with those beautiful fucking eyes of his, as he pushed the blade in and out of Suffer with a slow, sensual rhythm.

Suffer watched, stunned and fascinated in equal measure, a willing spectator to his own murder.

Seeing his skin receding into his hairless stomach on the inward thrust and then adhering to the blade on the outward stroke reminded me of pornography. Decadence maybe thought the same thing, if his growing arousal was anything to go by.

In my dreams since that night, the distinction between cock and blade is usually lost and I find myself with bits of burning church falling around my ears watching Decadence fuck slits into Suffer's stomach.

Blood was starting to gush from the wounds. Suffer's torso looked like a suburban water feature someone had filled with a glutinous black wine. Yet Decadence continued to stab him and Suffer continued to allow it. He even went as far as to twist round a little to expose some virgin flesh when Decadence began struggling to find suitable spots to stab at.

I had never seen Suffer so much at ease with himself and his environment. His breathing was regular, there were no spasms, no ticks, no face contorted with an over-supply of violent hatred. In being slain he had finally found something that assuaged his pain.

After perhaps two dozen drives of the sword he finally began to weaken. All three of us saw it together. We sighed and shared a tender moment of satisfaction, as you might with your close family as you simultaneously push away your plates upon the culmination of a good meal.

All good things come to an end!

Suffer closed his eyes contentedly.

And collapsed in a pool of blood on the altar.

As if in celebration that the Anti-Christ was slain, the stained-glass window behind the altar shattered into a thousand pieces of colored glass that rained down on his lifeless body like confetti. Heated to a sufficient degree, the other windows around the collapsing church followed in controlled bursts like sniper-fire. The gusts of air fed the fire anew, flames roaring higher around us.

"Let's get out of here!" Decadence yelled.

He made towards the Bible, but from what I could see through the flames the book had been reduced to a stained mess of blood-pulp. It was lodged under Suffer's body, which had itself been decorated with small shards of colored glass lodged in his back, transforming him into a psychedelic armadillo.

"Leave it," I said, pulling his arm back. "We have the sword."

He looked down, almost surprised to see it still in his shaking hand, wondering why it was there.

"I killed him," he said.

"You did," I replied and calmly took it from him.

The fabric of the building was deteriorating and beams and fixtures were beginning to fall all around us. Only when another small section of the roof fell to the ground close to where we were standing did Decadence come to his senses. Newly emerged into this pandemonium of our own making, he took my hand and, together, we ran at speed down the aisle.

I suspect the church had seen countless couples go hand in hand down that same aisle over hundreds of years. Who would have thought that the last couple to do so would be a pair of naked, murdering, church-burning Satanists?

When we got to the entrance, I slowed to a halt. Decadence kept a firm grip of my hand, but despite his straining to escape for the cool air of the churchyard, he let me yank him in close. Held there in my embrace, he looked down at me with such simple and enthusiastic delight that the heat and carnage surrounding us melted away to nothing. There it was again. A glimmer in his eyes of a straightforward, conventional life of pleasure. It was a life I had never known and one I did not deserve. But in the aisle of that collapsing church it was still there for the taking.

At least, for a moment.

I grabbed a fistful of hair at the back of his head and pulled him down into a kiss. In the inferno, his lips felt cool and moist. His tongue pulled and probed at mine, and we tied them into knots. His fingers dug hard into the flesh of my ass and shoulder while I held the sword so tightly against the flesh of his back that I drew blood, the hot liquid running across my fingers and soothing the heat-blistered skin. His dick grew into my stomach and I dampened at the mere thought of absorbing it into me.

I fell to the floor and pulled him on top of me. Decadence broke the kiss before I did. He looked up at the melting paintings being consumed by fire on the back wall. Generations of Dønnisal vicars. He seemed embarrassed to be performing any act of carnal love in front of them.

I didn't care. In fact, it seemed almost too perfect.

"Ignore them," I said.

In his child-like happiness Decadence didn't register the blood-soaked blade as it slid into his body even as he slid into mine. The ease with which the blade cleaved apart his flesh contrasted nicely with my memory of a sharper blade struggling against the bones of a skull. That had been a frenzied crime of passion. This was more like a sensitive mercy killing.

But they both had something in common. Neither of them resisted. They both had resigned themselves to their fate. They knew that it was inevitable. That I was inevitable.

I kissed Decadence again as I twisted the sword. He smiled back at me and closed those beautiful eyes for the last time.

Despite his massive blood loss he remained hard inside me. I allowed him that last indulgence. It's how he would have wanted to go.

As I lay there with the church collapsing around us and the ever-diminishing weight of Decadence pressing down on me, I thought about my journey. It was Peter who had set everything in motion. His decision to spurn Marta had brought me into existence. Poor Marta. She thought that she was pulling the strings but she was merely doing my bidding.

You know, I originally thought Baphomet's Agony was a silly idea. No offence, but in the grand scheme of things, who gives a fuck about teenage metal bands? But the more that it developed the more I came to see it as the perfect vehicle for my ambitions. Then when Peter died that pretty much destroyed what little there was left of Marta and I stepped into her place. The rest has been easy.

And here we are!

What's got into you two? You look like you've seen some sort of green-legged monster dredged up from the depths of Hel!

The New black

After the outrageous headlines of the last few months "Satanism" has been trending faster than any other word in the history of the internet and metal fans and journalists the world over have been descending on the picturesque Norwegian port of Kragerø.

Sigurd and Od caught up with Marta Skaði, one time manager of Baphomet's Agony and now VP of Satan's Spawn Records, to get a first-hand account of the macabre events that have shocked the world and seen this middle-class resort on the South coast of Telemark revealed as an unlikely den of iniquity.

Od: So, where to begin with this story? I guess we'll turn things on their head and start at the end! Tell us about the peculiar Norwegian pastime of church burning, Marta.

Sigurd: Well, historically, church fires have been quite common in Norway because so many of our churches are log-built.

Od: Thanks for that Sigurd but I was hoping that Marta would answer that question.

Sigurd: Just saying.

Od: Marta?

Marta: Sorry, boys, I'm afraid I've been advised by my lawyer not to discuss anything to do with church burning. I'm sure you can appreciate that.

Od: We can, of course. However, it has been widely reported that Baphomet's Agony, the band you used to be associated with, are thought to be involved in the destruction of the historic church at Dønnisal, which occurred four months ago.

Marta: I –

Sigurd: As I understand it, police investigating the fire found a van close-by belonging to the guitarist, Decadence. Isn't that right, Marta? They then found the remains of two members of the band inside the church.

Od: To clarify, the analysis of the badly burnt corpses is so far inconclusive on identity. That's my understanding.

Sigurd: But it doesn't look good, considering the proximity of the van and the subsequent disappearance of both Decadence and the vocalist Suffer, does it?

Od: No, it doesn't. However, Sigurd, while I'm much obliged for your ever-eloquent contribution please remember I'm interviewing Marta here.

Marta: I think you boys are doing just fine here without me. Perhaps I'll just go and leave you to it.

Sigurd: No, no, no! Tell us what was happening in Kragerø while the church was burning. We believe there was another fire?

Marta: Yes, from what I have been told, in the early hours of the same morning the Dønnisal Church burnt down, the Kragerø fire service was called out to another fire at a subterranean retail premises.

Sigurd: Those premises being a shop that served as a base for you and Baphomet's Agony, right?

Marta: I helped out there now and then, but I had no formal connection. It was the band's premises.

Sigurd: That's not what I've heard but carry on with your story.

Marta: Are you accusing me of something?

Od: He's not at all. He'd be a fool if he did, wouldn't you Sigurd! Sorry, Marta. We heard there were bodies discovered in those premises, too?

Marta: I believe so. It was quite a night for fires. They apparently found the charred skeletons of what appeared to be a paraplegic male and a female of East Asian extraction. They had been welded together with what was once probably a wheelchair.

Sigurd: Wasn't there a third body?

Marta: Oh yes. They also found the remains of another young adult male.

Od: I heard that Bolverk's bike was outside. The bassist. The police suspect it was him.

Sigurd: Can't they check the dental records to confirm it?

Marta: He'd had his head blown to bits by a shotgun so there was little to go on.

Sigurd: Self-inflicted?

Marta: Who's to say.

Od: And where were you when all of this was happening?

Marta: In Oslo with my boyfriend, Péjé Swartz.

Sigurd: The new CEO of Satan's Spawn?

Marta: The very same.

Sigurd: Weren't you with the vocalist, Suffer, at that time?

Marta: Fuck no! [Laughs] He was a talented black metal vocalist. One of the best, they say. But Suffer was not my type. Péjé and I had been seeing each other for a while by then. We were about to go public with our relationship.

Od: I see. Well can you tell us what you believe about how the fires started? I've heard it was Suffer who lost his mind, shot Bolverk in the shop, then tricked Decadence into the church burning where the two then died. Do you think that's true?

Marta: I think you've been hanging around on too many chatrooms.

Od: You don't believe it?

Marta: I didn't say that. Suffer's reputation was well known. Having spent time with them and seen the frictions in the ranks, I suppose it's entirely plausible he would lose his mind at some point.

Od: Let's not forget, aside from the three deaths that night, the police sought out the remaining member of the band, the drummer, Peter. Otherwise known as The Exorcist. They had to kick down the door of his apartment, where they then found his extensively decomposed remains with a dagger through his head. He was found in bed wrapped in the arms of his mother, who had apparently died of natural causes not long before the police arrived.

Marta: Your knowledge of these events far exceeds my own. I'll take your word for it.

Od: OK. Let's change the subject. The new album.

Marta: Out on Monday.

Od: That's right. It's out on Monday and has received rave reviews all over the world. I hear pre-orders for the CD alone would make it the highest grossing release from Scandinavia since records began.

Sigurd: I have to correct you there Od. As of this morning it was still some way behind 1992's "ABBA Gold".

Od: The highest grossing heavy metal release from Scandinavia since records began?

Sigurd: That's an interesting semantic question. I am quickly moving towards the position that contemporary Norwegian black metal is not –

Od: Sigurd, you might have noticed Marta is putting on her coat. Should we consider moving the focus of this interview away from you and back on to Marta and the posthumous release of Baphomet's Agony's new album?

Sigurd: As usual Od, I am trying to raise the caliber of metal journalism and, as usual, you are desperate to bring it back down to the level of the mundane.

Marta: What he's actually doing is trying to help you take your cock out of your mouth, so your readers can understand what the hell you're saying.

Od: Perhaps, Marta, you would like to tell us how well the new record is doing?

Marta: Let's just say that pre-orders have been healthy. The reviews have been even better. The label is excited.

Od: It's all pretty remarkable for a band whose members are all dead?

Marta: I guess you could say that.

Sigurd: You could say it's *because* of the infamy of the band and the horrific and captivating nature of their deaths that things are on the up? Suffer did you and Satan's Spawn Records a favor, clearly.

Marta: Suffer never did anything for anybody but himself. Anybody with half a brain could see that.

Sigurd: But you're the only ones left to benefit from –

Marta: The fans are the ones to benefit, Sigurd. They have this incredible new album and we at Satan's Spawn promises it will herald a new dawn for black metal. Are these really your questions? You don't want to talk about the music?

Od: Actually, we do. What is it you think the fans are going to get from this album, Marta?

Marta: Oh they're going to get what they've always craved. Devastation writ large. You see, when it's done right, black metal is like an anti-prism. You've seen that image of a line of white light hitting a prism and being refracted into its component parts? Splitting out into all the colors of the spectrum? Well black metal should do the opposite. This album takes all the goodness, beauty and variety in the world and condenses it down into a singular darkness forced out through a broken amp.

Od: You don't think the fans want a more polished and accessible sound from contemporary bands?

Marta: No. I'm sure there is a place for those bands that play accessible, bombastic, over-produced metal, but that's not what true black metal is about. Black metal is not supposed to be accessible, it's supposed to alienate. If you're not used to hearing it, all you can make out is tuneless noise. But, for the initiated, you can hear all the pain, the hatred and the truth of the universe. The true fans want their black metal to challenge, to hurt, to hate and to destroy. That's what this album is about. It's evil on a scale the world hasn't seen before.

Sigurd: Going back to your history with the band.

Marta: Come on, really?

Sigurd: Why not? This is the end for Baphomet's Agony. But where's the beginning? I get the sense there's a story behind all this you're not sharing with us.

Marta: Perhaps there is but I don't think you're ready.

Sigurd: [Laughs] This is Sigurd and Od you're talking to! We saw it all way before you came onto the scene. Come on, Marta, tell us everything. We'll get the drinks in. Get some food. See if you can shock us.

Marta: Stop staring at my tits for five seconds and *I'll* be shocked.

Sigurd: I was just admiring your necklace.

Marta: Sure you were.

Sigurd: Don't change the subject. You've talked a good game. All this "evil on a scale the world has never seen before". Fine. But where did that come from? Give us *the story*.

Marta: Are you prepared to accept the consequences of hearing my story?

Od: Erm, yes. Whatever that means.

Marta: Fuck it. But don't say I didn't warn you.

Od and Sigurd: Really?

Marta: You want a story? Sure. I'll give you a fucking story...

"Baphomet's Agony – *Burn in Hell"* will be available from all good record shops from Monday. A live album recorded in Bergen should be available by Christmas and a series of tribute concerts will be held across Europe next summer.